PLEASE RETURN THIS ITEM
BY THE DUE DATE TO ANY
TULSA CITY-COUNTY LIBRARY.

FINES ARE 5¢ PER DAY; A
MAXIMUM OF $1.00 PER ITEM.

SEP   1988

RSAC

HALLUCINATION ORBIT

HALLUCINATION ORBIT

PSYCHOLOGY IN SCIENCE FICTION

Edited by Isaac Asimov,
Charles G. Waugh,
& Martin H. Greenberg

Farrar·Straus·Giroux
New York

Copyright © 1983 by Nightfall, Inc.,
Charles G. Waugh, and Martin H. Greenberg
All rights reserved
First edition, 1983
Printed in the United States of America
Published simultaneously in Canada by
McGraw-Hill Ryerson Ltd., Toronto
Designed by Charlotte Staub

Library of Congress Cataloging in Publication Data
Main entry under title: Hallucination orbit.
  Summary: An anthology of twelve science fiction stories with psychological themes. Includes a brief analysis of each story.
  1. Science fiction, American. 2. Science fiction, English. 3. Children's stories, American. 4. Children's stories, English. 5. Psychology—Juvenile fiction. [1. Science fiction. 2. Short stories. 3. Psychology—Fiction] I. Asimov, Isaac. II. Waugh, Charles G. III. Greenberg, Martin Harry.
PZ5.H16 1983   [Fic]   82-21107
ISBN 0-374-32835-8

Christopher Anvil, *A Rose by Other Name* copyright © 1960 by Street & Smith Publications, Inc. Reprinted by permission of the author and his agents, The Scott Meredith Literary Agency, Inc., 845 Third Avenue, New York, NY 10022 / Jerome Bixby, *It's a Good Life* copyright © 1953 by Ballantine Books; copyright renewed 1981. Reprinted by arrangement with Forrest J. Ackerman, 2495 Glendower Avenue, Hollywood, CA 90027 / John Brunner, *What Friends Are For* copyright © 1974 by John Brunner. Reprinted by permission of Paul R. Reynolds, Inc., 12 East 41st Street, New York, NY 10017 / Roald Dahl, *The Sound Machine* copyright © 1949, by Roald Dahl, by permission of Alfred A. Knopf, Inc. This story first appeared in *The New Yorker* / Randall Garrett, *In Case of Fire* copyright © 1960 by Street and Smith Publications, Inc. Reprinted by permission of the author and his agents, The Scott Meredith Literary Agency, Inc. / Henry Kuttner, *Absalom* copyright © 1946 by Henry Kuttner; copyright renewed 1973. Reprinted by permission of The Harold Matson Co., Inc. / Edward Ludwig, *The Drivers* copyright © 1955 by Quinn Publishing Co., Inc. Reprinted by permission of the author / J. T. McIntosh, *Hallucination Orbit* copyright © 1952 by Galaxy Publishing Corporation; copyright renewed. Reprinted by permission of the author and his agents, The Scott Meredith Literary Agency, Inc. / Fred Saberhagen, *Wings Out of Shadow* copyright © 1974 by U.P.D. Publishing Corporation. Reprinted by permission of the author / Robert Silverberg, *The Man Who Never Forgot* copyright © 1957 by Fantasy House, Inc. From *Fantasy and Science Fiction*. Reprinted by permission of the author / Donald E. Westlake, *The Winner* copyright © 1970 by the author. Reprinted by permission of Knox Burger Associates, Ltd. This story first appeared in *Nova One*

CONTENTS

INTRODUCTION by Isaac Asimov		3
IT'S A GOOD LIFE by Jerome Bixby		9
THE SOUND MACHINE by Roald Dahl		33
HALLUCINATION ORBIT by J. T. McIntosh		51
THE WINNER by Donald E. Westlake		79
A ROSE BY OTHER NAME by Christopher Anvil		93
THE MAN WHO NEVER FORGOT by Robert Silverberg		107
RUNAROUND by Isaac Asimov		127
ABSALOM by Henry Kuttner		153
WINGS OUT OF SHADOW by Fred Saberhagen		173
IN CASE OF FIRE by Randall Garrett		199
WHAT FRIENDS ARE FOR by John Brunner		211
THE DRIVERS by Edward W. Ludwig		235
NOTES by Charles G. Waugh and Isaac Asimov		257

HALLUCINATION ORBIT

INTRODUCTION

The word *psyche*, in Greek, originally referred to *breath*, which, of course, the Greeks did not understand in the modern scientific sense. To them, breath was something invisible and mysterious that was, somehow, intimately related to life. Stones do not breathe, nor do dead human beings.

The word came to be translated into the English word *soul*, which is also viewed as something ethereal and insubstantial and somehow intimately related to life. Any closer definition, however, loses itself in theological subtleties and uncertainties.

If we define *psyche* or *soul* without reference to theology, we might think of it as the inner core of being that the physical body houses. It is the personality, the individuality, the thing you think of when you say "I." It is the thing that remains intact and whole, even though a limb is lost, eyes are blinded, or the body itself is ill, wounded, or dying.

Psychology, then, is the systematic study of that inner core that is you, and the word we are most apt to use to represent this in these nontheological times is, not *soul*, but *mind*. Psychology is the study of the mind and its relationship to behavior.

Psychology is fascinating in that it seems to exist at the end of two extremes of knowledge. In some ways, everyone understands it; in other ways, no one does. Other sciences may share these extremes, perhaps all sciences do, but surely none to the extent that psychology does.

For instance, to understand why a billiard ball behaves as it does, why it moves when struck, how it collides and rebounds with the cushion or with another billiard ball, how speed and direction alter as a result of collision—all this requires a good knowledge of the principles of that branch of physics known as *mechanics*. In reverse, the principles of mechanics can be worked out by a careful study of billiard-ball behavior.

And yet those who are expert at the art of billiards have not necessarily studied physics and mechanics, may never have heard of the conservation of momentum, may not appreciate the mathematical complexities of angular momentum produced by the placing of "curves" on balls by hitting them off center—yet they make billiard balls do everything but cook dinner, and they do it by meticulous attention to principles they do not know they know.

The same may be said of those who pitch baseballs with complex virtuosity, and batters who strike at those pitches with an artistry of timing. They may earn millions for their mastery of the applied science of mechanics even when (conceivably) they have never learned the simplest fundamentals of physical science.

You can understand the laws of science in a very useful sense merely through careful observation and practice; for science is an organized system of describing the real world, and *you live in the real world.* You can't help but learn to describe the world merely by virtue of that fact, even if your description is not in the conventional terms that scientists have worked out and agreed among themselves to use.

It is not surprising, then, that there are people who have come to understand the human mind well through having observed others, through living and interacting with them, through becoming aware of their habits, responses, and peculiarities. No one can read Shakespeare, Dostoevsky, Tolstoy, Dickens, Austen, Molière, Goethe, and any of innumerable others without seeing that each has a deep understanding of humanity in all its varieties and perplexities, even though not one of them may have studied psychology in any formal way.

This nonscientific understanding of psychology is undoubtedly more widespread than that of any other science. Sportspersons may deal unwittingly with physics, cooks with chemistry, gardeners with biology, sailors with meteorology, artists with mathematics—yet these are all specialized occupations.

Everyone, however, without exception, must deal with people. Even recluses must deal with themselves, and this might be enough, for each of us may well have within himself, or herself, all the virtues and vices, brilliance and foibles, aversions and tendencies of humanity in general.

Therefore we may conclude that in some ways psychology is the most widely understood science.

And yet...

The human mind, born, as it must be, of the human brain, is an extraordinarily complicated thing. The human brain is, with little doubt, the most complicated, subtly interrelated, lump of matter we know of (with the dubiously possible exception of the brain of the dolphin—which is both larger and more convoluted than the human brain).

In studying something as superlatively complex as the human brain, we should naturally expect ourselves to be frequently at a loss. That is all the more obvious when we stop to think that we study the human brain with nothing more than the human brain. We are asking complexity to comprehend equal complexity.

It is no wonder, then, that even though billions of human beings have, throughout the history of *Homo sapiens*, been studying themselves and others in a casual and unsystematic way—and even though extraordinary geniuses have illuminated the human condition in literature, art, philosophy, and, in these latter days, science, vast stretches of the uncertain and unknown remain. More so in psychology than in any other science. Even those areas most studied and expounded are bound to remain, to some degree, in dispute.

And so, in some ways, psychology is the least-understood science.

Consider, too, that the solution to all the problems that press, and have pressed, upon humanity through all its history rest, to a large extent, on the misfunctioning of the human mind. Some problems may seem totally independent of us, and intractable to any human effort—the coming of an ice age, for instance, or the explosion of the sun—and yet even there the human mind might conceivably foresee the event and choose actions that would help improve the situation, even if only by making death easier. Goodwill, reason, and ingenuity are needed (and are often lacking).

On the other hand, human folly—or, at the least, insufficient wisdom—presents us with ever-present and increasing danger. If we destroy ourselves through nuclear war, or overpopulation, or waste of resources, or pollution, or violence and alienation, then part—perhaps most—of the cause will rest with the inability of our minds to recognize the nature of the danger, and the reluctance of our minds to accept the necessity of taking those actions required to avert or ameliorate that danger.

There is no question, then, that psychology is the most important of the sciences. We can live, however primitively, with very little knowledge of any or all of the other sciences, but if we do not understand psychology, we are surely lost.

What role does science fiction play in all this?

Science fiction writers are not, on the whole, better or more understanding than other writers are, and there is no reason to look to them, as individuals, for a clearer illumination of the human condition.

However, in science fiction, human beings are pictured as facing unusual situations, bizarre societies, unorthodox problems. The effort to imagine the human response to such things may cast a light into the shadows in a new way, allowing us to see what had not been clear before.

The stories in this anthology have been selected with that in mind, and each has a special note written by myself and my co-editor Charles Waugh, who happens to be a professional psychologist.

Isaac Asimov

DEVELOPMENT

IT'S A *GOOD* LIFE
Jerome Bixby

Aunt Amy was out on the front porch, rocking back and forth in the highbacked chair and fanning herself, when Bill Soames rode his bicycle up the road and stopped in front of the house.

Perspiring under the afternoon "sun," Bill lifted the box of groceries out of the big basket over the front wheel of the bike, and came up the front walk.

Little Anthony was sitting on the lawn, playing with a rat. He had caught the rat down in the basement—he had made it think that it smelled cheese, the most rich-smelling and crumbly-delicious cheese a rat had ever thought it smelled, and it had come out of its hole, and now Anthony had hold of it with his mind and was making it do tricks.

When the rat saw Bill Soames coming, it tried to run, but Anthony thought at it, and it turned a flip-flop on the grass, and lay trembling, its eyes gleaming in small black terror.

Bill Soames hurried past Anthony and reached the front steps, mumbling. He always mumbled when he came to the Fremont house, or passed by it, or even thought of it. Everybody did. They thought about silly things, things that didn't mean very much, like two-and-two-is-four-and-twice-is-eight and so on; they tried to jumble up their thoughts and keep them skipping back and forth, so Anthony couldn't read their minds. The mumbling helped. Because if Anthony got anything strong out of your thoughts, he might take a notion to do something about it—like curing your wife's sick headaches or your kid's mumps, or getting your old milk cow back on schedule, or fixing the privy. And while Anthony mightn't actually mean any harm, he couldn't be expected to have much notion of what was the right thing to do in such cases.

That was if he liked you. He might try to help you, in his way. And that could be pretty horrible.

If he didn't like you . . . well, that could be worse.

Bill Soames set the box of groceries on the porch railing, and stopped his mumbling long enough to say, "Everythin' you wanted, Miss Amy."

"Oh, fine, William," Amy Fremont said lightly. "My, ain't it terrible hot today?"

Bill Soames almost cringed. His eyes pleaded with her. He shook his head violently *no*, and then interrupted his mumbling again, though obviously he didn't want to: "Oh, don't say that, Miss Amy . . . it's fine, just fine. A real good day!"

Amy Fremont got up from the rocking chair, and came across the porch. She was a tall woman, thin, a smiling vacancy in her eyes. About a year ago, Anthony had gotten mad at her, because she'd told him he shouldn't have turned the cat into a cat-rug, and although he had always obeyed her more than anyone else, which was hardly at all, this time he'd snapped at her. With his mind. And that had been the end of Amy Fremont's bright eyes, and the end of Amy Fremont as everyone had known her. And that was when word got around in Peaksville (population: 46) that even the members of Anthony's own family weren't safe. After that, everyone was twice as careful.

Someday Anthony might undo what he'd done to Aunt Amy. Anthony's Mom and Pop hoped he would. When he was older, and maybe sorry. If it was possible, that is. Because Aunt Amy had changed a lot, and besides, now Anthony wouldn't obey anyone.

"Land alive, William," Aunt Amy said, "you don't have to mumble like that. Anthony wouldn't hurt you. My goodness, Anthony likes you!" She raised her voice and called to Anthony, who had tired of the rat and was making it eat itself. "Don't you, dear? Don't you like Mr. Soames?"

Anthony looked across the lawn at the grocery man—a bright, wet, purple gaze. He didn't say anything. Bill Soames tried to smile at him. After a second Anthony returned his attention to the rat. It had already devoured its tail, or at least chewed it off—for Anthony had made it bite faster than it could swallow, and little pink and red furry pieces lay around it on the green grass. Now the rat was having trouble reaching its hindquarters.

Mumbling silently, thinking of nothing in particular as hard as he could, Bill Soames went stiff-legged down the walk, mounted his bicycle and pedaled off.

"We'll see you tonight, William," Aunt Amy called after him.

As Bill Soames pumped the pedals, he was wishing deep down that he could pump twice as fast, to get away from Anthony all the faster, and away from Aunt Amy, who sometimes just forgot how *careful* you had to be. And he shouldn't have thought that. Because Anthony caught it. He caught the desire to get away from the Fremont house as if it was something *bad*, and his purple gaze blinked, and he snapped a small, sulky thought after Bill Soames—just a small one, because he was in a good mood today, and besides, he liked Bill Soames, or at least didn't dislike him, at least today. Bill Soames wanted to go away—so, petulantly, Anthony helped him.

Pedaling with superhuman speed—or rather, appearing to, because in reality the bicycle was pedaling *him*—Bill Soames vanished down the road in a cloud of dust, his thin, terrified wail drifting back across the summer-like heat.

Anthony looked at the rat. It had devoured half its belly, and had died from pain. He thought it into a grave out deep in the cornfield—his father had once said, smiling, that he might do that with the things he killed—and went around the house, casting his odd shadow in the hot, brassy light from above.

In the kitchen, Aunt Amy was unpacking the groceries. She put the Mason-jarred goods on the shelves, and the meat and milk in the icebox, and the beet sugar and coarse flour in big cans under the sink. She put the cardboard box in the corner, by the door, for Mr. Soames to pick up next time he came. It was stained and battered and torn and worn fuzzy, but it was one of the few left in Peaksville. In faded red letters it said *Campbell's Soup*. The last cans of soup, or of anything else, had been eaten long ago, except for a small communal hoard which the villagers dipped into for special occasions—but the box lingered on, like a coffin, and when it and the other boxes were gone, the men would have to make some out of wood.

Aunt Amy went out in back, where Anthony's Mom—Aunt Amy's sister—sat in the shade of the house, shelling peas. The peas, every time Mom ran a finger along a pod, went *lollop-lollop-lollop* into the pan on her lap.

"William brought the groceries," Aunt Amy said. She sat down wearily in the straightbacked chair beside Mom, and began fanning herself again. She wasn't really old; but ever since Anthony had snapped at her with his mind, something had seemed to be wrong with her body as well as her mind, and she was tired all the time.

"Oh, good," said Mom. *Lollop* went the fat peas into the pan.

Everybody in Peaksville always said "Oh, fine," or "Good," or "Say, that's swell!" when almost anything happened or was mentioned—even unhappy things like accidents or even deaths. They'd always say "Good," because if they didn't try to cover up how they really felt, Anthony might overhear with his mind, and then nobody knew what might happen. Like the time Mrs. Kent's husband, Sam, had come walking back from the graveyard, because Anthony liked Mrs. Kent and had heard her mourning.

Lollop.

"Tonight's television night," said Aunt Amy. "I'm glad. I look forward to it so much every week. I wonder what we'll see tonight?"

"Did Bill bring the meat?" asked Mom.

"Yes." Aunt Amy fanned herself, looking up at the

featureless brassy glare of the sky. "Goodness, it's so hot. I wish Anthony would make it just a little cooler—"

"Amy!"

"Oh!" Mom's sharp tone had penetrated, where Bill Soames's agonized expression had failed. Aunt Amy put one thin hand to her mouth in exaggerated alarm. "Oh . . . I'm sorry, dear." Her pale blue eyes shuttled around, right and left, to see if Anthony was in sight. Not that it would make any difference if he was or wasn't—he didn't have to be near you to know what you were thinking. Usually, though, unless he had his attention on somebody, he would be occupied with thoughts of his own.

But some things attracted his attention—you could never be sure just what.

"This weather's just fine," Mom said.

Lollop.

"Oh, yes," Aunt Amy said. "It's a wonderful day. I wouldn't want it changed for the world!"

Lollop.

Lollop.

"What time is it?" Mom asked.

Aunt Amy was sitting where she could see through the kitchen window to the alarm clock on the shelf above the stove. "Four-thirty," she said.

Lollop.

"I want tonight to be something special," Mom said. "Did Bill bring a good lean roast?"

"Good and lean, dear. They butchered just today, you know, and sent us over the best piece."

"Dan Hollis will be so surprised when he finds out that tonight's television party is a birthday party for him too!"

"Oh *I* think he will! Are you sure nobody's told him?"

"Everybody swore they wouldn't."

"That'll be real nice," Aunt Amy nodded, looking off across the cornfield. "A birthday party."

"Well—" Mom put the pan of peas down beside her, stood up, and brushed her apron. "I'd better get the roast on. Then we can set the table." She picked up the peas.

Anthony came around the corner of the house. He didn't look at them, but continued on down through the carefully kept garden—all the gardens in Peaksville were carefully kept, very carefully kept—and went past the rustling, useless hulk that had been the Fremont family car, and went smoothly over the fence and out into the cornfield.

"Isn't this a lovely day!" said Mom, a little loudly, as they went toward the back door.

Aunt Amy fanned herself. "A beautiful day, dear. Just fine!"

Out in the cornfield, Anthony walked between the tall, rustling rows of green stalks. He liked to smell the corn. The alive corn overhead, and the old dead corn underfoot. Rich Ohio earth, thick with weeds and brown, dry-rotting ears of corn, pressed between his bare toes with every step— he had made it rain last night so everything would smell and feel nice today.

He walked clear to the edge of the cornfield, and over to where a grove of shadowy green trees covered cool, moist, dark ground, and lots of leafy undergrowth, and jumbled moss-covered rocks, and a small spring that made a clear, clean pool. Here Anthony liked to rest and watch the birds and insects and small animals that rustled and scampered and chirped about. He liked to lie on the cool ground and look up through the moving greenness overhead, and watch the insects flit in the hazy soft sunbeams that stood like slanting, glowing bars between ground and treetops. Somehow, he liked the thoughts of the little creatures in this place better than the thoughts outside; and while the thoughts he picked up here weren't very strong or very clear, he could get enough out of them to know what the little creatures liked and wanted, and he spent a lot of time making the grove more like what they wanted it to be. The spring hadn't always been here; but one time he had found thirst in one small furry mind, and had brought subterranean water to the surface in a clear cold flow, and had watched blinking as the creature drank, feeling its pleasure. Later he had made the pool, when he found a small urge to swim.

He had made rocks and trees and bushes and caves, and sunlight here and shadows there, because he had felt in all the tiny minds around him the desire—or the instinctive want—for this kind of resting place, and that kind of mating place, and this kind of place to play, and that kind of home.

And somehow the creatures from all the fields and pastures around the grove had seemed to know that this was a good place, for there were always more of them coming in—every time Anthony came out here there were more creatures than the last time, and more desires and needs to be tended to. Every time there would be some kind of creature he had never seen before, and he would find its mind, and see what it wanted, and then give it to it.

He liked to help them. He liked to feel their simple gratification.

Today, he rested beneath a thick elm, and lifted his purple gaze to a red and black bird that had just come to the grove. It twittered on a branch over his head, and hopped back and forth, and thought its tiny thoughts, and Anthony made a big, soft nest for it, and pretty soon it hopped in.

A long, brown, sleek-furred animal was drinking at the pool. Anthony found its mind next. The animal was thinking about a smaller creature that was scurrying along the ground on the other side of the pool, grubbing for insects. The little creature didn't know that it was in danger. The long, brown animal finished drinking and tensed its legs to leap, and Anthony thought it into a grave in the cornfield.

He didn't like those kinds of thoughts. They reminded him of the thoughts outside the grove. A long time ago some of the people outside had thought that way about *him*, and one night they'd hidden and waited for him to come back from the grove—and he'd just thought them all into the cornfield. Since then, the rest of the people hadn't thought that way—at least, very clearly. Now their thoughts were all mixed up and confusing whenever they thought about him or near him, so he didn't pay much attention.

He liked to help them too, sometimes—but it wasn't simple, or very gratifying either. They never thought happy thoughts when he did—just the jumble. So he spent more time out here.

He watched all the birds and insects and furry creatures for a while, and played with a bird, making it soar and dip and streak madly around tree trunks until, accidentally, when another bird caught his attention for a moment, he ran it into a rock. Petulantly, he thought the rock into a grave in the cornfield; but he couldn't do anything more with the bird. Not because it was dead, though it was; but because it had a broken wing. So he went back to the house. He didn't feel like walking back through the cornfield, so he just *went* to the house, right down into the basement.

It was nice down here. Nice and dark and damp and sort of fragrant, because once Mom had been making preserves in a rack along the far wall, and then she'd stopped coming down ever since Anthony had started spending time here, and the preserves had spoiled and leaked down and spread over the dirt floor, and Anthony liked the smell.

He caught another rat, making it smell cheese, and after he played with it, he thought it into a grave right beside the long animal he'd killed in the grove. Aunt Amy hated rats, and so he killed a lot of them, because he liked Aunt Amy most of all and sometimes did things that Aunt Amy wanted. Her mind was more like the little furry minds out in the grove. She hadn't thought anything bad at all about him for a long time.

After the rat, he played with a big black spider in the corner under the stairs, making it run back and forth until its web shook and shimmered in the light from the cellar window like a reflection in silvery water. Then he drove fruit flies into the web until the spider was frantic trying to wind them all up. The spider liked flies, and its thoughts were stronger than theirs, so he did it. There was something bad in the way it liked flies, but it wasn't clear—and besides, Aunt Amy hated flies too.

He heard footsteps overhead—Mom moving around in the kitchen. He blinked his purple gaze, and almost decided to make her hold still—but instead he *went* up to the attic, and, after looking out the circular window at the front end of the long V-roofed room for a while at the front lawn and the dusty road and Henderson's tip-waving wheatfield beyond, he curled into an unlikely shape and went partly to sleep.

Soon people would be coming for television, he heard Mom think.

He went more to sleep. He liked television night. Aunt Amy had always liked television a lot, so one time he had thought some for her, and a few other people had been there at the time, and Aunt Amy had felt disappointed when they wanted to leave. He'd done something to them for that—and now everybody came to television.

He liked all the attention he got when they did.

Anthony's father came home around six-thirty, looking tired and dirty and bloody. He'd been over in Dunn's pasture with the other men, helping pick out the cow to be slaughtered this month and doing the job, and then butchering the meat and salting it away in Soames's icehouse. Not a job he cared for, but every man had his turn. Yesterday, he had helped scythe down old McIntyre's wheat. Tomorrow, they would start threshing. By hand. Everything in Peaksville had to be done by hand.

He kissed his wife on the cheek and sat down at the kitchen table. He smiled and said, "Where's Anthony?"

"Around someplace," Mom said.

Aunt Amy was over at the wood-burning stove, stirring the big pot of peas. Mom went back to the oven and opened it and basted the roast.

"Well, it's been a *good* day," Dad said. By rote. Then he looked at the mixing bowl and breadboard on the table. He sniffed at the dough. "M'm," he said. "I could eat a loaf all by myself, I'm so hungry."

"No one told Dan Hollis about its being a birthday party, did they?" his wife asked.

"Nope. We kept as quiet as mummies."

"We've fixed up such a lovely surprise!"

"Um? What?"

"Well . . . you know how much Dan likes music. Well, last week Thelma Dunn found a *record* in her attic!"

"No!"

"Yes! And we had Ethel sort of ask—you know, without really *asking*—if he had that one. And he said no. Isn't that a wonderful surprise?"

"Well, now, it sure is. A record, imagine! That's a real nice thing to find! What record is it?"

"Perry Como, singing *You Are My Sunshine*."

"Well, I'll be darned. I always liked that tune." Some raw carrots were lying on the table. Dad picked up a small one, scrubbed it on his chest, and took a bite. "How did Thelma happen to find it?"

"Oh, you know—just looking around for new things."

"M'm." Dad chewed the carrot. "Say, who has that picture we found a while back? I kind of liked it—that old clipper sailing along—"

"The Smiths. Next week the Sipichs get it, and they give the Smiths old McIntyre's music-box, and we give the Sipichs—" and she went down the tentative order of things that would exchange hands among the women at church this Sunday.

He nodded. "Looks like we can't have the picture for a while, I guess. Look, honey, you might try to get that detective book back from the Reillys. I was so busy the week we had it, I never got to finish all the stories—"

"I'll try," his wife said doubtfully. "But I hear the van Husens have a stereoscope they found in the cellar." Her voice was just a little accusing. "They had it two whole months before they told anybody about it—"

"Say," Dad said, looking interested. "That'd be nice, too. Lots of pictures?"

"I suppose so. I'll see on Sunday. I'd like to have it—but we still owe the van Husens for their canary. I don't know why that bird had to pick *our* house to die . . . it must have been sick when we got it. Now there's just no satisfying Betty van Husen—she even hinted she'd like our *piano* for a while!"

"Well, honey, you try for the stereoscope—or just anything you think we'll like." At last he swallowed the carrot. It had been a little young and tough. Anthony's whims about the weather made it so that people never knew what crops would come up, or what shape they'd be in if they did. All they could do was plant a lot; and always enough of something came up any one season to live on. Just once there had been a grain surplus; tons of it had been hauled to the edge of Peaksville and dumped off into the nothingness. Otherwise, nobody could have breathed, when it started to spoil.

"You know," Dad went on. "It's nice to have the new things around. It's nice to think that there's probably still a lot of stuff nobody's found yet, in cellars and attics and barns and down behind things. They help, somehow. As much as anything can help—"

"Sh-h!" Mom glanced nervously around.

"Oh," Dad said, smiling hastily. "It's all right! The new things are *good!* It's *nice* to be able to have something around you've never seen before, and know that something you've given somebody else is making them happy . . . that's a real *good* thing."

"A good thing," his wife echoed.

"Pretty soon," Aunt Amy said, from the stove, "there won't be any more new things. We'll have found everything there is to find. Goodness, that'll be too bad—"

"*Amy!*"

"Well—" her pale eyes were shallow and fixed, a sign of her recurrent vagueness. "It will be kind of a shame—no new things—"

"Don't *talk* like that," Mom said, trembling. "Amy, be quiet!"

"It's *good,*" said Dad, in the loud, familiar, wanting-to-be-overheard tone of voice. "Such talk is *good.* It's okay, honey

—don't you see? It's good for Amy to talk any way she wants. It's good for her to feel bad. Everything's good. Everything *has* to be good . . ."

Anthony's mother was pale. And so was Aunt Amy—the peril of the moment had suddenly penetrated the clouds surrounding her mind. Sometimes it was difficult to handle words so that they might not prove disastrous. You just never *knew*. There were so many things it was wise not to say, or even think—but remonstration for saying or thinking them might be just as bad, if Anthony heard and decided to do anything about it. You could just never tell what Anthony was liable to do.

Everything had to be good. Had to be fine just as it was, even if it wasn't. Always. Because any change might be worse. So terribly much worse.

"Oh, my goodness, yes, of course it's good," Mom said. "You talk any way you want to, Amy, and it's just fine. Of course, you want to remember that some ways are *better* than others . . ."

Aunt Amy stirred the peas, fright in her pale eyes.

"Oh, yes," she said. "But I don't feel like talking right now. It . . . it's *good* that I don't feel like talking."

Dad said tiredly, smiling, "I'm going out and wash up."

They started arriving around eight o'clock. By that time, Mom and Aunt Amy had the big table in the dining room set, and two more tables off to the side. The candles were burning, and the chairs situated, and Dad had a big fire going in the fireplace.

The first to arrive were the Sipichs, John and Mary. John wore his best suit, and was well-scrubbed and pink-faced after his day in McIntyre's pasture. The suit was neatly pressed, but getting threadbare at elbows and cuffs. Old McIntyre was working on a loom, designing it out of schoolbooks, but so far it was slow going. McIntyre was a capable man with wood and tools, but a loom was a big order when you couldn't get metal parts. McIntyre had been one of the ones who, at first, had wanted to try to get Anthony to make things the villagers needed, like clothes and canned goods and medical supplies and gasoline. Since then, he felt that what had happened to the whole Terrance family and Joe Kinney was his fault, and he worked hard trying to make it up to the rest of them. And since then, no one had tried to get Anthony to do anything.

Mary Sipich was a small, cheerful woman in a simple dress. She immediately set about helping Mom and Aunt Amy put the finishing touches on the dinner.

The next arrivals were the Smiths and the Dunns, who lived right next to each other down the road, only a few yards from the nothingness. They drove up in the Smiths' wagon, drawn by their old horse.

Then the Reillys showed up, from across the darkened wheatfield, and the evening really began. Pat Reilly sat down at the big upright in the front room, and began to play from the popular sheet music on the rack. He played softly, as expressively as he could—and nobody sang. Anthony liked piano playing a whole lot, but not singing; often he would come up from the basement, or down from the attic, or just come, and sit on top of the piano, nodding his head as Pat played *Lover* or *Boulevard of Broken Dreams* or *Night and Day*. He seemed to prefer ballads, sweet-sounding songs—but the one time somebody had started to sing, Anthony had looked over from the top of the piano and done something that made everybody afraid of singing from then on. Later, they'd decided that the piano was what Anthony had heard first, before anybody had ever tried to sing, and now anything else added to it didn't sound right and distracted him from his pleasure.

So, every television night, Pat would play the piano, and that was the beginning of the evening. Wherever Anthony was, the music would make him happy, and put him in a good mood, and he would know that they were gathering for television and waiting for him.

By eight-thirty everybody had shown up, except for the seventeen children and Mrs. Soames who was off watching them in the schoolhouse at the far end of town. The children of Peaksville were never, never allowed near the Fremont house—not since little Fred Smith had tried to play with Anthony on a dare. The younger children weren't even told about Anthony. The others had mostly forgotten about him, or were told that he was a nice, nice goblin but they must never go near him.

Dan and Ethel Hollis came late, and Dan walked in not suspecting a thing. Pat Reilly had played the piano until his hands ached—he'd worked pretty hard with them today—and now he got up, and everybody gathered around to wish Dan Hollis a happy birthday.

"Well, I'll be darned," Dan grinned. "This is swell. I wasn't expecting this at all . . . gosh, this is *swell!*"

They gave him his presents—mostly things they had made by hand, though some were things that people had possessed as their own and now gave him as his. John Sipich gave him a watch charm, hand-carved out of a piece of hickory wood. Dan's watch had broken down a year or so ago, and there was nobody in the village who knew how to fix it, but he still carried it around because it had been his grandfather's and was a fine old heavy thing of gold and silver. He attached the charm to the chain, while everybody laughed and said John had done a nice job of carving. Then Mary Sipich gave him a knitted necktie, which he put on, removing the one he'd worn.

The Reillys gave him a little box they had made, to keep

things in. They didn't say what things, but Dan said he'd keep his personal jewelry in it. The Reillys had made it out of a cigar box, carefully peeled of its paper and lined on the inside with velvet. The outside had been polished, and carefully if not expertly carved by Pat—but his carving got complimented too. Dan Hollis received many other gifts— a pipe, a pair of shoelaces, a tie pin, a knit pair of socks, some fudge, a pair of garters made from old suspenders.

He unwrapped each gift with vast pleasure, and wore as many of them as he could right there, even the garters. He lit up the pipe, and said he'd never had a better smoke; which wasn't quite true, because the pipe wasn't broken in yet. Pete Manners had had it lying around ever since he'd received it as a gift four years ago from an out-of-town relative who hadn't known he'd stopped smoking.

Dan put the tobacco into the bowl very carefully. Tobacco was precious. It was only pure luck that Pat Reilly had decided to try to grow some in his backyard just before what had happened to Peaksville had happened. It didn't grow very well, and then they had to cure it and shred it and all, and it was just precious stuff. Everybody in town used wooden holders old McIntyre had made, to save on butts.

Last of all, Thelma Dunn gave Dan Hollis the record she had found.

Dan's eyes misted even before he opened the package. He knew it was a record.

"Gosh," he said softly. "What one is it? I'm almost afraid to look . . ."

"You haven't got it, darling," Ethel Hollis smiled. "Don't you remember, I asked about *You Are My Sunshine?*"

"Oh, gosh," Dan said again. Carefully he removed the wrapping and stood there fondling the record, running his big hands over the worn grooves with their tiny, dulling crosswise scratches. He looked around the room, eyes shining, and they all smiled back, knowing how delighted he was.

"Happy birthday, darling!" Ethel said, throwing her arms around him and kissing him.

He clutched the record in both hands, holding it off to one side as she pressed against him. "Hey," he laughed, pulling back his head. "Be careful . . . I'm holding a priceless object!" He looked around again, over his wife's arms, which were still around his neck. His eyes were hungry. "Look . . . do you think we could play it? Lord, what I'd give to hear some new music . . . just the first part, the orchestra part, before Como sings?"

Faces sobered. After a minute, John Sipich said, "I don't think we'd better, Dan. After all, we don't know just where the singer comes in—it'd be taking too much of a chance. Better wait till you get home."

Dan Hollis reluctantly put the record on the buffet with all his other presents. "It's good," he said automatically, but disappointedly, " that I can't play it here."

"Oh, yes," said Sipich. "It's good." To compensate for Dan's disappointed tone, he repeated, "It's good."

They ate dinner, the candles lighting their smiling faces, and ate it all right down to the last delicious drop of gravy. They complimented Mom and Aunt Amy on the roast beef, and the peas and carrots, and the tender corn on the cob. The corn hadn't come from the Fremonts' cornfield, naturally—everybody knew what was out there; and the field was going to weeds.

Then they polished off the dessert—homemade ice cream and cookies. And then they sat back, in the flickering light of the candles, and chatted, waiting for television.

There never was a lot of mumbling on television night—

everybody came and had a good dinner at the Fremonts', and that was nice, and afterward there was television, and nobody really thought much about that—it just had to be put up with. So it was a pleasant enough get-together, aside from your having to watch what you said just as carefully as you always did everyplace. If a dangerous thought came into your mind, you just started mumbling, even right in the middle of a sentence. When you did that, the others just ignored you until you felt happier again and stopped.

Anthony liked television night. He had done only two or three awful things on television night in the whole past year.

Mom had put a bottle of brandy on the table, and they each had a tiny glass of it. Liquor was even more precious than tobacco. The villagers could make wine, but the grapes weren't right, and certainly the techniques weren't, and it wasn't very good wine. There were only a few bottles of real liquor left in the village—four rye, three Scotch, three brandy, nine real wine and half a bottle of Drambuie belonging to old McIntyre (only for marriages)—and when those were gone, that was it.

Afterward, everybody wished that the brandy hadn't been brought out. Because Dan Hollis drank more of it than he should have, and mixed it with a lot of the homemade wine. Nobody thought anything about it at first, because he didn't show it much outside, and it was his birthday party and a happy party, and Anthony liked these get-togethers and shouldn't see any reason to do anything even if he was listening.

But Dan Hollis got high, and did a fool thing. If they'd seen it coming, they'd have taken him outside and walked him around.

The first thing they knew, Dan stopped laughing right in

the middle of the story about how Thelma Dunn had found the Perry Como record and dropped it and it hadn't broken because she'd moved faster than she ever had before in her life and caught it. He was fondling the record again, and looking longingly at the Fremonts' gramophone over in the corner, and suddenly he stopped laughing and his face got slack, and then it got ugly, and he said, "Oh, *Christ!*"

Immediately the room was still. So still they could hear the whirring movement of the grandfather's clock out in the hall. Pat Reilly had been playing the piano, softly. He stopped, his hands poised over the yellowed keys.

The candles on the dining-room table flickered in a cool breeze that blew through the lace curtains over the bay window.

"Keep playing, Pat," Anthony's father said softly.

Pat started again. He played *Night and Day*, but his eyes were sidewise on Dan Hollis, and he missed notes.

Dan stood in the middle of the room, holding the record. In his other hand he held a glass of brandy so hard his hand shook.

They were all looking at him.

"*Christ*," he said again, and he made it sound like a dirty word.

Reverend Younger, who had been talking with Mom and Aunt Amy by the dining-room door, said "Christ" too —but he was using it in a prayer. His hands were clasped, and his eyes were closed.

John Sipich moved forward. "Now, Dan . . . it's good for you to talk that way. But you don't want to talk too much, you know."

Dan shook off the hand Sipich put on his arm.

"Can't even play my record," he said loudly. He looked down at the record, and then around at their faces. "Oh, my *God* . . ."

He threw the glassful of brandy against the wall. It splattered and ran down the wallpaper in streaks.

Some of the women gasped.

"Dan," Sipich said in a whisper. "Dan, cut it out—"

Pat Reilly was playing *Night and Day* louder, to cover up the sounds of the talk. It wouldn't do any good, though, if Anthony was listening.

Dan Hollis went over to the piano and stood by Pat's shoulder, swaying a little.

"Pat," he said. "Don't play *that*. Play *this*." And he began to sing. Softly, hoarsely, miserably: "Happy birthday to me . . . Happy birthday to me . . ."

"*Dan!*" Ethel Hollis screamed. She tried to run across the room to him. Mary Sipich grabbed her arm and held her back. "Dan," Ethel screamed again. "Stop—"

"My God, be quiet!" hissed Mary Sipich, and pushed her toward one of the men, who put his hand over her mouth and held her still.

"—Happy birthday, dear Danny," Dan sang. "Happy birthday to me!" He stopped and looked down at Pat Reilly. "Play it, Pat. Play it, so I can sing right . . . you know I can't carry a tune unless somebody plays it!"

Pat Reilly put his hands on the keys and began *Lover*—in a slow waltz tempo, the way Anthony liked it. Pat's face was white. His hands fumbled.

Dan Hollis stared over at the dining-room door. At Anthony's mother, and at Anthony's father who had gone to join her.

"You had him," he said. Tears gleamed on his cheeks as the candlelight caught them. "*You* had to go and *have* him . . ."

He closed his eyes, and the tears squeezed out. He sang loudly, "You are my sunshine . . . my only sunshine . . . you make me happy . . . when I am blue . . ."

Anthony came into the room.

Pat stopped playing. He froze. Everybody froze. The breeze rippled the curtains. Ethel Hollis couldn't even try to scream—she had fainted.

"Please don't take my sunshine . . . away . . ." Dan's voice faltered into silence. His eyes widened. He put both hands out in front of him, the empty glass in one, the record in the other. He hiccupped, and said, "No—"

"Bad man," Anthony said, and thought Dan Hollis into something like nothing anyone would have believed possible, and then he thought the thing into a grave deep, deep in the cornfield.

The glass and record thumped on the rug. Neither broke.

Anthony's purple gaze went around the room.

Some of the people began mumbling. They all tried to smile. The sound of mumbling filled the room like a far-off approval. Out of the murmuring came one or two clear voices:

"Oh, it's a very good thing," said John Sipich.

"A good thing," said Anthony's father, smiling. He'd had more practice in smiling than most of them. "A wonderful thing."

"It's swell . . . just swell," said Pat Reilly, tears leaking from eyes and nose, and he began to play the piano again, softly, his trembling hands feeling for *Night and Day*.

Anthony climbed up on top of the piano, and Pat played for two hours.

Afterward, they watched television. They all went into the front room, and lit just a few candles, and pulled up chairs around the set. It was a small-screen set, and they couldn't all sit close enough to it to see, but that didn't matter. They didn't even turn the set on. It wouldn't have worked anyway, there being no electricity in Peaksville.

They just sat silently, and watched the twisting, writhing shapes on the screen, and listened to the sounds that came out of the speaker, and none of them had any idea of what it was all about. They never did. It was always the same.

"It's real nice," Aunt Amy said once, her pale eyes on the meaningless flickers and shadows. "But I liked it a little better when there were cities outside and we could get real—"

"Why, Amy!" said Mom. "It's good for you to say such a thing. Very good. But how can you mean it? Why, this television is *much* better than anything we ever used to get!"

"Yes," chimed in John Sipich. "It's fine. It's the best show we've ever seen!"

He sat on the couch, with two other men, holding Ethel Hollis flat against the cushions, holding her arms and legs and putting their hands over her mouth, so she couldn't start screaming again.

"It's really *good!*" he said again.

Mom looked out of the front window, across the darkened road, across Henderson's darkened wheatfield to the vast, endless, gray nothingness in which the little village of Peaksville floated like a soul—the huge nothingness that was most evident at night, when Anthony's brassy day had gone.

It did no good to wonder where they were . . . no good at all. Peaksville was just someplace. Someplace away from the world. It was wherever it had been since that day three years ago when Anthony had crept from her womb and old Doc Bates—God rest him—had screamed and dropped him and tried to kill him, and Anthony had whined and done the thing. Had taken the village someplace. Or had destroyed the world and left only the village, nobody knew which.

It did no good to wonder about it. Nothing at all did any

good—except to live as they must live. Must always, always live, if Anthony would let them.

These thoughts were dangerous, she thought.

She began to mumble. The others started mumbling too. They had all been thinking, evidently.

The men on the couch whispered and whispered to Ethel Hollis, and when they took their hands away, she mumbled too.

While Anthony sat on top of the set and made television, they sat around and mumbled and watched the meaningless, flickering shapes far into the night.

Next day it snowed, and killed off half the crops—but it was a *good* day.

Jerome Bixby (1923–)
Jerome Bixby started out to be a musician. But he began working as a science fiction editor in the late 1940's, then turned to screenplays and, after a brief period as a realtor, teleplays. Though he is a prolific writer of over one thousand shorter works, readers tend to remember short-story plots and not authors. So his concentration on this length has probably caused him to receive far less recognition than he deserves.

SENSATION

THE SOUND MACHINE
Roald Dahl

It was a hot summer evening and Klausner walked quickly through the front gate and around the side of the house and into the garden at the back. He went on down the garden until he came to a wooden shed and he unlocked the door, went inside, and closed the door behind him.

The interior of the shed was an unpainted room. Against one wall, on the left, there was a long wooden workbench, and on it, among a littering of wires and batteries and small sharp tools, there stood a black box about three feet long, the shape of a child's coffin.

Klausner moved across the room to the box. The top of the box was open, and he bent down and began to poke and peer inside it among a mass of different-colored wires and silver tubes. He picked up a piece of paper that lay beside the box, studied it carefully, put it down, peered inside the box, and started running his fingers along the wires, tugging gently at them to test the connections, glancing back at the paper, then into the box, then at the paper again, checking each wire. He did this for perhaps an hour.

Then he put a hand around to the front of the box where there were three dials, and he began to twiddle them, watching at the same time the movement of the mechanism inside the box. All the while he kept speaking softly to himself, nodding his head, smiling sometimes, his hands always moving, the fingers moving swiftly, deftly, inside the box, his mouth twisting into curious shapes when a thing was delicate or difficult to do, speaking to himself, saying, "Yes . . . Yes . . . And now this one . . . Yes . . . Yes . . . But is this right? . . . Is it—where's my diagram? . . . Ah, yes . . . Of course . . . Yes, yes . . . That's right . . . And now . . . Good . . . Yes . . . Yes, yes, yes." His concentration was intense; his movements were quick; there was an air of urgency about the way he worked, of breathlessness, of strong suppressed excitement.

Suddenly he heard footsteps on the gravel path outside and he straightened and turned swiftly as the door opened and a tall man came in. It was Scott. It was only Scott, the doctor.

"Well, well, well," the Doctor said. "So this is where you hide yourself in the evenings."

"Hullo, Scott," Klausner said.

"I happened to be passing," the Doctor told him, "so I dropped in to see how you were. There was no one in the house, so I came down here. How's that throat of yours been behaving?"

"It's all right. It's fine."

"Now I'm here I might as well have a look at it."

"Please don't trouble. I'm quite cured. I'm fine."

The Doctor began to feel the tension in the room. He looked at the black box on the bench; then he looked at the man. "You've got your hat on," he said.

"Oh, have I?" Klausner reached up, removed the hat, and put it on the bench.

The Doctor came up closer and bent down to look into the box. "What's this?" he said. "Making a radio?"

"No. Just fooling around."

"It's got rather complicated-looking innards."

"Yes." Klausner seemed tense and distracted.

"What is it?" the Doctor asked. "It's rather a frightening-looking thing, isn't it?"

"It's just an idea."

"Yes?"

"It has to do with sound, that's all."

"Good heavens, man! Don't you get enough of that sort of thing all day in your work?"

"I like sound."

"So it seems." The Doctor went to the door, turned, and said, "Well, I won't disturb you. Glad your throat's not worrying you any more." But he kept standing there, looking at the box, intrigued by the remarkable complexity of its insides, curious to know what this strange patient of his was up to. "What's it really for?" he asked. "You've made me inquisitive."

Klausner looked down at the box, then at the Doctor, and he reached up and began gently to scratch the lobe of his right ear. There was a pause. The Doctor stood by the door, waiting, smiling.

"All right, I'll tell you, if you're interested." There was

another pause, and the Doctor could see that Klausner was having trouble about how to begin. He was shifting from one foot to the other, tugging at the lobe of his ear, looking at his feet, and then at last, slowly, he said, "Well, it's like this ... It's ... the theory is very simple, really. The human ear ... You know that it can't hear everything. There are sounds that are so low-pitched or so high-pitched that it can't hear them."

"Yes," the Doctor said. "Yes."

"Well, speaking very roughly, any note so high that it has more than fifteen thousand vibrations a second—we can't hear it. Dogs have better ears than us. You know you can buy a whistle whose note is so high-pitched that you can't hear it at all. But a dog can hear it."

"Yes, I've seen one," the Doctor said.

"Of course you have. And up the scale, higher than the note of that whistle, there is another note—a vibration, if you like, but I prefer to think of it as a note. You can't hear that one either. And above that there is another and another rising right up the scale for ever and ever and ever, an endless succession of notes ... an infinity of notes ... there is a note—if only our ears could hear it—so high that it vibrates a million times a second ... and another a million times as high as that ... and on and on, higher and higher, as far as numbers go, which is ... infinity ... eternity ... beyond the stars. ..."

Klausner stood next to the workbench, fluttering his hands, becoming more animated every moment. He was a small, frail man, nervous and twitchy, with always moving hands. His large head inclined toward his left shoulder, as though his neck were not quite strong enough to support it rigidly. His face was smooth and pale, almost white, and the pale-gray eyes that blinked and peered from behind a pair of thick-lensed steel spectacles were bewildered, unfocused, remote. He was a frail, nervous, twitchy little man, a moth of a man, dreamy and distracted, suddenly fluttering and animated; and now the Doctor, looking at that strange pale face and those pale-gray eyes, felt that somehow there was about this little person a quality of distance, of immense, immeasurable distance, as though the mind were far away from where the body was.

The Doctor waited for him to go on. Klausner sighed and clasped his hands tightly together. "I believe," he said, speaking more slowly now, "that there is a whole world of sound about us all the time that we cannot hear. It is possible that up there in those high-pitched, inaudible regions there is a new, exciting music being made, with subtle harmonies and fierce grinding discords, a music so powerful that it would drive us mad if only our ears were tuned to hear the sound of it. There may be anything . . . for all we know there may—"

"Yes," the Doctor said. "But it's not very probable."

"Why not? Why not?" Klausner pointed to a fly sitting on a small roll of copper wire on the workbench. "You see that fly? What sort of a noise is that fly making now? None —that one can hear. But for all we know the creature may be whistling like mad on a very high note, or barking or croaking or singing a song. It's got a mouth, hasn't it? It's got a throat!"

The Doctor looked at the fly and he smiled. He was still standing by the door with his hand on the doorknob. "Well," he said. "So you're going to check up on that?"

"Some time ago," Klausner said, "I made a simple instrument that proved to me the existence of many odd, inaudible sounds. Often I have sat and watched the needle of my instrument recording the presence of sound vibrations in the air when I myself could hear nothing. And *those* are the sounds I want to listen to. I want to know where they come from and who or what is making them."

"And that machine on the table, there," the Doctor said, "is that going to allow you to hear these noises?"

"It may. Who knows? So far, I've had no luck. But I've made some changes in it, and tonight I'm ready for another trial. This machine," he said, touching it with his hands, "is designed to pick up sound vibrations that are too high-pitched for reception by the human ear and to convert them to a scale of audible tones. I tune it in, almost like a radio."

"How d'you mean?"

"It isn't complicated. Say I wish to listen to the squeak of a bat. That's a fairly high-pitched sound—about thirty thousand vibrations a second. The average human ear can't quite hear it. Now, if there were a bat flying around this room and I tuned in to thirty thousand on my machine, I would hear the squeaking of that bat very clearly. I would even hear the correct note—F sharp, or B flat, or whatever it might be—but merely at a much *lower pitch*. Don't you understand?"

The Doctor looked at the long, black coffin-box. "And you're going to try it tonight?"

"Yes."

"Well, I wish you luck." He glanced at his watch. "My goodness!" he said. "I must fly. Goodbye, and thank you for telling me. I must call again sometime and find out what happened." The Doctor went out and closed the door behind him.

For a while longer, Klausner fussed about with the wires in the black box; then he straightened up and, in a soft, excited whisper, said, "Now we'll try again . . . We'll take it out into the garden this time . . . and then perhaps . . .

perhaps . . . the reception will be better. Lift it up now . . . carefully . . . Oh, my God, it's heavy!" He carried the box to the door, found that he couldn't open the door without putting it down, carried it back, put it on the bench, opened the door, and then carried it with some difficulty into the garden. He placed the box carefully on a small wooden table that stood on the lawn. He returned to the shed and fetched a pair of earphones. He plugged the wire connections from the earphones into the machine and put the earphones over his ears. The movements of his hands were quick and precise. He was excited, and breathed loudly and quickly through his mouth. He kept on talking to himself with little words of comfort and encouragement, as though he were afraid—afraid that the machine might not work and afraid also of what might happen if it did.

He stood there in the garden beside the wooden table, so pale, small, and thin that he looked like an ancient, consumptive, bespectacled child. The sun had gone down. There was no wind, no sound at all. From where he stood, he could see over a low fence into the next garden, and there was a woman walking down the garden with a flower basket on her arm. He watched her for a while without thinking about her at all. Then he turned to the box on the table and pressed a switch on its front. He put his left hand on the volume control and his right hand on the knob that moved a needle across a large central dial, like the wavelength dial of a radio. The dial was marked with many numbers, in a series of bands, starting at 15,000 and going on up to 1,000,000.

And now he was bending forward over the machine. His head was cocked to one side in a tense, listening attitude. His right hand was beginning to turn the knob. The needle was traveling slowly across the dial, so slowly that he could hardly see it move, and in the earphones he could hear a faint, spasmodic crackling.

Behind this crackling sound, he could hear a distant humming tone, which was the noise of the machine itself, but that was all. As he listened, he became conscious of a curious sensation, a feeling that his ears were stretching out away from his head, that each ear was connected to his head by a thin, stiff wire, like a tentacle, and that the wires were lengthening, that the ears were going up and up toward a secret and forbidden territory, a dangerous, ultrasonic region where ears had never been before and had no right to be.

The little needle crept slowly across the dial, and suddenly he heard a shriek, a frightful piercing shriek, and he jumped and dropped his hands, catching hold of the edge of the table. He stared around him as if expecting to see the person who had shrieked. There was no one in sight except the woman in the garden next door, and it was certainly not she. She was bending down, cutting yellow roses and putting them in her basket.

Again it came—a throatless, inhuman shriek, sharp and short, very clear and cold. The note itself possessed a minor, metallic quality that he had never heard before. Klausner looked around him, searching instinctively for the source of the noise. The woman next door was the only living thing in sight. He saw her reach down, take a rose stem in the fingers of one hand, and snip the stem with a pair of scissors. Again he heard the scream.

It came at the exact moment when the rose stem was cut.

At this point, the woman straightened up, put the scissors in the basket with the roses, and turned to walk away.

"Mrs. Saunders!" Klausner shouted, and his voice was high and shrill with excitement. "Oh, Mrs. Saunders!"

The woman looked around, and she saw her neighbor standing on his lawn—a fantastic, arm-waving little person with a pair of earphones on his head—calling to her in a voice so high and loud that she became alarmed.

"Cut another one! Please cut another one quickly!"

She stood still, staring at him. "Why, Mr. Klausner," she said, "what's the matter?"

"Please do as I ask," he said. "Cut just one more rose!"

Mrs. Saunders had always believed her neighbor to be a rather peculiar person; now it seemed . . . it seemed that he had gone completely crazy. She wondered whether she should run into the house and fetch her husband. No, she thought. No, he's harmless. I'll just humor him. "Certainly, Mr. Klausner, if you like," she said. She took her scissors from the basket, bent down, and snipped another rose.

Again Klausner heard that frightful throatless shriek in the earphones; again it came at the exact moment the rose stem was cut. He took off the earphones and ran to the fence that separated the two gardens. "All right," he said. "That's enough. No more. Please, no more."

The woman stood there holding the yellow rose that she had just cut, looking at him.

"I'm going to tell you something, Mrs. Saunders," he said, "something that you won't believe." He put his hands on the top of the fence and peered at her intently through his thick spectacles. "You have, this evening, cut a basketful of roses. You have, with a sharp pair of scissors, cut through the stems of living things and each rose that you cut screamed in the most terrible way. Did you know that, Mrs. Saunders?"

"No," she said. "I certainly didn't know that."

"It happens to be true," he said. He was breathing rather rapidly, but he was trying to control his excitement. "I heard them shrieking. Each time you cut one I heard the cry of pain. A very high-pitched sound, approximately one hundred and thirty-two thousand vibrations a second. You couldn't possibly have heard it yourself. But I heard it."

"Did you really, Mr. Klausner?" She decided she would make a dash for the house in about five seconds.

"You might say," he went on, "that a rosebush has no nervous system to feel with, no throat to cry with. You'd be right. It hasn't. Not like ours, anyway. But *how do you know*, Mrs. Saunders"—and there he leaned far over the fence and spoke in a fierce whisper—"*how do you know* that a rosebush doesn't feel as much pain when someone cuts its stem in two as you would feel if someone cut your wrist off with a garden shears? *How do you know that?* It's alive, isn't it?"

"Yes, Mr. Klausner. Oh, yes—and good night," and quickly she turned and ran up the garden to her house. Klausner went back to the table. He put on the earphones and stood for a while listening. He could still hear the faint spasmodic crackling sound and the humming noise of the machine. But nothing more. Slowly he bent down and took hold of a small white daisy growing on the lawn. He took it between thumb and forefinger and slowly pulled it upward and sideways until the stem broke.

From the moment that he started pulling to the moment when the stem broke, he heard—he distinctly heard in the earphones—a faint, high-pitched cry, curiously inanimate. He took another daisy and did it again. Once more he heard the cry, but he wasn't so sure now that it expressed *pain*. No, it wasn't pain; it was surprise. Or was it? It didn't really express any of the feelings or emotions known to a human being. It was just crying, a neutral, stony cry—a single, emotionless note, expressing nothing. It had been the same with the roses. He had been wrong in calling it a cry of pain. A flower probably didn't feel pain. It felt something else which we didn't know about—something called toin or spurl or plinuckment, or anything you like.

He stood up and removed the earphones. It was getting dark and he could see pricks of light shining in the windows of the dark houses all around him. Carefully, he picked up the black box from the table, carried it into the shed, and put it on the workbench. Then he went out, locked the door behind him, and walked up to the house.

The next morning, Klausner was up as soon as it was light. He dressed and went straight to the shed. He picked the machine up and carried it outside, clasping it to his chest with both hands, walking unsteadily under its weight. He went past the house, out through the front gate, and across the road to the park. There he paused and looked around him; then he went on until he came to a large tree, a beech tree, and placed the machine on the ground, close to the trunk of the tree. Quickly he went back to the house and got an axe from the coal cellar and carried it across the road into the park. He put the axe on the ground beside the tree.

Then he looked around him again, peering nervously through his thick glasses in every direction. There was no one about. It was six in the morning.

He put the earphones on his head and switched on the machine. He listened for a moment to the faint familiar humming sound; then he picked up the axe, took a stance with his legs wide apart, and swung the axe as hard as he could at the base of the tree trunk. The blade cut deep into the wood and stuck there, and at the instant of impact he heard a most extraordinary noise in the earphones. It was a new noise, unlike any he had heard before—a harsh, noteless, enormous noise, a growling, low-pitched, screaming sound, not quick and short like the noise of the roses, but drawn out, like a sob, lasting for fully a minute, loudest at the moment when the axe struck, fading gradually, fainter and fainter, until it was gone.

Klausner stared in horror at the place where the blade of the axe had sunk into the woodflesh of the tree; then gently, he took the axe handle, worked the blade loose, and threw the thing on the ground. With his fingers he touched the gash that the axe had made in the wood, touching the edges of the gash, trying to press them together to close the wound, and he kept saying, "Tree . . . oh, tree . . . I am sorry . . . I am so sorry . . . but it will heal . . . It will heal fine . . ."

For a while he stood there with his hands upon the trunk of the great tree; then suddenly he turned away and hurried off out of the park, across the road, through the front gate, and back into his house. He went to the telephone, consulted the book, dialed a number, and waited. He held the receiver tightly in his left hand and tapped the table impatiently with his right. He heard the telephone buzzing at the other end, and then the click of a lifted receiver and a man's voice, a sleepy voice, saying, "Hullo. Yes?"

"Dr. Scott?" he said.

"Yes. Speaking."

"Dr. Scott. You must come at once—quickly please."

"Who is it speaking?"

"Klausner here, and you remember what I told you last night about my experiments with sound and how I hoped I might—"

"Yes, yes, of course, but what's the matter? Are you ill?"

"No, I'm not ill, but—"

"It's half past six in the morning," said the Doctor, "and you call me, but you are not ill."

"Please come. Come quickly. I want someone to hear it. It's driving me mad! I can't believe it . . ."

The Doctor heard the frantic, almost hysterical note in the man's voice, the same note he was used to hearing in the voices of people who called up and said, "There's been an accident. Come quickly." He said slowly, "You really want me to get out of bed and come over now?"

"Yes, now. At once please."

"All right then, I'll come."

Klausner sat down beside the telephone and waited. He tried to remember what the shriek of the tree had sounded like, but he couldn't. He could remember only that it had made him feel sick with horror. He tried to imagine what sort of noise a human would make if he had to stand anchored to the ground while someone deliberately swung a small sharp thing at his leg so that the blade cut in deep and wedged itself in the cut. Same sort of noise perhaps? No. Quite different. The noise of the tree was worse than any known human noise, because of that frightening, toneless, throatless quality. He began to wonder about other living things, and he thought immediately of a field of wheat, a field of wheat standing up straight and yellow and alive, with the mower going through it, cutting the stems, five hundred stems a second, every second. Oh, my God, what would the noise be like? Five hundred wheat plants screaming together, and every second another five hundred being cut and screaming and no, he thought, no I do not want to go to a wheat field with my machine. I would never eat bread after that. But what about potatoes and cabbages and carrots and onions? And what about apples? Ah, no! Apples are all right. They fall off naturally when they are ripe. Apples are all right if you let them fall off instead of tearing them from the tree branch. But not vegetables. Not a potato for example. A potato would surely shriek; so would a carrot and an onion and a cabbage . . .

He heard the click of the front-gate latch and he jumped

up and went out and saw the tall doctor coming down the path, his little black bag in hand.

"Well," the Doctor said. "Well, what's all the trouble?"

"Come with me, Doctor. I want you to hear it. I called you because you're the only one I've told. It's over the road in the park. Will you come now?"

The Doctor looked at him. He seemed calmer now. There was no sign of madness or hysteria; he was merely disturbed and excited. "All right, I'll come," the Doctor said. They went across the road, into the park and Klausner led the way to the great beech tree at the foot of which stood the long, black coffin-box of the machine—and the axe.

"Why did you bring the machine out here?" asked the Doctor.

"I wanted a tree. There aren't any big trees in the garden."

"And why the axe?"

"You'll see in a moment. But now please put on these earphones and listen. Listen carefully and tell me afterwards precisely what you hear. I want to make quite sure . . ."

The Doctor smiled and took the earphones, which he put over his ears.

Klausner bent down and flicked the switch on the panel of the machine; then he picked up the axe and took his stance with his legs apart, ready to swing. For a moment, he paused. "Can you hear anything?" he said to the Doctor.

"Can I what?"

"Can you *hear* anything?"

"Just a humming noise."

Klausner stood there with the axe in his hands, trying to bring himself to swing, but the thought of the noise that the tree would make made him pause again.

"What are you waiting for?" the Doctor asked.

"Nothing," Klausner answered, and then he lifted the axe and swung it at the tree; and as he swung, he thought he felt, he could swear he felt a movement of the ground on which he stood. He felt a slight shifting of the earth beneath his feet, as though the roots of the tree were moving underneath the soil, but it was too late to check the blow, and the axe blade struck the tree and wedged deep into the wood. At that moment, high overhead, there was the cracking sound of wood splintering and the swishing sound of leaves brushing against other leaves and they both looked up and the Doctor cried, "Watch out! Run, man! Quickly run!"

The Doctor had ripped off the earphones and was running away fast, but Klausner stood spellbound, staring up at the great branch, sixty feet long at least, that was bending slowly downward, breaking and cracking and splintering at its thickest point, just where it joined the main trunk of the tree. The branch came crashing down, and Klausner leaped just in time. It fell upon the machine and smashed it into pieces.

"Great heavens!" shouted the Doctor as he came running back. "That was a near one! I thought it had got you!"

Klausner was staring at the tree. His large head was leaning to one side and upon his smooth white face there was a tense, horrified expression. Slowly he walked up to the tree and gently he pried the blade loose from the trunk.

"Did you hear it?" he said, turning to the Doctor. His voice was barely audible.

The Doctor was still out of breath from the running and the excitement. "Hear what?"

"In the earphones. Did you hear anything when the axe struck?"

The Doctor began to rub the back of his neck. "Well," he said, "as a matter of fact . . ." He paused and frowned and bit his lower lip. "No, I'm not sure. I couldn't be sure. I don't suppose I had the earphones on for more than a second after the axe struck."

"Yes, yes, but what did you hear?"

"I don't know," the Doctor said. "I don't know what I heard. Probably the noise of the branch breaking." He was speaking rapidly, rather irritably.

"What did it sound like?" Klausner leaned forward slightly, staring hard at the Doctor. "Exactly what did it sound like?"

"Oh, hell!" the Doctor said. "I really don't know. I was more interested in getting out of the way. Let's leave it."

"Dr. Scott, what—did—it—sound—like?"

"For God's sake, how could I tell, what with half the tree falling on me and having to run for my life?" The Doctor certainly seemed nervous. Klausner had sensed it now. He stood quite still, staring at the Doctor, and for fully half a minute he didn't speak. The Doctor moved his feet, shrugged his shoulders, and half turned to go. "Well," he said, "we'd better get back."

"Look," said the little man, and now his smooth white face became suddenly suffused with color. "Look," he said, "you stitch this up." He pointed to the last gash the axe had made in the tree trunk. "You stitch this up quickly."

"Don't be silly," the Doctor said.

"You do as I say. Stitch it up." Klausner was gripping the axe handle and he spoke softly, in a curious, almost a threatening tone.

"Don't be silly," the Doctor said. "I can't stitch through wood. Come on. Let's get back."

"So you can't stitch through wood?"

"No, of course not."

"Have you got any iodine in your bag?"

"Yes, of course."

"Then paint the cut with iodine. It'll sting, but that can't be helped."

"Now, look," the Doctor said, and again he turned as if to go. "Let's not be ridiculous. Let's get back to the house and then . . ."

"Paint—the—cut—with—iodine."

The Doctor hesitated. He saw Klausner's hands tightening on the handle of the axe. He decided that his only alternative was to run away fast, and he certainly wasn't going to do that.

"All right," he said. "I'll paint it with iodine."

He got his black bag which was lying on the grass about ten yards away, opened it, and took out a bottle of iodine and some cotton. He went up to the tree trunk, uncorked the bottle, tipped some of the iodine onto the cotton wool, bent down, and began to dab it into the cut. He kept one eye on Klausner, who was standing motionless with the axe in his hands, watching the Doctor.

"Make sure you get it right in."

"Yes," the Doctor said.

"Now do the other one, the one just above it!"

The Doctor did as he was told. "There you are," he said. "It's done."

He straightened up and surveyed his work in a very serious manner. "That should do nicely."

Klausner came closer and gravely examined the two wounds.

"Yes," he said, nodding his huge head slowly up and down. "Yes, yes, yes, that will do nicely." He stepped back a pace. "You'll come and look at them tomorrow?"

"Oh, yes," the Doctor said. "Of course."

"And put some more iodine on?"

"If necessary, yes."

"Thank you, Doctor," Klausner said, and he nodded his

head again and he dropped the axe and all at once he smiled, a wild, excited smile, and quickly the Doctor went over to him and gently he took him by the arm and he said, "Come on, we must go now," and suddenly they were walking away, the two of them, walking silently, rather hurriedly, across the park, over the road, back to the house.

Roald Dahl (1916–   )
Born in Wales of Norwegian parents, Roald Dahl is now a resident of Britain. He has, however, spent much of his life in the United States. He was transferred to Washington, D.C., during World War II, as a result of injuries suffered in the Royal Air Force, and began writing flying stories. But he soon changed over to the type of poisonously chilling story, such as "Man from the South" (1953) and "Royal Jelly" (1960), for which he has become famous. In a much lighter vein, he has also produced several children's novels such as The Gremlins (1943) and Charlie and the Chocolate Factory (1964)—the latter of which was filmed as Willie Wonka and the Chocolate Factory (1971).

PERCEPTION

HALLUCINATION ORBIT
J. T. McIntosh

Ord sat in his swivel chair and surveyed the Solar System. The clarity of vision, unimpeded by the two-hundred-mile curtain of Earth's atmosphere, was such that, from his position in Pluto's orbit, he could see with the naked eye every one of the planets except Pluto itself, hiding in a cluster of bright stars, and Mercury, eclipsed at the moment by the Sun.

But then, Ord knew exactly where to look. Every day, for over two thousand days, he had looked out on the Solar System. He had seen Mercury scuttle round the Sun twenty-five times; Venus, more sedately, nine; Earth had made six of the familiar trips through space that meant years; Mars was on its fourth journey; but Jupiter wasn't more than halfway around yet.

"It helps, I suppose, to be able to see them," said a light, whimsical voice behind him. Even when Una said the most serious things, which was often, her voice laughed. "If you hadn't been able to see the planets, you'd have been a straitjacket case long ago."

"Who knows I'm not one now?" Ord asked. "You don't, anyway."

He didn't turn yet. He postponed the moment when he would, dragging it out almost ecstatically from second to second—like a heavy smoker halting, pausing deliberately in anticipation, cigarette in mouth, before lighting it.

"I think," she retorted, the laughter in her voice as ever, "that so long as you talk sanely about madness, you can't be so far gone."

The moment came. He couldn't wait forever. He swung around and looked at her with a slow, ironical smile. He had known more beautiful women, but none, perhaps, who knew their limitations as well as she did.

Una always wore that spotless white shirt, open-necked and tucked tightly into the waistband of her sharply creased bottle-green slacks. Perhaps it was pessimistic to think the worst of what one didn't know, but Ord took it for granted that Una's only good points of figure were the neat waist and upper half and the length of leg that her customary outfit displayed.

There was a slight irregularity about her forehead which she treated adroitly by always having a cascade of her beautiful ash-blonde hair over one side of her face. Her teeth were splendid in a subtle half-smile; she never allowed herself more. There was just a hint at the top button of her chaste, impeccable shirt that her skin wasn't all of a uniform satin smoothness, but suspicion was never allowed to grow to certainty.

"How long now, Colin?" Una asked. "I don't watch time as you do. Where could they be, if they started whenever the beam failed?"

"I haven't worked it out since you asked the last time." He couldn't still the tremor in his voice. "But they could be very close."

There was a hint of regret in her nod.

Ord looked past her at the blank wall opposite the observation windows. He wasn't cramped.

The space station three billion six hundred million miles from the Sun was designed for one man who would always be alone, who would spend two years in his own company for the somewhat fabulous salary of a space station officer, and everything had been done to make the quarters seem roomy and comfortable without giving a chilling impression of emptiness. There was the observatory, the machine room, the lounge, the workshop, the bedroom, the bathroom, the storerooms, even a spare room into which Una disappeared, though it had not been provided for Una or anyone like her.

As Ord looked at the blank wall, he was thinking of the activity on Earth, six years before, when one of the three Pluto directional radio beams had failed. There were plenty of beams left to guide ships through space, but the sudden failure of Station Two's beam must have had some effect on almost every interplanetary trip. Five minutes on the Moon trip, at certain times; two or three days on journeys to Mars or Venus, depending on the relative positions of the starting point, destination, and the two remaining Pluto beams; weeks, even months more required for the run to some of the asteroids and the satellites of the outer planets.

Two spokes of the directional wheel remained, but that left a great gaping angle of a hundred and twenty degrees, served only feebly by the beams from ships' destinations, with no powerful universal beam to reinforce them.

The situation was not new. Someday there would be so many line-of-flight beams in the Solar System that ships wouldn't have to know the beams they were on. They would merely point their noses where they wanted to go and cast off, like so many galleons sailing before the wind. But as yet there was not enough interplanetary travel to make the duplication of beams practicable.

If a beam failed, it failed, and more than six years had to pass before it could be put in operation again, unless the failure occurred at a convenient time—when a ship was well on the way to relieve a station officer and check the equipment, say. Through history, however, failure of anything man-made had tended to come almost always at the most inconvenient times.

Ord followed the ship in his mind through its six-year journey. A week to prepare. Two days to reach the Moon. Three weeks for the run to Mars, which would have been sixteen days if Station Two had been sending out its beam. Then trouble. Only the little Ganymede beam, in the positions of the planets and their satellites at the time, to help the repair ship on its way from Mars. Almost nine months to Jupiter. But at least, by that time, the ship would have some velocity to help the rockets on the remaining three billion two hundred million miles . . . and the long, dreary search for the silent speck in space that was the space station.

Eleven months altogether, with the beam; over six years without it.

One thing that helped Ord bear the extra five years of solitude he had to spend aboard the station, thousands of millions of miles from the nearest man, was the thought of the accumulated pay he would collect. The station officers were necessary, and the various space lines had to accept responsibility for them.

He would be set up for life, at twenty-nine, when he got back to Earth at last.

Una shrugged. "Oh, well, it's been nice knowing you. And I mean that."

"It would be for you, Una. But that was because of the others before you. I learned a lot."

"You've just broken rule one," she said lightly. "Never talk of 'the others.' Just be careful you don't break rule two."

"What rule is that?"

"You should know. You want me to break it? Most particularly, never talk of any others to come."

She made a gesture of dismissal, as if she were tearing the whole subject out of a notebook, crumpling it, and throwing it away.

"Shall we play chess?" she asked lightly. "It's a long time since we did."

"All right. But not here. Let's go into the lounge."

He led the way through the station as if she didn't know it as well as he did. He set up the pieces rapidly, through long practice. Una didn't sit down opposite him, but poised on the edge of the sofa. She always kept her long, graceful line intact.

They had just made the first oblique reference to something which had been growing for a long time. Undoubtedly Ord was growing tired of Una. It was nobody's fault, or his, insofar as it was anyone's. There was a hint of farewell in the chess game. One for the road, so to speak.

Una played quickly and decisively. One particularly rapid move brought the usual complaint from Ord.

"I wish you'd pay more attention," he protested. "If you win, I look silly, taking so much time to think things out. And if I win, you lose nothing because you obviously weren't trying."

Una laughed. "It's just a game," she answered.

She won the first game. "Luck," Ord grunted, without heat. "You never saw the danger of that rook to bishop's fourth."

"Perhaps not. But look how well I followed it up, so it really doesn't matter, does it?"

They played the inevitable second game, and inevitably, also, Ord won it. Like all chess players who have won a game they knew they could win when and how they wished, he felt relaxed and pleased with himself.

He yawned.

Una rose. "I can take a hint," she said.

"No, please . . ."

She smiled at him and disappeared into her room.

Ord spent a long time looking at the blank door. He had been warned against solitosis (Latin *solitarius*, from *solus*, and the Greek *-osis*), but for him it wasn't so bad. He still knew the truth; perhaps that was it. After all this time, he was still in no danger of really believing what was not so. For example . . .

He got up and went through to the machine room. Among other things, this room presented a complete picture of conditions throughout the entire station from moment to moment. He could sit before the dials and switches and meters and check on everything from the outside temperature to the air pressure in the farthest storeroom.

He could see quite plainly, for example, that the temperature in Una's room, as of that moment, was minus 110 degrees Centigrade. A long way above absolute zero, certainly—but a long way below comfortable bedroom temperature. Moreover, the air pressure was only eight pounds.

In a word, though he had seen Una enter the room, he might see her come out of it again. But Una wasn't there. The door had never been open.

There was no Una.

Knowing that fact was a big factor. Long ago, he had feared a time when he wouldn't know such things. He still feared it now and then.

Yet if he pressurized the spare room, raised its temperature, and then walked in, he would see Una asleep in the bed. If he touched her, she would be real. If he slapped her face with his hand, his palm would sting, and she would awaken, resentful. If he stabbed her, she would die, and he would have to take the trouble of burying her out in space.

That was all real—to him.

But he could see and appreciate the facts indicated by the dials. Even though he was tired of Una, however, he could not merely tell her to vanish and she would be gone. He had had to provide a ship to bring her here, and he would have to provide another to take her away.

Solitosis was no new thing; it had been discovered soon after space flight. Unfortunately, no one had so far discovered what to do about it, except remove the conditions that produced it. Space is not merely a void; it's emptier than that—empty of horizon, sky, soft sunlight, ground and greenery and buildings, empty of time and continuity of one's history, either as an individual or member of the human race. Worst of all, it's empty of people. A hermit may deliberately escape civilization, but leave him alone on a deserted world and he turns psychotic. That, in short, is solitosis.

There was a reason for the fact that there was a space station officer—he could handle the maintenance of the station—and a reason for the fact that there was only one. Two men together were not enough to protect each other from solitosis. The critical number was about forty. But to leave forty men on a space station was uneconomic. To leave fewer, yet more than one, was dangerous to all, for solitosis could be homicidal.

The natural solution was to leave one man, who would naturally become a solitosis victim, but generally didn't harm himself and could be restored to complete sanity when he was relieved—simply by returning him to Earth.

It was simple. It worked. Of course, station officers had to be paid to take two years of insanity. It was rarely completely pleasant or completely unpleasant. The result took different forms, but always there were pleasures and pains.

No station officer was ever in a position to know what he was in for before he signed on, for no man was allowed to subject himself to solitosis twice.

But Ord was more interested in the problem of Una. He knew, of course, that he wouldn't work any solution out and do something about it. His particular brand of solitosis didn't work like that. Certainly, somewhere in his mind, a decision was being reached. But what that was was hidden from him. He had to wait and see what happened. But being tired of Una, he knew the general lines.

Putting on his suit, Ord went outside. Fifty years before, scores of ships had come in on the beam from the station, which had been held on its course by six freighters. Each ship in the fleet had dragged or pushed a lump of rock that nobody wanted, for the station, when complete, had to have mass. Gradually, a planet was built—a very small planet, but enough to form a base for the station and enable it to follow Pluto in its orbit with a minimum expenditure of power. The station on Pluto itself was already in operation, and Station Three was being set up concurrently.

Bouncing gently over the rocks of the dark, airless world that was only big enough to hold a small ship to its surface, Ord paused at the tiny cruiser Una had used. It was as real as she was, no more, no less. He forgot the details of the story that explained Una's arrival. It was so completely preposterous that any girl should arrive alone at any space station, in any kind of ship, that he hadn't bothered to think up a convincing explanation. Una, like the others, just appeared. She had had a story which she was prepared to tell, but he had cut it short. That was most satisfactory all around.

The ship, he saw, was not obviously damaged. He jumped up on the hull experimentally. He thought that he landed on it and stood twelve feet above the surface of the planet.

He searched hazily for an explanation. Perhaps he had picked a spur of rock and made it the ship. Perhaps his eyes manufactured twelve feet of height. He had never inspected the ship closely, and he didn't now; it would only demand a lot of tiring mental effort. He wouldn't know consciously that he was constructing everything he saw, but that was what he would be doing.

He bounced back to the station and into the airless machine room to examine the beam equipment once more. There was nothing seriously wrong with it. He could repair it in a few hours if he had the tools and six hands, which was more than most space station officers could say.

That was the difficulty about a job like Ord's—station

officers had to be experienced. But how could they be experienced when they could never have done the job before?

He cast a last glance around the machine room and left.

Ord did think of going back to Una's ship, finding something wrong, and repairing it, so that it would be possible for her to go. But that would be humoring his solitosis. He still preferred to be as sane as possible.

He had involuntarily produced men as companions once, but it hadn't worked. He could never become sufficiently interested in their physical appearance to make them real. He might talk with them and enjoy talking, but they were always ghosts and looked it. The women had never been ghosts.

In fact, he had been afraid, once, that the time would come when he would actually believe in them. And, of course, he had often explored the possibility that when someone *actually* came, he would think it was part of another hallucination. But there seemed little reason to fear that while it was still so easy to prove to himself that he was alone at the station.

He took off his suit and washed and shaved carefully, having decided, long since, that the normal habits of human existence should be carefully preserved. He dressed neatly, though the station was warm and there was no real need for clothes, and, when he slept, he wore pajamas.

There had been a time—the time of Suzy and Margo— when the apparent life at the station was what might have been expected of a solitary man. But he discovered, quite plainly and simply, that there were too many complications. Una had perhaps been too much of a swing in the other direction. His relations with her, Ord thought wryly, wouldn't have been out of place in a Victorian book for boys or girls, except that he didn't mind her smoking.

He slept for twelve hours. Once he wakened, half convinced he had heard something, but he was sleepy, didn't want to move, and had no intention of pandering to his own neurosis.

It was not until he had been up for hours that he began to wonder why Una didn't appear. Perhaps she was ill. Perhaps, though he didn't think of it that way, he had decided unconsciously to have her die on him, lingeringly and effectively.

He sighed, went to the machine room, and brought the temperature and air pressure of Una's room to normal. Then he went in.

She was gone, but her perfume lingered in the air. He went to the observation room and looked for her ship. It was gone, too.

He was a little disgusted, but he didn't blame himself. It was easier and more satisfactory to blame Una. She might at least have said good-by. All in all, he had liked her. He would have liked to meet the real Una, if there was one somewhere. He had tired of her chiefly because she had never become a genuine, credible character. She had always been true to style, whereas real people weren't.

He stayed in the observatory and looked for a ship. He smiled at the thought that what he believed to be a ship, bringing another girl with another fantastic story of being lost in space, might turn out to be the relief ship.

He was glad his solitosis had not taken the form that Benson's had. Benson had lost all sense of time. He had spent millions of subjective years waiting for the relief ship, though Benson only had to wait the regulation two years. Benson hadn't minded much. He thought he had turned into a mental giant. As it turned out, his functioning IQ had really gone up fifteen points. It came down again eleven points, but certainly Benson had no reason to regret his two years of solitude. Nevertheless, Ord was glad it hadn't taken him the same way.

As he expected, the ship was there, curving in for a landing. It wasn't the relief ship, since it was too small. It was, in fact, far too small to be capable of the trip from Earth with no beam to assist it.

Ord was on the merry-go-round again. If he hadn't done a good job on the last hours of Una, he had made up for it with the first few hours of whoever it was. The little ship overshot, handled exactly as women often handled spacecraft. It took a long, five-hour sweep that had Ord biting his nails. Moreover, it wasn't a rocket ship at all. Perhaps this time the girl—naturally, it would be a girl—had an explanation for the impossible to beat all explanations. She was certainly keeping him in suspense.

But at last the ship was down, and Ord, already in his spacesuit, hurried out to it. A figure emerged as he reached it, and through the faceplate he saw a face which was clear from the start.

The girl gestured toward the ship, uselessly. He indicated the space station. She shook her head inside the huge helmet, pointing to the ship. He was puzzled. This was new.

Suddenly, to indicate her meaning, she bent down and lifted the end of the ship, then looked up at him. He understood at last. She was afraid it wasn't safe to leave the ship there. She thought it might blow away.

He laughed and tried to reassure her without words. It was true enough that even a light breeze might be enough to break the feeble attraction of the planet for the ship. But on a tiny man-made world, with no atmosphere, that was no problem. He demonstrated, getting below the ship and heaving it. It sailed up slowly, and for a moment Ord almost shared the girl's fear that it would never return. But then gravity caught it and the ship returned gently. It was clear that it would take considerable force to break the hold of the small world on it.

The girl turned from it, ready to go with Ord to the space station.

Ord shut the airlock and began to divest himself of his suit. The girl, however, still wasn't satisfied. She looked about for meters to assure herself that the pressure was sufficient. Gravely, Ord pointed them out. Then she opened her helmet and took a slow, cautious breath.

"You must be Baker," she said.

That was another shock. Baker was the previous officer, and Ord had all but forgotten his name—actually, until she mentioned it, the name had been forgotten. For a moment, Ord wondered wildly if the girl was one of Baker's dreams, seven years late. But Baker's solitosis hadn't taken that form.

"No, Ord," he said. "Colin Ord."

"Before we go any further," she said, "just how does solitosis affect you?"

This, too, was new.

"Just makes me see things that aren't there," replied Ord cautiously.

"And you know there's nothing there?"

"Sometimes."

"Do you know I'm here?"

Ord grinned. "I'm not even wondering about it."

Suddenly the girl was holding a gun pointed at him.

"One thing you can be sure of," she told him. "This gun is here. I don't want to be unpleasant, but I think we should remove misunderstandings. I'm not God's little gift to lonely space station officers, and any time you do anything that indicates you think I am, this comes out and it may do some damage. That clear?"

"Very. I told you my name. What's yours?"

"Elsa Catterline. You want to know why I'm here, of course."

"Not particularly."

She looked up warily at that. But she went on lifting off her helmet and removing her spacesuit. Ord made no move to help her. There was always the possibility that it might really be dangerous.

"I'll tell you all the same," she continued. "I killed a man—why and how doesn't matter. I had access to an experimental ship. That one out there. I thought if I disappeared for about two years . . ."

"Don't labor over it," said Ord. "I'm not asking questions."

"I know. I wonder why."

She won her battle with the suit and emerged. Ord's eyes widened. She was beautiful, really beautiful, but he had expected that. The unexpected thing was that she wore the kind of outfit girls in magazine stories wore in similar circumstances—white nylon shorts and what might have been called the minimum bra.

Once there would have been nothing surprising in that, but for years he had been very careful and restrained. He had tried sex undiluted, and then had gone back to diluting it in self-protection. It was a long time since any of his girls had been so feminine and made it so obvious.

In fact, for the first time, he seriously considered the possibility that she was real. Real people were sometimes more fantastic than the wildest imaginings.

"I wonder," he said.

"Don't," she snapped.

"I was only thinking," he went on easily, "that you're going to have a tough time with that gun when you get tired of holding it. It's a heavy gun. Want me to get a gunbelt for you?"

She flushed angrily. She looked the kind of sweet-natured kid who could kill a man, at that. Her nose and eyes and mouth were exactly where she would have placed them herself for the best effect, if she could have done so, and everything about her was compact and perfect and made for efficiency. Not efficiency in handling a spaceship or even a gun, but efficiency in always getting what she wanted. Another thing to add to Ord's growing list of points of interest about Elsa Catterline was that she wasn't the kind of girl he would normally go for.

"The gun, if you don't mind my saying so," he said, "is a silly idea. What do you hope to accomplish with it? How long will it be before I take it from you? Two hours, perhaps, before you get careless. Even then I might wait for a still better chance. Sooner or later you have to sleep. Can you lock any door in my station and be sure I can't get in? I won't keep you in suspense—you can't." He shrugged. "But by all means try."

Unexpectedly, she threw away the gun and smiled at him.

"I'm not dumb," she told him. "That was for the time when I still wasn't sure you weren't violent. I think I can get on with you, Ord."

He nodded coldly. The pattern was clear now.

"I get it," he said.

The trouble was that it did nothing to settle the question of whether she was real or not. That she could be merely Una's successor was so obvious that there was no need to go into it. But it was also possible—unlikely, yet possible—that a girl of the type she seemed to be could have picked a space station as a hideout and could have acted as she had acted, was acting, and would act.

He was suddenly tired of the whole business. He wanted Earth. It had been a dull throb all this time, but now it flared to a mad longing, as it did every few months. It was all very well for Wordsworth to talk about that inward eye which is the bliss of solitude. Get Wordsworth out there and let him run a space station.

Ord wanted the presence of people about him that would keep him sane. He wanted to put women back in their place in his life. He wanted to be able to forget for hours, even days at a time, that there were such things as women.

Only twenty-four hours before, he had been congratulating himself that solitosis hadn't really got him. And now he didn't know whether Elsa was real or not. Either way, it was as bad. If she was real, he should have known it at once. If she was just another ghost, he should have known that, too.

"I'm going out to have a look at your ship," he said.

He thought she would object, but she merely shrugged.

"You might have left your suit on, then," she told him.

Twenty minutes later he was inside the little ship. He made no examination. That could come after he had settled something else. There was light and there was air. Fourteen pounds per square inch, the meters said.

He found a gasoline lighter and manipulated it clumsily with his big, semi-rigid gloves. The flame flared. But that meant nothing. If there was no lighter, and he saw it, he might also see it burn where there was no air.

There was a valve on his suit to test air pressure. He opened it. The little dial swung around to fourteen pounds. The question was, had he really opened the valve? He tried again, concentrating, making sure he really had hold of the valve. A half-turn was all that was necessary. Slowly, painfully, he turned it. He saw it turn. There was still cigarette smoke in the small, cramped quarters. He watched it swirl into the little box at his hip. The needle registered fourteen pounds.

He felt the sweat on his forehead. Trying to deceive

himself, to get a jump ahead of his own mind, he lunged out into the open and twisted the valve again. He told himself he was only testing it. He looked down.

No pressure.

He raised his heavy arms and stumbled like a sleepwalker back to the ship's airlock. Still keeping his arms raised, he entered the control room again. Only then did he look down.

The dial, untouched, still read no pressure. There was no air on the ship. There was no ship. Now that he knew that, he was able to open and close the valve.

Elsa was no more real than Una.

It was easier, then, to check and doublecheck. Very soon he was walking through the walls of the ship she had come in. It was simpler to check on it than on Elsa. She would remain real to the last, but the ship was only a minor part of the illusion.

He had had some bad moments in the last hour. It had become all too clear that he was losing his last defenses in his fight for sanity in insanity. He had won his battle again, but perhaps this was the last time he would win it. The next time he might fail to prove the illusion. That, after this, wouldn't necessarily prove the reality.

Elsa was finished. She had been too real and not real enough. Why had he ever let Una go?

He plodded back to the station and removed his suit. He found Elsa in the lounge, squatting on her heels and looking like a magazine cover.

"Out," he said bluntly. "It was a mistake your coming here. I'm sorry."

There was a flash of movement as she dived for the gun. Just in time he tensed himself, reminding himself of what he had learned, and when she fired at him he felt nothing.

He grinned back at her.

"The instinct of self-preservation is too strong," he said. "I can't let myself be shot, whatever happens."

He stepped forward. She fought him for the gun. She bit his wrist, and it hurt. But he got the gun.

"If you shoot me, nothing happens," he pointed out. "But if I shoot you, you die. You know that?"

She nodded sullenly and got up, put on her suit, and left.

In twenty minutes, her ship took off. Ord didn't even watch it out of sight.

He still held the gun in his hand. He threw it in a drawer. It would remain there until he forgot it. Then there would be no gun.

From now on, he decided, there would be no surrender to solitosis. There would be no more Elsas or Suzys or Margos. When he weakened, he would bring Una back, or he might have another try at male companionship.

For days, he thought he was winning his battle. He slept well, and he remained alone. He spent a lot of time in the observation room, but he never saw a ship.

The trouble was that the fight was not on the conscious level of his mind. There would be no warning before he would suddenly see a ship, without having taken any conscious decision. Then it would be too late to tell himself there was no ship.

It came at last. There was a tiny point of light moving visibly. As soon as he saw it, he left the observation room and fought with himself. He might convince the other part of his mind that it was a mistake, and when he went back to the observation room it would be a mistake—the moving point of light would be gone. It had happened before.

But solitosis was progressive, he thought dully, as he stood in the observation room four hours later and saw the ship. If it didn't get you under in one year, it did it in two.

Or four or six. Una, intelligent and restrained, had been the last stand of a mind under constant fire. Una was part of the disease, yes, but disease still controlled firmly and confidently. When he let Una go, he had been giving up.

The ship this time was a lifeboat from a larger vessel. That wasn't new. Suzy had come in a lifeboat. So had Dorothy, later, from the same mythical ship.

Ord stood and watched it land, concentrating so that his hair tingled with sweat. He wasn't trying to exorcise the ship; that would have been impossible. He was merely building into himself a powerful, binding resolve to know on this and all future occasions the truth from the lie. He would not drive the new visitor away as he had driven Elsa when he discovered she was another phantom. But he must know. Until Elsa came, he had always known. He mustn't lose that, whatever else he lost.

He saw a spacesuit figure emerge from the lifeboat, and then he went down to the airlock and waited.

He must be a hopeless romantic, he thought while he waited. Solitosis showed people a lot about themselves. There had been plenty of opportunity for realism, as opposed to romance, but he had never taken it.

The airlock opened. For a moment the face behind the plate of the helmet was shadowy and ill-defined. Then it cleared gradually like a lantern slide carefully focused, sharp and clear, on a screen.

Ord sighed in relief. He hadn't proved yet that the new girl was another wraith, but it was going to be possible, after all. With Elsa's face as clear from the first second as his own in a mirror, how could he know?

The girl opened her faceplate. "Colin Ord?" she said briskly. "I'm Dr. Lynn of Four Star Lines. Marilyn Lynn." She grinned, a friendly, put-you-at-your-ease grin. A professional grin—part of the bedside manner of a good doctor, male or female, young or old. "Cacophanous," she added, "but I've had quite a while to get used to it."

"Very nice," he said. "First remark of second castaway on desert island. Do you tell me the rest of the story straight away, or are you going to be coy?"

She frowned—putting the fresh patient in his place.

"I'm not going to tell you anything," she said, "until I've found out a little more about you."

"Excellent!" Ord answered. "Tone, inflection, and diction just right. It all fits."

He saw with further relief that she was of the Una type. She was beautiful, naturally, but not fantastic. And as she stripped off her suit, he saw that she wore slacks and a tunic, which was reasonable. She looked intelligent. She wasn't too young—at least his own age. Perhaps he was still the master.

She looked at him, too, with the eye of a diagnostician.

"Don't bother," he told her. "I see things that aren't there. Particularly people."

She nodded. "I see. So you don't believe I'm here?"

"Well, I ask you," he said skeptically. "Would you, if you were me?" He remembered a line of nonsense verse—Lear, probably—and quoted, "What would you do if you were me to prove that you were you?"

She was weighing the situation calmly. She didn't seem to mind Ord seeing what she was doing.

"Do you *know* I'm not real?" she asked.

"No. That comes with time. At least, it always has so far."

"You mean you've always proved to yourself that your—visitors were mere fantasy?"

"With a struggle," he admitted.

"Interesting. That looks like a case of controlled solitosis. I never heard of one before."

Ord laughed cynically. "That's right, feed my ego. It always comes to that in the end."

The girl gestured at her discarded suit. "You can't tell whether that's real or not?"

"Not at once. Eventually, yes—I hope."

He led her to the lounge. She looked around and nodded. She seemed pleased.

"Everything neat and tidy. You have no idea what a pleasure it is to meet you, Mr. Ord."

"That doesn't make you real," replied Ord rudely. "They all say that."

She looked at him in surprise. "Why should I want to make you accept me as real?" she asked.

It was like a physical blow. Ord had no idea why, but that didn't lessen the effect.

"That's right," he said slowly. "Why should you?"

"Tell me about the others," she suggested.

Like any good doctor, she gave the impression that what motivated her questions was not clinical but personal interest. The practicing doctor, Ord mused, was primarily an artist, not a scientist.

He told her. He edited the story a little, but he told it fairly, with particular detail on Elsa and Una, his most recent companions.

"Una is interesting," Marilyn said. "She was the only one who knew everything that you do. She didn't let you talk about it, but she knew."

Automatically, Ord began to make coffee. Marilyn watched him.

"When will you know whether I'm real or not?" she asked casually.

"Can't say. Perhaps in five minutes, perhaps not for hours. I—"

"Don't tell me how you do it," she said quickly. "Not yet. Do it first. Does it involve me? I mean, you don't shoot me to see if I die, or anything, do you?"

He grinned. "Nothing like that. If I shot you, you would die—like the witches in history. They died if they were, and they died if they weren't."

"Your mind has remained agile enough."

"Naturally. I never heard of solitosis inhibiting intelligence. Did you?"

She was significantly silent.

He raised his eyebrows. "You mean it often happens? Or always?"

"Not always. Frequently. It's pretty obvious, isn't it? The mind unbalanced naturally functions less well than the normal mind."

"Benson was the exception that proves the rule?"

She nodded. She knew who Benson was. That, like almost everything else, proved nothing.

She held up her cup before her. "Is this part of the test?" she asked. "Whether more coffee is actually drunk than you drink yourself?"

"No, that doesn't help. It would be very easy for me to make half what I thought I made, to bring out one cup and think I brought two, to take a nonexistent cup from a nonexistent girl, like this." He took it. "To fill it with nothing and pass it back, and later to . . ."

His words died, for he had seen something strange in her face. Horror or sadness or understanding, he couldn't be sure.

"What's the matter?" he asked.

"I don't know. Perhaps I misunderstood."

"Something I said?" he continued. "Easy to make half

what I thought I made . . . you knew about that, surely. And bringing out one cup when I thought I brought two. Nonexistent cup, nonexistent girl—it can't be because I called you a nonexistent girl, for we've been into that before. Naturally, if there's no cup I'd be careful, with part of my mind, not to pour coffee in it . . ."

He frowned. "There it is again. You tried not to show it this time. But I caught a faint shadow of it. Something I said or did frightened you, or makes you unhappy, or maybe just interests you. I'm not handing you imaginary coffee, am I? It seems real."

She was completely in control of herself again. She laughed. "No, not that. You're handing me real coffee, which means that part of your mind already knows I'm real. But it's the part you don't trust and can't touch."

"I'm not doing anything I don't know I'm doing, am I?"

She shook her head. "Since you're bound to think about it, whatever I say—it was just something you said. What you know you said. And it is not horrible or frightening and there's no earthly reason why it should make me sad. It's just something I didn't know."

"You won't tell me any more than that?"

She answered the question with another. "Don't your puppets do what you tell them?"

"No. You know that."

She put down the cup. "I'll wash the dishes," she said lightly. "Will that prove anything?"

"Sometimes, for an intelligent girl, you're very dumb," he said gloomily. "Next time they were used, I could just imagine they were washed, couldn't I?"

"Of course." Her eyes—brown eyes, deep-set under thin eyebrows—followed him as he rose suddenly. "Where are you going?"

"To find out if you're real."

"My ship. Go ahead."

Ord went to the airlock and put on his spacesuit. He thought for a while about what he might have said that brought that curious expression on Marilyn's face. But it was very clear that he could never, unaided, work out the problem. What he had said was so simple, so obviously true . . . and eventually she would tell him about it. It didn't matter.

There was nothing in what had happened so far, or what she had said, that settled the problem of the moment. Possibly, to add to all the other arguments against the possibility of Marilyn being a real woman, there was the consideration that, if she were, she would insist on it. But, after all, would she? She was a doctor, perhaps a psychiatrist. She knew solitosis.

A doctor of any kind, he told himself decidedly, encountering anyone with solitosis, would most certainly play along with him, telling him nothing, denying nothing, insisting on nothing.

That, he realized vaguely, was of vital importance. He was not at all sure why.

The test which had worked on Elsa's ship was as good as any, he thought. It might not work twice, but he would do his best to see that it did.

He opened the valve on his suit, making quite certain it registered atmosphere nil. Then he grasped his gloves together and strained his arms to pull them apart. When he opened the lifeboat's airlock, he kept his hands linked by his thumbs. In a few moments he stood in the control room of the little ship, which was the only room there, and his hands were still linked.

The needle registered fifteen pounds. A dull feeling of failure numbed him.

He had concentrated with all his power, making sure the

valve was really open and that he never had a chance to close it. He tried again, opening and closing it.

He might have known that each new scheme only worked once. He thought, trying to be calm.

Solitosis wasn't a suicidal psychosis, or at least he had heard it was never. He had seen it in books. One small indication of that had been when Elsa shot him and he felt nothing, though she had looked perfectly real. He could be hurt, as when she bit him, but not seriously.

He battered his fist against the bulkhead. There was no straight spur of rock that height where the ship had landed. A bulkhead was there, or there was nothing.

His glove was made to resist a vacuum, but it wasn't cushioned against impact. His hand hurt and went on hurting.

Grimly, he continued beating the bulkhead until he could not force himself to bear any more pain.

There was a bulkhead there. Therefore, there was a ship. His undamaged hand went to his faceplate. He hesitated, then reminded himself that solitosis wasn't suicidal. He opened the plate. He felt his nose, his eyes, his chin. He pinched his cheek.

The faceplate was open and he could breathe.

Only two possibilities were left. Either Marilyn and all that went with her were real, or he was over the top at last, absolutely in the grip of solitosis, so that he couldn't even be certain he had left the space station.

And if Marilyn was real . . .

He collapsed weakly as an insidious thought beat the spirit out of him. He was ready to believe in Marilyn, but there was one thing he could not ignore. Solitosis got everyone. People could fight it, but they could never hold it off. Yet it had very clearly not affected Marilyn. You knew solitosis when you saw it. Even he would know.

He could not say whether she existed subjectively or objectively—could he say whether the station existed, whether Earth existed, whether there was a Galaxy? Was there any essential difference between Una and his mother or his sister? Were they all creatures of his mind?

Life itself might be a thought in his mind. Matter could be merely a concept. He existed. "*I think, therefore I am.*" He could accept that. Could he accept anything else?

He forced himself fiercely back to normalcy, limiting himself to Marilyn. She existed, and because she came in a ship in which he could open his faceplate, she existed more than Una had.

Hanging determinedly on to that idea, he closed the plate and stumbled back to the station. It seemed very far away. He had taken too much out of himself. Mental effort could be even more exhausting than physical exertion. Whatever the truth might be, he had fought too hard toward it or away from it.

He got through the airlock into the station and, safely inside, fell on his face.

Twenty-four hours later, he knew that he had proved Marilyn's existence beyond reasonable doubt. He had been ill, and she had tended him.

"You proved what you wanted to prove," she told him, when the worst was over. "But was it worth it?"

"It was worth it," he said, sitting up in bed. "No wonder whole philosophies have been founded on reality. It's the most important thing there is to a man."

She shook her head, smiling.

"Merely to you," she said. "Solitosis naturally affects what matters most to the individual. But we needn't talk about that."

There was a warmth, a kindness about her that none of

the phantoms could ever have had, because they were all reflections of himself. He had made them what they were.

"How did you avoid solitosis?" he asked.

She smiled again. "The only way. There are fifty men and women in the Lioness, the relief ship. That number is well above the critical point. It will still be a while before they can land a big ship on this little world, but all the time while they're maneuvering, they'll be keeping me sane by being there. I know they are, you see. When you do, you'll improve."

Ord relaxed. Long, involved explanations were never satisfying. It was the simple explanation that one could instantly believe.

"That will take a while," he said. "I don't mind how long it takes."

He saw the same shadow pass across her face.

"Tell me," he said quietly.

"Look at me."

He looked. She was strong, quietly beautiful. She still wore her tunic and slacks. He even saw, with faint regret, that, while she wore no wedding ring, there was a white band on her finger where one would have been.

"Yes?" he urged.

"I didn't realize until you talked of a nonexistent girl," Marilyn said quietly. "I was real, yes, but not your picture of me.

"No, it's not so terrible," Marilyn went on. "Almost everything was as you thought. It's natural to send a doctor first to visit any sick person. I'm a doctor, and I was a girl once. But that was forty years ago. And you had to make me young and beautiful."

With an effort, Ord laughed naturally. "Was that all? You had me thinking—"

The old doctor didn't hear him. She wasn't thinking of her courage in coming to him alone, but remembered that all doctors take risks.

"It was pleasant to be a girl again," she said reflectively. "I could see myself in your eyes, and—almost—I was young again. I like you. If it hadn't been too completely ridiculous, I'd have fallen in love with you.

"As I grow old in the next few weeks, Ord," she told him, "you'll be recovering. It will show you how your case is progressing. When you see me as I really am, you'll be all right."

He put his hand gently on her arm. He was thinking of her courage in coming on ahead of the relief ship, alone, because she might be able to help a man who could not be quite sane.

"I think," he said, "I see you now as you really are."

J. T. McIntosh (1925–)

J. T. McIntosh is the pen name of Scottish author and newspaper editor James Murdoch MacGregor. He has also been a professional musician and schoolteacher. Since beginning to write in 1950, he has published approximately twenty science fiction novels and a hundred shorter works. He possesses considerable narrative skills, as well as an ability to delineate characters. Perhaps someday a publisher will be wise enough to issue a collection of his best work, but until then, readers should keep an eye out for "First Lady," "Made in U.S.A.," and "Immortality . . . for Some."

LEARNING
THE WINNER
Donald E. Westlake

Wordman stood at the window, looking out, and saw Revell walk away from the compound. "Come here," he said to the interviewer. "You'll see the Guardian in action."

The interviewer came around the desk and stood beside Wordman at the window. He said, "That's one of them?"

"Right." Wordman smiled, feeling pleasure. "You're lucky," he said. "It's rare when one of them even makes the attempt. Maybe he's doing it for your benefit."

The interviewer looked troubled. He said, "Doesn't he know what it will do?"

"Of course. Some of them don't believe it, not till they've tried it once. Watch."

They both watched. Revell walked without apparent haste, directly across the field toward the woods on the other side. After he'd gone about two hundred yards from the edge of the compound he began to bend forward slightly at the middle, and a few yards farther on he folded his arms across his stomach as though it ached him. He tottered, but kept moving forward, staggering more and more, appearing to be in great pain. He managed to stay on his feet nearly all the way to the trees, but finally crumpled to the ground, where he lay unmoving.

Wordman no longer felt pleasure. He liked the theory of the Guardian better than its application. Turning to his desk, he called the infirmary and said, "Send a stretcher out to the east, near the woods. Revell's out there."

The interviewer turned at the sound of the name, saying, "Revell? Is that who that is? The poet?"

"If you can call it poetry." Wordman's lips curled in disgust. He'd read some of Revell's so-called poems; garbage, garbage.

The interviewer looked back out the window. "I'd heard he was arrested," he said thoughtfully.

Looking over the interviewer's shoulder, Wordman saw that Revell had managed to get back up onto hands and knees, was now crawling slowly and painfully toward the woods. But a stretcher team was already trotting toward him and Wordman watched as they reached him, picked up the pain-weakened body, strapped it to the stretcher, and carried it back to the compound.

As they moved out of sight, the interviewer said, "Will he be all right?"

"After a few days in the infirmary. He'll have strained some muscles."

The interviewer turned away from the window. "That was very graphic," he said carefully.

"You're the first outsider to see it," Wordman told him, and smiled, feeling good again. "What do they call that? A scoop?"

"Yes," agreed the interviewer, sitting back down in his chair. "A scoop."

They returned to the interview, just the most recent of dozens Wordman had given in the year since this pilot project of the Guardian had been set up. For perhaps the fiftieth time he explained what the Guardian did and how it was of value to society.

The essence of the Guardian was the miniature black box, actually a tiny radio receiver, which was surgically inserted into the body of every prisoner. In the center of this prison compound was the Guardian transmitter, perpetually sending its message to these receivers. As long as a prisoner stayed within the hundred-and-fifty-yard range of that transmitter, all was well. Should he move beyond that range, the black box inside his skin would begin to send messages of pain throughout his nervous system. This pain increased as the prisoner moved farther from the transmitter, until at its peak it was totally immobilizing.

"The prisoner can't hide, you see," Wordman explained. "Even if Revell had reached the woods, we'd have found him. His screams would have led us to him."

The Guardian had been initially suggested by Wordman himself, at that time serving as assistant warden at a more ordinary penitentiary in the Federal system. Objections, mostly from sentimentalists, had delayed its acceptance for several years, but now at last this pilot project had been established, with a guaranteed five-year trial period, and Wordman had been placed in charge.

"If the results are as good as I'm sure they will be," Wordman said, "all prisons in the Federal system will be converted to the Guardian method."

The Guardian method had made jailbreaks impossible, riots easy to quell—by merely turning off the transmitter for a minute or two—and prisons simplicity to guard. "We have no guards here as such," Wordman pointed out. "Service employees only are needed here, people for the mess hall, infirmary, and so on."

For the pilot project, prisoners were only those who had committed crimes against the State rather than against individuals. "You might say," Wordman said, smiling, "that here are gathered the Disloyal Opposition."

"You mean, political prisoners," suggested the interviewer.

"We don't like that phrase here," Wordman said, his manner suddenly icy. "It sounds Commie."

The interviewer apologized for his sloppy use of terminology, ended the interview shortly afterward, and Wordman, once again in a good mood, escorted him out of the building. "You see," he said, gesturing. "No walls. No machine guns in towers. Here at last is the model prison."

The interviewer thanked him again for his time, and went away to his car. Wordman watched him leave, then went over to the infirmary to see Revell. But he'd been given a shot, and was already asleep.

Revell lay flat on his back and stared at the ceiling. He kept thinking, over and over again, "I didn't know it would be as bad as that. I didn't know it would be as bad as that." Mentally, he took a big brush of black paint and wrote the words on the spotless white ceiling: *"I didn't know it would be as bad as that."*

"Revell."

He turned his head slightly and saw Wordman standing beside the bed. He watched Wordman, but made no sign.

Wordman said, "They told me you were awake."

Revell waited.

"I tried to tell you when you first came," Wordman reminded him. "I told you there was no point trying to get away."

Revell opened his mouth and said, "It's all right, don't feel bad. You do what you have to do, I do what I have to do."

"Don't *feel* bad!" Wordman stared at him. "What have *I* got to feel bad about?"

Revell looked up at the ceiling, and the words he had painted there just a minute ago were gone already. He wished he had paper and pencil. Words were leaking out of him like water through a sieve. He needed paper and pencil to catch them in. He said, "May I have paper and pencil?"

"To write more obscenity? Of course not."

"Of course not," echoed Revell. He closed his eyes and watched the words leaking away. A man doesn't have time both to invent and memorize, he has to choose, and long ago Revell had chosen invention. But now there was no way to put the inventions down on paper and they trickled through his mind like water and eroded away into the great outside world. "Twinkle, twinkle, little pain," Revell said softly, "in my groin and in my brain, down so low and up so high, will you live or will I die?"

"The pain goes away," said Wordman. "It's been three days, it should be gone already."

"It will come back," Revell said. He opened his eyes and wrote the words on the ceiling. "It will come back."

Wordman said, "Don't be silly. It's gone for good unless you run away again."

Revell was silent.

Wordman waited, half-smiling, and then frowned. "You aren't," he said.

Revell looked at him in some surprise. "Of course I am," he said. "Didn't you know I would?"

"No one tries it twice."

"I'll never stop leaving. Don't you know that? I'll never stop leaving, I'll never stop being, I'll not stop believing I'm who I must be. You had to know that."

Wordman stared at him. "You'll go through it *again?*"

"Ever and ever," Revell said.

"It's a bluff." Wordman pointed an angry finger at Revell, saying, "If you want to die, I'll let you die. Do you know if we don't bring you back you'll die out there?"

"That's escape, too," Revell said.

"Is that what you want? All right. Go out there again, and I won't send anyone after you, that's a promise."

"Then you lose," Revell said. He looked at Wordman finally, seeing the blunt angry face. "They're your rules," Revell told him, "and by your own rules you're going to lose. You say your black box will make me stay, and that means the black box will make me stop being me. I say you're wrong. I say as long as I'm leaving you're losing, and if the black box kills me you've lost forever."

Spreading his arms, Wordman shouted, "Do you think this is a *game?*"

"Of course," said Revell. "That's why you invented it."

"You're insane," Wordman said. He started for the door. "You shouldn't be here, you should be in an asylum."

"That's losing, too," Revell shouted after him, but Wordman had slammed the door and gone.

Revell lay back on the pillow. Alone again, he could dwell once more on his terrors. He was afraid of the black box, much more now that he knew what it could do to him, afraid to the point where his fear made him sick to his stomach. But he was afraid of losing himself, too, this a more abstract and intellectual fear but just as strong. No, it was even stronger, because it was driving him to go out again.

"But I didn't know it would be as bad as that," he whispered. He painted it once more on the ceiling, this time in red.

Wordman had been told when Revell would be released from the infirmary, and he made a point of being at the door when Revell came out. Revell seemed somewhat leaner, perhaps a little older. He shielded his eyes from the sun with his hand, looked at Wordman, and said, "Good-bye, Wordman." He started walking east.

Wordman didn't believe it. He said, "You're bluffing, Revell."

Revell kept walking.

Wordman couldn't remember when he'd ever felt such anger. He wanted to run after Revell and kill him with his bare hands. He clenched his hands into fists and told himself he was a reasonable man, a rational man, a merciful man. As the Guardian was reasonable, was rational, was merciful. It required only obedience, and so did he. It punished only such purposeless defiance as Revell's, and so did he. Revell was antisocial, self-destructive, he had to learn. For his own sake, as well as for the sake of society. Revell had to be taught.

Wordman shouted, "What are you trying to get out of this?" He glared at Revell's moving back, listened to Revell's silence. He shouted, "I won't send anyone after you! You'll crawl back yourself!"

He kept watching until Revell was far out from the compound, staggering across the field toward the trees, his arms folded across his stomach, his legs stumbling, his head bent forward. Wordman watched, and then gritted his teeth, and turned his back, and returned to his office to work on the monthly report. Only two attempted escapes last month.

Two or three times in the course of the afternoon he looked out the window. The first time, he saw Revell far across the field, on hands and knees, crawling toward the trees. The last time, Revell was out of sight, but he could be heard screaming. Wordman had a great deal of trouble concentrating his attention on the report.

Toward evening he went outside again. Revell's screams sounded from the woods, faint but continuous. Wordman stood listening, his fists clenching and relaxing at his sides. Grimly he forced himself not to feel pity. For Revell's own good he had to be taught.

A staff doctor came to him a while later and said, "Mr. Wordman, we've got to bring him in."

Wordman nodded. "I know. But I want to be sure he's learned."

"For God's sake," said the doctor, "*listen* to him."

Wordman looked bleak. "All right, bring him in."

As the doctor started away, the screaming stopped. Wordman and the doctor both turned their heads, listened —silence. The doctor ran for the infirmary.

Revell lay screaming. All he could think of was the pain, and the need to scream. But sometimes, when he managed a scream of the very loudest, it was possible for him to have a fraction of a second for himself, and in those fractions of seconds he still kept moving away from the prison, inching along the ground, so that in the last hour he had moved approximately seven feet. His head and right arm were now visible from the country road that passed through these woods.

On one level, he was conscious of nothing but the pain and his own screaming. On another level, he was totally, even insistently, aware of everything around him, the blades of grass near his eyes, the stillness of the woods, the tree branches high overhead. And the small pickup truck, when it stopped on the road beyond him.

The man who came over from the truck and squatted beside Revell had a lined and weathered face and the rough clothing of a farmer. He touched Revell's shoulder and said, "You hurt, fella?"

"Eeeeast!" screamed Revell. "Eeeeast!"

"Is it okay to move you?" asked the man.

"Yesssss!" shrieked Revell. "Eeeeast!"

"I'd best take you to a doctor."

There was no change in the pain when the man lifted him and carried him to the truck and laid him down on the floor in back. He was already at optimum distance from the transmitter; the pain now was as bad as it could get.

The farmer tucked a rolled-up wad of cloth into Revell's open mouth. "Bite on this," he said. "It'll make it easier."

It made nothing easier, but it muffled his screams. He was grateful for that; the screams embarrassed him.

He was aware of it all, the drive through increasing darkness, the farmer carrying him into a building that was of colonial design on the outside but looked like the infirmary on the inside, and a doctor who looked down at him and touched his forehead and then went to one side to thank the farmer for bringing him. They spoke briefly over there, and then the farmer went away and the doctor came back to look at Revell again. He was young, dressed in laboratory white, with a pudgy face and red hair. He seemed sick and angry. He said, "You're from that prison, aren't you?"

Revell was still screaming through the cloth. He managed a head-spasm which he meant to be a nod. His armpits felt as though they were being cut open with knives of ice. The sides of his neck were being scraped by sandpaper. All of his joints were being ground back and forth, back and forth, the way a man at dinner separates the bones of a chicken wing. The interior of his stomach was full of acid. His body was stuck with needles, sprayed with fire. His skin was being peeled off, his nerves cut with razor blades, his muscles pounded with hammers. Thumbs were pushing his eyes out from inside his head. And yet the genius of this pain, the brilliance that had gone into its construction, it permitted his mind to work, to remain constantly aware. There was no unconsciousness for him, no oblivion.

The doctor said, "What beasts some men are. I'll try to get it out of you. I don't know what will happen, we aren't supposed to know how it works, but I'll try to take the box out of you."

He went away, and came back with a needle. "Here. This will put you to sleep."

Ahhhhh.

"He isn't there. He just isn't anywhere in the woods."

Wordman glared at the doctor, but knew he had to accept what the man reported. "All right," he said. "Someone took him away. He had a confederate out there, someone who helped him get away."

"No one would dare," said the doctor. "Anyone who helped him would wind up here themselves."

"Nevertheless," said Wordman. "I'll call the State Police," he said, and went on into his office.

Two hours later the State Police called back. They'd checked the normal users of that road, local people who might have seen or heard something, and had found a farmer who'd picked up an injured man near the prison and taken him to a Dr. Allyn in Boonetown. The State Police were convinced the farmer had acted innocently.

"But not the doctor," Wordman said grimly. "He'd have to know the truth almost immediately."

"Yes, sir, I should think so."

"And he hasn't reported Revell."

"No, sir."

"Have you gone to pick him up yet?"

"Not yet. We just got the report."

"I'll want to come with you. Wait for me."

"Yes, sir."

Wordman traveled in the ambulance in which they'd bring Revell back. They arrived without siren at Dr. Allyn's with two cars of state troopers, marched into the tiny operating room, and found Allyn washing instruments at the sink.

Allyn looked at them all calmly and said, "I thought you might be along."

Wordman pointed at the man who lay, unconscious, on the table in the middle of the room. "There's Revell," he said.

Allyn glanced at the operating table in surprise. "Revell? The poet?"

"You didn't know? Then why help him?"

Instead of answering, Allyn studied his face and said, "Would you be Wordman himself?"

Wordman said, "Yes, I am."

"Then I believe this is yours," Allyn said, and put into Wordman's hands a small and bloody black box.

The ceiling was persistently bare. Revell's eyes wrote on it words that should have singed the paint away, but nothing ever happened. He shut his eyes against the white at last and wrote in spidery letters on the inside of his lids the single word *oblivion*.

He heard someone come into the room, but the effort of making a change was so great that for a moment longer he permitted his eyes to remain closed. When he did open them he saw Wordman there, standing grim and mundane at the foot of the bed.

Wordman said, "How are you, Revell?"

"I was thinking about oblivion," Revell told him. "Writing a poem on the subject." He looked up at the ceiling, but it was empty.

Wordman said, "You asked, one time, you asked for pencil and paper. We've decided you can have them."

Revell looked at him in sudden hope, but then understood, "Oh," he said. "Oh, *that*."

Wordman frowned and said, "What's wrong? I said you can have pencil and paper."

"If I promise not to leave any more."

Wordman's hands gripped the foot of the bed. He said, "What's the matter with you? You can't get away, you have to know that by now."

"You mean I can't win. But I won't lose. It's your game, your rules, your home ground, your equipment; if I can manage a stalemate, that's pretty good."

Wordman said, "You still think it's a game. You think none of it matters. Do you want to see what you've done?" He stepped back to the door, opened it, made a motion, and Dr. Allyn was led in. Wordman said to Revell, "You remember this man?"

"I remember," said Revell.

Wordman said, "He just arrived. They'll be putting the Guardian in him in about an hour. Does it make you proud, Revell?"

Looking at Allyn, Revell said, "I'm sorry."

Allyn smiled and shook his head. "Don't be. I had the idea the publicity of a trial might help rid the world of things like the Guardian." His smile turned sour. "There wasn't very much publicity."

Wordman said, "You two are cut out of the same cloth. The emotions of the mob, that's all you can think of. Revell in those so-called poems of his, and you in that speech you made in court."

Revell, smiling, said, "Oh? You made a speech? I'm sorry I didn't get to hear it."

"It wasn't very good," Allyn said. "I hadn't known the trial would only be one day long, so I didn't have much time to prepare it."

Wordman said, "All right, that's enough. You two can talk later, you'll have years."

At the door Allyn turned back and said, "Don't go anywhere till I'm up and around, will you? After my operation."

Revell said, "You want to come along next time?"

"Naturally," said Allyn.

Donald E. Westlake (1933-   )

An accomplished and prolific mystery novelist, Donald Westlake won an Edgar Award for his novel God Save the Mark *(1967). Many of his humorous works, such as* The Busy Body *(1966) and* The Hot Rock *(1970), have been made into films. He also writes tough-guy stories under the pseudonym of Richard Stark. Most of his fifteen science fiction stories were published early in his career, with "Or Not to Die" being written before his twenty-first birthday. And except for "The Winner," which first appeared in an original anthology (Nova 1) in 1970, he has not worked in the field since 1963.*

LANGUAGE

A ROSE BY OTHER NAME
Christopher Anvil

A tall man in a tightly belted trenchcoat carried a heavy brief case toward the Pentagon building.

A man in a black overcoat strode with a bulky suitcase toward the Kremlin.

A well-dressed man wearing a dark-blue suit stepped out of a taxi near the United Nations building, and paid the driver. As he walked away, he leaned slightly to the right, as if the attaché case under his left arm held lead instead of paper.

On the sidewalk nearby, a discarded newspaper lifted in the wind to lie face-up before the entrance to the building. Its big black headline read: U.S. WILL FIGHT!

A set of diagrams in this newspaper showed United States and Soviet missiles, with comparisons of ranges, payloads, and explosive powers, and with the Washington Monument sketched into the background to give an idea of their size.

The well-dressed man with the attaché case strode across the newspaper to the entrance, his heels ripping the tables of missile comparisons as he passed.

Inside the building, the Soviet delegate was at this moment saying:

"The Soviet Union is the most scientifically advanced nation on Earth. The Soviet Union is the most powerful nation on Earth. It is not up to you to say to the Soviet Union, 'Yes' or 'No.' The Soviet Union has told you what it is going to do. All I can suggest for you is, you had better agree with us."

The United States delegate said, "That is the view of the Soviet government?"

"That is the view of the Soviet government."

"In that case, I will have to tell you the view of the United States government. If the Soviet Union carries out this latest piece of brutal aggression, the United States will consider it a direct attack upon its own security. I hope you know what that means."

There was an uneasy stir in the room.

The Soviet delegate said slowly, "I am sorry to hear you say that. I am authorized to state that the Soviet Union will not retreat on this issue."

The United States delegate said, "The position of the United States is already plain. If the Soviet Union carries this out, the United States will consider it as a direct attack. There is nothing more I can say."

In the momentary silence that followed, a guard with a

rather stuporous look opened the door to let in a well-dressed man, who was just sliding something back into his attaché case. This man glanced thoughtfully around the room, where someone was just saying:

"Now what do we do?"

Someone else said hesitantly, "A conference, perhaps?"

The Soviet delegate said coolly, "A conference will not settle this. The United States must correct its provocative attitude."

The United States delegate looked off at a distant wall. "The provocation is this latest Soviet aggression. All that is needed is for the Soviet Union not to do it."

"The Soviet Union will not retreat on this issue."

The United States delegate said, "The United States will not retreat on this issue."

There was a dull silence that lasted for some time.

As the United States and Soviet delegates sat unmoving, there came an urgent plea, "Gentlemen, doesn't anyone have an idea? However implausible?"

The silence continued long enough to make it plain that now no one could see any way out.

A well-dressed man in dark blue, carrying an attaché case, stepped forward and set the case down on a table with a solid *clunk* that riveted attention.

"Now," he said, "we are in a real mess. Very few people on Earth want to get burned alive, poisoned, or smashed to bits. We don't want a ruinous war. But from the looks of things, we're likely to get one whether we want it or not.

"The position we are in is like that of a crowd of people locked in a room. Some of us have brought along for our protection large savage dogs. Our two chief members have trained tigers. This menagerie is now straining at the leash. Once the first blow lands, no one can say where it will end.

"What we seem to need right now is someone with the skills of a lion tamer. The lion tamer controls the animals by understanding, timing, and *distraction*."

The United States and Soviet delegates glanced curiously at each other. The other delegates shifted around with puzzled expressions. Several opened their mouths as if to interrupt, glanced at the United States and Soviet delegates, shut their mouths, and looked at the attaché case.

"Now," the man went on, "a lion tamer's tools are a pistol, a whip, and a chair. They are used to distract. The pistol contains blank cartridges, the whip is snapped above the animal's head, and the chair is held with the points of the chair legs out, so that the animal's gaze is drawn first to one point, then another, as the chair is shifted. The sharp noise of gun and whip distract the animal's attention. So does the chair. And so long as the animal's attention is distracted, its terrific power isn't put into play. This is how the lion tamer keeps peace.

"The thought processes of a war machine are a little different from the thought processes of a lion or a tiger. But the principle is the same. What we need is something corresponding to the lion tamer's whip, chair, and gun."

He unsnapped the cover of the attaché case, and lifted out a dull gray slab with a handle on each end, several dials on its face, and beside them a red button and a blue button.

"It's generally known," he said, looking around at the scowling delegates, "that certain mental activities are associated with certain areas of the brain. Damage a given brain area, and you disrupt the corresponding mental action. Speech may be disrupted, while writing remains. A man who speaks French and German may lose his ability to speak French, but still be able to speak German. These things are well-known, but not generally used. Now, who knows if, perhaps, there is a special section of the brain which handles the vocabulary *related to military subjects?*"

He pushed in the blue button.

The Soviet delegate sat up straight. "What is that button you just pushed?"

"A demonstration button. It actuates when I release it."

The United States delegate said, "Actuates *what?*"

"I will show you, if you will be patient just a few minutes."

"What's this about brain areas? We can't open the brain of every general in the world."

"You won't have to. Of course, you have heard of resonant frequencies and related topics. Take two tuning forks that vibrate at the same rate. Set one in vibration, and the other across the room will vibrate. Soldiers marching across a bridge break step, lest they start the bridge in vibration and bring it down. The right note on a violin will shatter a glass. Who knows whether minute electrical currents in a particular area of the brain, associated with a certain characteristic mental activity, may not tend to induce a similar activity in the corresponding section of another brain? And, in that case, if it were possible to induce a sufficiently *strong* current, it might actually overload that particular—"

The United States delegate tensely measured with his eyes the distance to the gray slab on the table.

The Soviet delegate slid his hand toward his waistband.

The man who was speaking took his finger from the blue button.

The Soviet delegate jerked out a small black automatic. The United States delegate shot from his chair in a flying leap. Around the room, men sprang to their feet. There was an instant of violent activity.

Then the automatic fell to the floor. The United States

delegate sprawled motionless across the table. Around the room, men crumpled to the floor in the nerveless fashion of the dead drunk.

Just one man remained on his feet, leaning forward with a faintly dazed expression as he reached for the red button. He said, "You have temporarily overloaded certain mental circuits, gentlemen. I have been protected by a . . . you might say, a jamming device. You will recover from the effects of *this* overload. The next one you experience will be a different matter. I am sorry, but there are certain conditions of mental resonance that the human race can't afford at the moment." He pressed the red button.

The United States delegate, lying on the table, experienced a momentary surge of rage. In a flash, it was followed by an intensely clear vision of the map of Russia, the polar regions adjoining it, and the nations along its long southern border. Then the map was more than a map, as he saw the economic complexes of the Soviet Union, and the racial and national groups forcibly submerged by the central government. The strong and weak points of the Soviet Union emerged, as in a transparent anatomical model of the human body laid out for an operation.

Not far away, the Soviet delegate could see the submarines off the coasts of the United States, the missiles arcing down the vital industrial areas, the bombers on their long one-way missions, and the unexpected land attack to settle the problem for once and for all. As he thought, he revised the plan continuously, noting an unexpected American strength here, and the possibility of a dangerous counter blow there.

In the minds of another delegate, Great Britain balanced off the United States against the Soviet Union, then by a series of carefully planned moves acquired the moral leadership of a bloc of uncommitted nations. Next, with this as a basis for maneuver—

Another delegate saw leading a Europe small in area but immense in productive power. After first isolating Britain—

At nearly the same split fraction of an instant, all these plans became complete. Each delegate saw his nation's way to the top with a dazzling, more than human clarity.

And then there was an impression like the brief glow of an overloaded wire. There was a sensation similar to pain.

This experience repeated itself in a great number of places around the globe.

In the Kremlin, a powerfully built marshal blinked at the members of his staff.

"Strange. For a minute there, I seemed to see—" He shrugged, and pointed at the map. "Now, along the North German Plain here, where we intend to . . . to—" He scowled, groping for a word. "Hm-m-m. Where we want to . . . ah . . . destabilize the . . . the ridiculous NATO protective counterproposals—" He stopped, frowning.

The members of his staff straightened up and looked puzzled. A general said, "Marshal, I just had an idea. Now, one of the questions is: Will the Americans . . . ah— Will they . . . hm-m-m—" He scowled, glanced off across the room, bit his lip, and said, "Ah . . . what I'm trying to say is: Will they forcibly demolecularize Paris, Rome, and other Allied centers when we . . . ah . . . inundate them with the integrated hyperarticulated elements of our—" He cut himself off suddenly, a look of horror on his face.

The marshal said sharply, "What are you talking about —'demolecularize'? You mean, will they . . . hm-m-m . . . deconstitute the existent structural pattern by application of intense energy of nuclear fusion?" He stopped and blinked several times as this last sentence played itself back in his mind.

Another member of the staff spoke up hesitantly, "Sir, I'm not exactly sure what you have in mind, but I had a thought back there that struck me as a good workable plan to deconstitutionalize the whole American government in five years by instructing their political organization through intrasocietal political action simultaneously on all levels. Now—"

"Ah," said another general, his eyes shining with an inward vision, "I have a better plan. Banana embargo. Listen—"

A fine beading of perspiration appeared on the marshal's brow. It had occurred to him to wonder if the Americans had somehow just landed the ultimate in foul blows. He groped mentally to try to get his mind back on the track.

At this moment, two men in various shades of blue were sitting by a big globe in the Pentagon building staring at a third man in an olive-colored uniform. There was an air of embarrassment in the room.

At length, one of the men in blue cleared his throat. "General, I hope your plans are based on something a little clearer than that. I don't see how you can expect us to co-operate with you in recommending *that* kind of a thing to the President. But now, I just had a remarkable idea. It's a little unusual; but if I do say so, it's the kind of thing that can clarify the situation instead of sinking it in hopeless confusion. Now, what I propose is that we immediately proceed to layerize the existent trade routes in *depth*. This will counteract the Soviet potential nullification of our seaborne surface-level communications through their underwater superiority. Now, this involves a fairly unusual concept. But what I'm driving at—"

"Wait a minute," said the general, in a faintly hurt tone. "You didn't get my point. It may be that I didn't express it quite as I intended. But what I mean is, we've got to really bat those bricks all over the lot. Otherwise, there's bound to be trouble. Look—"

The man in Air Force blue cleared his throat. "Frankly, I've always suspected there was a certain amount of confusion in both your plans. But I never expected anything like this. Fortunately, *I* have an idea—"

At the United Nations, the American and Russian delegates were staring at the British delegate, who was saying methodically, "Agriculture, art, literature, science, engineering, medicine, sociology, botany, zoology, beekeeping, tinsmithing, speleology, wa . . . w . . . milita . . . mili . . . mil . . . hm-m-m . . . sewing, needlework, navigation, law, business, barrister, batt . . . bat . . . ba— Can't say it."

"In other words," said the United States delegate, "we're mentally hamstrung. Our vocabulary is gone as regards . . . ah— That is, we can talk about practically anything, except subjects having to do with . . . er . . . strong disagreements."

The Soviet delegate scowled. "That is bad. I just had a good idea, too. Maybe—" He reached for pencil and paper.

A guard came in scowling. "Sorry, sir. There's no sign of any such person in the building now. He must have gotten away."

The Soviet delegate was looking glumly at his piece of paper. "Well," he said, "I do not think I would care to trust the safety of my country to this method of communication."

Staring up at him from the paper were the words:

"Instructions to head man of Forty-fourth Ground-Walking Club. Seek to interpose your club along the high ground between the not-friendly-to-us fellows and the railway station. Use repeated strong practical urging procedures to obtain results desired."

The United States delegate had gotten hold of a typewriter, slid in a piece of paper, typed rapidly, and was now scowling in frustration at the result.

The Soviet delegate shook his head. "What's the word for it? We've been bugged. The section of our vocabulary dealing with . . . with . . . you know what I mean . . . that section has been burned out."

The United States delegate scowled. "Well, we can still stick pins in maps and draw pictures. Eventually we can get across what we mean."

"Yes, but that is no way to run a wa . . . wa . . . a strong disagreement. We will have to build up a whole new vocabulary to deal with the subject."

The United States delegate thought it over, and nodded. "All right," he said. "Now, look. If we're each going to have to make new vocabularies, do we want to end up with . . . say . . . sixteen different words in sixteen different languages all for the same thing? Take a . . . er . . . 'strong disagreement.' Are you going to call it 'gosnik' and we call it 'gack' and the French call it 'gouk' and the Germans call it 'Gunck'? And then we have to have twenty dozen different sets of dictionaries and hundreds of interpreters so we can merely get some idea what each other is talking about?"

"No," said the Soviet delegate grimly. "Not that. We should have an international commission to settle that. Maybe there, at least, is something we can agree on. Obviously, it is to everyone's advantage not to have innumerable new words for the same thing. Meanwhile, perhaps . . . ah . . . perhaps for now we had better postpone a final settlement of the present difficulty."

Six months later, a man wearing a tightly belted trenchcoat approached the Pentagon building.

A man carrying a heavy suitcase strode along some distance from the Kremlin.

A taxi carrying a well-dressed man with an attaché case cruised past the United Nations building.

Inside the United Nations building, the debate was getting hot. The Soviet delegate said angrily:

"The Soviet Union is the most scientifically advanced and unquestionably the most gacknik nation on Earth. The Soviet Union will not take dictation from anybody. We have given you an extra half-year to make up your minds, and now we are going to put it to you bluntly:

"If you want to cush a gack with us over this issue, we will mongel you. We will grock you into the middle of next week. No running dog of a capitalist imperialist will get out in one piece. You may hurt us in the process, but we will absolutely bocket you. The day of decadent capitalism is over."

A rush of marvelous dialectic burst into life in the Soviet delegate's mind. For a split instant he could see with unnatural clarity not only why, but how, his nation's philosophy was bound to emerge triumphant—if handled properly—and even without a ruinous gack, too.

Unknown to the Soviet delegate, the United States delegate was simultaneously experiencing a clear insight into the stunning possibilities of basic American beliefs, which up to now had hardly been tapped at all.

At the same time, other delegates were sitting straight, their eyes fixed on distant visions.

The instant of dazzling certainty burnt itself out.

"Yes," said the Soviet delegate, as if in a trance. "No need to even cush a gack. Inevitably, victory must go to communi . . . commu . . . comm . . . com—" He stared in horror.

The American delegate shut his eyes and groaned. "Capitalis . . . capita . . . capi . . . cap . . . rugged individu . . . rugged indi . . . rugge . . . rug . . . rug—" He looked up. "Now we've got to have *another* conference. And then, on top of that, we've got to somehow cram our new definitions down the throats of the thirty per cent of the people they *don't* reach with their device."

The Soviet delegate felt for his chair and sat down heavily. "Dialectic materia . . . dialecti . . . dial . . . dia—" He put his head in both hands and drew in a deep shuddering breath.

The British delegate was saying, "Thin red li . . . thin re . . . thin . . . thin— This *hurts*."

"Yes," said the United States delegate. "But if this goes on, we may end up with a complete, new, unified language. Maybe that's the idea."

The Soviet delegate drew in a deep breath and looked up gloomily. "Also, this answers one long-standing question."

"What's that?"

"One of your writers asked it long ago: 'What's in a name?' "

The delegates all nodded with sickly expressions.

"Now we know."

Christopher Anvil (? -)
Christopher Anvil is the pen name of Harry C. Crosby, Jr. He is the author of five novels and over one hundred shorter stories. His stories are essentially intellectual exercises, often presented as a series of letters or memos and featuring a rather

droll sense of humor. They usually either suggest an ingenuous solution to a social problem (such as "The Troublemaker" [1960] and "Philosopher's Stone" [1963]) or point out the foolishness of a particular social policy (such as "Positive Feedback" [1965] and "Behind the Sandrat Hoax" [1968]).

MEMORY

THE MAN WHO NEVER FORGOT
Robert Silverberg

He saw the girl waiting in line outside a big Los Angeles movie house, on a mildly foggy Tuesday morning. She was slim and pale, barely five-three, with stringy flaxen hair, and she was alone. He remembered her, of course.

He knew it would be a mistake, but he crossed the street anyway and walked up along the theater line to where she stood.

"Hello," he said.

She turned, stared at him blankly, flicked the tip of her tongue out for an instant over her lips. "I don't believe I—"

"Tom Niles," he said. "Pasadena, New Year's Day, 1955.

You sat next to me. Ohio State 20, Southern Cal 7. You don't remember?"

"A football game? But I hardly ever—I mean—I'm sorry, mister. I—"

Someone else in the line moved forward toward him with a tight hard scowl on his face. Niles knew when he was beaten. He smiled apologetically and said, "I'm sorry, miss. I guess I made a mistake. I took you for someone I knew—a Miss Bette Torrance. Excuse me."

And he strode rapidly away. He had not gone more than ten feet when he heard the little surprised gasp and the "But I am Bette Torrance!"—but he kept going.

I should know better after twenty-eight years, he thought bitterly. *But I forget the most basic fact—that even though I remember people, they don't necessarily remember me—*

He walked wearily to the corner, turned right, and started down a new street, one whose shops were totally unfamiliar to him and which, therefore, he had never seen before. His mind, stimulated to its normal pitch of activity by the incident outside the theater, spewed up a host of tangential memories like the good machine it was:

January 1 1955 Rose Bowl Pasadena California Seat G126; warm day, high humidity, arrived in stadium 12:03 P.M., PST. Came alone. Girl in next seat wearing blue cotton dress, white oxfords, carrying Southern Cal pennant. Talked to her. Name Bette Torrance, senior at Southern Cal, government major. Had a date for the game but he came down with flu symptoms night before, insisted she see game anyway. Seat on other side of her empty. Bought her a hot dog, 20¢ (no mustard)—

There was more, much more. Niles forced it back down. There was the virtually stenographic report of their conversation all that day:

("... I hope we win. I saw the last Bowl game we won, two years ago ...."

"... Yes, that was 1953. Southern Cal 7, Wisconsin 0 ... and two straight wins in 1944–45 over Washington and Tennessee ...."

"... Gosh, you know a lot about football! What did you do, memorize the record book?")

And the old memories. The jeering yell of freckled Joe Merritt that warm April day in 1937—*Who are you, Einstein?* And Buddy Call saying acidly on November 8, 1939, *Here come Tommy Niles, the human adding machine. Get him!* And then the bright stinging pain of a snowball landing just below his left clavicle, the pain that he could summon up as easily as any of the other pain-memories he carried with him. He winced and closed his eyes suddenly, as if struck by the icy pellet here on a Los Angeles street on a foggy Tuesday morning.

They didn't call him the human adding machine any more. Now it was the human tape recorder; the derisive terms had to keep pace with the passing decades. Only Niles himself remained unchanging, The Boy with the Brain Like a Sponge grown up into The Man with the Brain Like a Sponge, still cursed with the same terrible gift.

His data-cluttered mind ached. He saw a diminutive yellow sports car parked on the far side of the street, recognized it by its make and model and color and license number as the car belonging to Leslie F. Marshall, twenty-six, blond hair, blue eyes, television actor with the following credits—

Wincing, Niles applied the cutoff circuit and blotted out the upwelling data. He had met Marshall once, six months ago, at a party given by a mutual friend—an erstwhile mutual friend; Niles found it difficult to keep friends for long. He had spoken with the actor for perhaps ten minutes and had added that much more baggage to his mind.

It was time to move on, Niles decided. He had been in Los Angeles ten months. The burden of accumulated memories was getting too heavy; he was greeting too many people who had long since forgotten him (*curse my John Q. Average build, 5 feet 9, 163 pounds, brownish hair, brownish eyes, no unduly prominent physical features, no distinguishing scars except those inside,* he thought). He contemplated returning to San Francisco, and decided against it. He had been there only a year ago; Pasadena, two years ago. The time had come, he realized, for another eastward jaunt.

Back and forth across the face of America goes Thomas Richard Niles, der fliegende Holländer, the Wandering Jew, the Ghost of Christmas Past, the Human Tape Recorder. He smiled at a newsboy who had sold him a copy of the *Examiner* on May 13 past, got the usual blank stare in return, and headed for the nearest bus terminal.

For Niles the long journey had begun on October 11, 1929, in the small Ohio town of Lowry Bridge. He was third of three children, born of seemingly normal parents, Henry Niles (b. 1896), Mary Niles (b. 1899). His older brother and sister had shown no extraordinary manifestations. Tom had.

It began as soon as he was old enough to form words; a neighbor woman on the front porch peered into the house where he was playing, and remarked to his mother, "Look how *big* he's getting, Mary!"

He was less than a year old. He had replied, in virtually the same tone of voice, "*Look how big he's getting, Mary!*" It caused a sensation, even though it was only mimicry, not even speech.

He spent his first twelve years in Lowry Bridge, Ohio.

In later years, he often wondered how he had been able to last there so long.

He began school at the age of four, because there was no keeping him back; his classmates were five and six, vastly superior to him in physical coordination, vastly inferior in everything else. He could read. He could even write, after a fashion, though his babyish muscles tired easily from holding the pen. And he could remember.

He remembered everything. He remembered his parents' quarrels and repeated the exact words of them to anyone who cared to listen, until his father whipped him and threatened to kill him if he ever did *that* again. He remembered that too. He remembered the lies his brother and sister told, and took great pains to set the record straight. He learned eventually not to do that, either. He remembered things people had said, and corrected them when they later deviated from their earlier statements.

He remembered everything.

He read a textbook once and it stayed with him. When the teacher asked a question based on the day's assignment, Tommy Niles's skinny arm was in the air long before the others had ever really assimilated the question. After a while, his teacher made it clear to him that he could *not* answer every question, whether he had the answer first or not; there were twenty other pupils in the class. The other pupils in the class made that abundantly clear to him, after school.

He won the verse-learning contest in Sunday school. Barry Harman had studied for weeks in hopes of winning the catcher's mitt his father had promised him if he finished first—but when it was Tommy Niles's turn to recite, he began with *In the beginning God created the heaven and the earth*, continued through *Thus the heavens and the earth were finished, and all the host of them*, headed on into *Now the serpent was more subtil than any beast of the field which the Lord God had made,* and presumably would have continued clear through Genesis, Exodus, and on to Joshua if the dazed proctor hadn't shut him up and declared him the winner.

Barry Harman didn't get his glove; Tommy Niles got a black eye instead.

He began to realize he was different. It took time to make the discovery that other people were always forgetting things, and that instead of admiring him for what he could do they hated him for it. It was difficult for a boy of eight, even Tommy Niles, to understand why they hated him, but eventually he did find it out, and then he started learning how to hide his gift.

Through his ninth and tenth years he practiced being normal, and almost succeeded; the after-school beatings stopped, and he managed to get a few B's on his report cards at last, instead of straight rows of A's. He was growing up; he was learning to pretend. Neighbors heaved sighs of relief, now that that terrible Niles boy was no longer doing all those crazy things.

But inwardly he was the same as ever. And he realized he'd have to leave Lowry Bridge soon.

He knew everyone too well. He would catch them in lies ten times a week, even Mr. Lawrence, the minister, who once turned down an invitation to pay a social call to the Nileses one night, saying, "I really have to get down to work and write my sermon for Sunday," when only three days before Tommy had heard him say to Miss Emery, the church secretary, that he had had a sudden burst of inspiration and had written three sermons all at one sitting, and now he'd have some free time for the rest of the month.

Even Mr. Lawrence lied, then. And he was the best of them. As for the others—

Tommy waited until he was twelve; he was big for his age by then and figured he could take care of himself. He borrowed twenty dollars from the supposedly secret cashbox in the back of the kitchen cupboard (his mother had mentioned its existence five years before, in Tommy's hearing) and tiptoed out of the house at three in the morning. He caught the night freight for Chillicothe, and was on his way.

There were thirty people on the bus out of Los Angeles. Niles sat alone in the back, by the seat just over the rear wheel. He knew four of the people in the bus by name—but he was confident they had forgotten who he was by now, and so he kept to himself.

It was an awkward business. If you said hello to someone who had forgotten you, they thought you were a troublemaker or a panhandler. And if you passed someone by, thinking he had forgotten you, and he hadn't—well, then you were a snob. Niles swung between both those poles five times a day. He'd see someone, such as that girl Bette Torrance, and get a cold, unrecognizing stare; or he'd go by someone else, believing the other person did not remember him but walking rapidly just in case he did, and there would be the angry, "Well! Who the blazes do you think you are!" floating after him as he retreated.

Now he sat alone, bouncing up and down with each revolution of the wheel, with the one suitcase containing his property thumping constantly against the baggage rack over his head. That was one advantage of his talent: he could travel light. He didn't need to keep books, once he had read them, and there wasn't much point in amassing belongings of any other sort either; they became overfamiliar and dull too soon.

He eyed the road signs. They were well into Nevada by now. The old, wearisome retreat was on.

He could never stay in the same city too long. He had to move on to new territory, to some new place where he had no old memories, where no one knew him, where he knew no one. In the sixteen years since he had left home, he'd covered a lot of ground.

He remembered the jobs he had held.

He had been a proofreader for a Chicago publishing firm, once. He did the jobs of two men. The way proofreading usually worked, one man read the copy from the manuscript, the other checked it against the galleys. Niles had a simpler method: he would scan the manuscript once, thereby memorizing it, and then merely check the galleys for discrepancies. It brought him fifty dollars a week for a while, before the time came to move along.

He once held a job as a sideshow freak in a traveling carnie that made a regular Alabama–Mississippi–Georgia circuit. Niles had really been low on cash, then. He remembered how he had gotten the job: by buttonholing the carnie boss and demanding a tryout. "Read me anything—anything at all! I can remember it!" The boss had been skeptical, and didn't see any use for such an act anyway, but finally gave in when Niles practically fainted of malnutrition in his office. The boss read him an editorial from a Mississippi county weekly, and when he was through, Niles recited it back, word-perfect. He got the job, at fifteen dollars a week plus meals, and sat in a little booth under a sign that said THE HUMAN TAPE RECORDER. People read or said things to him, and he repeated them. It was dull work; sometimes the things they said were filthy, and most of the time they couldn't even remember what they had said to him a minute later. He stayed with the show four weeks, and when he left no one missed him much.

The bus rolled on into the fogbound night.

There had been other jobs: good jobs, bad jobs. None

of them had lasted very long. There had been some girls too, but none of them had lasted too long. They had all, even those he had tried to conceal it from, found out about his special ability, and soon after that they had left. No one could stay with a man who never forgot, who could always dredge yesterday's foibles out of the reservoir that was his mind and hurl then unanswerable into the open. And the man with the perfect memory could never live long among imperfect human beings.

To forgive is to forget, he thought. The memory of old insults and quarrels fades, and a relationship starts anew. But for him there could be no forgetting, and hence little forgiving.

He closed his eyes after a while and leaned back against the hard leather cushion of his seat. The steady rhythm of the bus lulled him to sleep. In sleep, his mind could rest; he found ease from memory. He never dreamed.

In Salt Lake City he paid his fare, left the bus, suitcase in hand, and set out in the first direction he faced. He had not wanted to go any farther east on that bus. His cash reserve was only sixty-three dollars now, and he had to make it last.

He found a job as a dishwasher in a downtown restaurant, held it long enough to accumulate a hundred dollars, and moved on again, this time hitchhiking to Cheyenne. He stayed there a month and took a night bus to Denver, and when he left Denver it was to go to Wichita.

Wichita to Des Moines, Des Moines to Minneapolis, Minneapolis to Milwaukee, then down through Illinois, carefully avoiding Chicago, and on to Indianapolis. It was an old story for him, this traveling. Gloomily he celebrated his twenty-ninth birthday alone in an Indianapolis rooming house on a drizzly October day, and for the purpose of brightening the occasion, summoned up his old memories of his fourth birthday party, in 1933 . . . one of the few unalloyedly happy days of his life.

They were all there, all his playmates, and his parents, and his brother Hank, looking gravely important at the age of eight, and his sister Marian, and there were candles and favors and punch and cake. Mrs. Heinsohn from next door stopped in and said, "He looks like a regular little man," and his parents beamed at him, and everyone sang and had a good time. And afterward, when the last game had been played, the last present opened, when the boys and girls had waved good-bye and disappeared up the street, the grown-ups sat around and talked of the new President and the many strange things that were happening in the country, and little Tommy sat in the middle of the floor, listening and recording everything and glowing warmly, because somehow during the whole afternoon no one had said or done anything cruel to him. He was happy that day, and he went to bed still happy.

Niles ran through the party twice, like an old movie he loved well; the print never grew frayed, the registration always remained as clear and sharp as ever. He could taste the sweet tang of the punch, he could relive the warmth of that day when through some accident the others had allowed him a little happiness.

Finally he let the brightness of the party fade, and once again he was in Indianapolis on a gray, bleak afternoon, alone in an eight-dollar-a-week furnished room.

Happy birthday to me, he thought bitterly. *Happy birthday.*

He stared at the blotchy green wall with the cheap Corot print hung slightly askew. I could have been something special, he brooded, one of the wonders of the world. Instead I'm a skulking freak who lives in dingy third-floor back rooms, and I don't dare let the world know what I can do.

He scooped into his memory and came up with the Toscanini performance of Beethoven's Ninth he had heard in Carnegie Hall once while he was in New York. It was infinitely better than the later performance Toscanini had approved for recording, yet no microphones had taken it down; the blazing performance was as far beyond recapture as a flame five minutes snuffed, except in one man's mind. Niles had it all: the majestic downcrash of the tympani, the resonant, perspiring basso bringing forth the great melody of the finale, even the French-horn bobble that must have enraged the maestro so, the infuriating cough from the dress circle at the gentlest moment of the adagio, the sharp pinching of Niles's shoes as he leaned forward in his seat—

He had it all, in highest fidelity.

He arrived in the small town on a moonless night three months later, a cold, crisp January evening, when the wintry wind swept in from the north, cutting through his thin clothing and making the suitcase an almost impossible burden for his numb, gloveless hand. He had not meant to come to this place, but he had run short of cash in Kentucky, and there had been no helping it. He was on his way to New York, where he could live in anonymity for months unbothered, and where he knew his rudeness would go unnoticed if he happened to snub someone on the street or if he greeted someone who had forgotten him.

But New York was still hundreds of miles away, and it might have been millions on this January night. He saw a sign: BAR. He forced himself forward toward the sputtering neon; he wasn't ordinarily a drinker, but he needed the warmth of alcohol inside him now, and perhaps the barkeep would need a man to help out, or could at least rent him a room for what little he had in his pockets.

There were five men in the bar when he reached it. They looked like truck drivers. Niles dropped his valise to the left of the door, rubbed his stiff hands together, exhaled a white cloud. The bartender grinned jovially at him.

"Cold enough for you out there?"

Niles managed a grin. "I wasn't sweating much. Let me have something warming. Double shot of bourbon, maybe."

That would be ninety cents. He had $7.34.

He nursed the drink when it came, sipped it slowly, let it roll down his gullet. He thought of the summer he had been stranded for a week in Washington, a solid week of 97-degree temperature and 97 percent humidity, and the vivid memory helped to ease away some of the psychological effects of the coldness.

He relaxed; he warmed. Behind him came the penetrating sound of argument.

"—I tell you Joe Louis beat Schmeling to a pulp the second time! Kayoed him in the first round!"

"You're nuts! Louis just barely got him down in a fifteen-round decision, the second bout."

"Seems to me—"

"I'll put money on it. Ten bucks says it was a decision in fifteen, Mac."

Sound of confident chuckles. "I wouldn't want to take your money so easy, pal. Everyone knows it was a knockout in one."

"Ten bucks, I said."

Niles turned to see what was happening. Two of the truck drivers, burly men in dark pea jackets, stood nose to nose. Automatically the thought came: *Louis knocked Max Schmeling out in the first round at Yankee Stadium, New*

York, June 22, 1938. Niles had never been much of a sports fan, and particularly disliked boxing—but he had once glanced at an almanac page cataloguing Joe Louis' title fights, and the data had, of course, remained.

He watched detachedly as the bigger of the two truck drivers angrily slapped a ten-dollar bill down on the bar; the other matched it. Then the first glanced up at the barkeep and said, "Okay, Bud. You're a shrewd guy. Who's right about the second Louis-Schmeling fight?"

The barkeep was a blank-faced cipher of a man, middle-aged, balding, with mild, empty eyes. He chewed at his lip a moment, shrugged, fidgeted, finally said, "Kinda hard for me to remember. That musta been twenty-five years ago."

Twenty, Niles thought.

"Lessee now," the bartender went on. "Seems to me I remember—yeah, sure. It went the full fifteen, and the judges gave it to Louis. I seem to remember a big stink being made over it; the papers said Joe should've killed him a lot faster'n that."

A triumphant grin appeared on the bigger driver's face. He deftly pocketed both bills.

The other man grimaced and howled, "Hey! You two fixed this thing up beforehand! I know damn well that Louis kayoed the German in one."

"You heard what the man said. The money's mine."

"No," Niles said suddenly, in a quiet voice that seemed to carry halfway across the bar. *Keep your mouth shut,* he told himself frantically. *This is none of your business. Stay out of it!*

But it was too late.

"What you say?" asked the one who'd dropped the tenspot.

"I say you're being rooked. Louis won the fight in one

round, like you say. June 22, 1938, Yankee Stadium. The barkeep's thinking of the Arturo-Godoy fight. *That* went the full fifteen in 1940. February 9."

"There—told you! Gimme back my money!"

But the other driver ignored the cry and turned to face Niles. He was a cold-faced, heavy-set man, and his fists were starting to clench. "Smart man, eh? Boxing expert?"

"I just didn't want to see anybody get cheated," Niles said stubbornly. He knew what was coming now. The truck driver was weaving drunkenly toward him; the barkeep was yelling, the other patrons were backing away.

The first punch caught Niles in the ribs; he grunted and staggered back, only to be grabbed by the throat and slapped three times. Dimly he heard a voice saying, "Hey, let go the guy! He didn't mean anything! You want to kill him?"

A volley of blows doubled him up; a knuckle swelled his right eyelid, a fist crashed stunningly into his left shoulder. He spun, wobbled uncertainly, knowing that his mind would permanently record every moment of this agony.

Through half-closed eyes he saw them pulling the enraged driver off him; the man writhed in the grip of three others, aimed a last desperate kick at Niles's stomach and grazed a rib, and finally was subdued.

Niles stood alone in the middle of the floor, forcing himself to stay upright, trying to shake off the sudden pain that drilled through him in a dozen places.

"You all right?" a solicitous voice asked. "Hell, those guys play rough. You oughtn't mix up with them."

"I'm all right," Niles said hollowly. "Just . . . let me . . . catch my breath."

"Here. Sit down. Have a drink. It'll fix you up."

"No," Niles said. *I can't stay here. I have to get moving.* "I'll be all right," he muttered unconvincingly. He picked up his suitcase, wrapped his coat tight about him, and left the bar, step by step by step.

He got fifteen feet before the pain became unbearable. He crumpled suddenly and fell forward on his face in the dark, feeling the cold iron-hard frozen turf against his cheek, and struggled unsuccessfully to get up. He lay there, remembering all the various pains of his life, the beatings, the cruelty, and when the weight of memory became too much to bear he blanked out.

The bed was warm, the sheets clean and fresh and soft. Niles woke slowly, feeling a temporary sensation of disorientation, and then his infallible memory supplied the data on his blackout in the snow and he realized he was in a hospital.

He tried to open his eyes; one was swollen shut, but he managed to get the other's lids apart. He was in a small hospital room—no shining metropolitan hospital pavilion, but a small county clinic with gingerbread molding on the walls and homey lace curtains, through which afternoon sunlight was entering.

So he had been found and brought to a hospital. That was good. He could easily have died out there in the snow; but someone had stumbled over him and brought him in. That was a novelty, that someone had bothered to help him; the treatment he had received in the bar last night—was it last night?—was more typical of the world's attitude toward him. In twenty-nine years he had somehow failed to learn adequate concealment, camouflage, and every day he suffered the consequences. It was hard for him to remember, he who remembered everything else, that the other people were not like him, and hated him for what he was.

Gingerly he felt his side. There didn't seem to be any

broken ribs—just bruises. A day or so of rest and they would probably discharge him and let him move on.

A cheerful voice said, "Oh, you're awake, Mr. Niles. Feeling better now? I'll brew some tea for you."

He looked up and felt a sudden sharp pang. She was a nurse—twenty-two, twenty-three, new at the job perhaps, with a flowing tumble of curling blond hair and wide, clear blue eyes. She was smiling, and it seemed to Niles it was not merely a professional smile. "I'm Miss Carroll, your day nurse. Everything okay?"

"Fine," Niles said hesitantly. "Where am I?"

"Central County General Hospital. You were brought in late last night—apparently you'd been beaten up and left by the road out on Route 32. It's a lucky thing Mark McKenzie was walking his dog, Mr. Niles." She looked at him gravely. "You remember last night, don't you? I mean—the shock—amnesia—"

Niles chuckled. "That's the last ailment in the world I'd be afraid of," he said. "I'm Thomas Richard Niles, and I remember pretty well what happened. How badly am I damaged?"

"Superficial bruises, mild shock and exposure, slight case of frostbite," she summed up. "You'll live. Dr. Hammond'll give you a full checkup a little later, after you've eaten. Let me bring you some tea."

Niles watched the trim figure vanish into the hallway.

She was certainly an attractive girl, he thought, fresh-eyed, alert . . . *alive*.

Old cliché: patient falling for his nurse. But she's not for me, I'm afraid.

Abruptly the door opened and the nurse reentered, bearing a little enameled tea tray. "You'll never guess! I have a surprise for you, Mr. Niles. A visitor. Your mother."

"My moth—"

"She saw the little notice about you in the county paper. She's waiting outside, and she told me she hasn't seen you in seventeen years. Would you like me to send her in now?"

"I guess so," Niles said, in a dry, feathery voice.

A second time the nurse departed. *My God*, Niles thought! *If I had known I was this close to home—*
I should have stayed out of Ohio altogether.

The last person he wanted to see was his mother. He began to tremble under the covers. The oldest and most terrible of his memories came bursting up from the dark compartment of his mind where he thought he had imprisoned it forever. The sudden emergence from warmth into coolness, from darkness to light, the jarring slap of a heavy hand on his buttocks, the searing pain of knowing that his security was ended, that from now on he would be alive, and therefore miserable—

The memory of the agonized birth-shriek sounded in his mind. He could never forget being born. And his mother was, he thought, the one person of all he could never forgive, since she had given him forth into the life he hated. He dreaded the moment when—

"Hello, Tom. It's been a long time."

Seventeen years had faded her, had carved lines in her face and made the cheeks more baggy, the blue eyes less bright, the brown hair a mousy gray. She was smiling. And to his own astonishment Niles was able to smile back.

"Mother."

"I read about it in the paper. It said a man of about thirty was found just outside town with papers bearing the name Thomas R. Niles, and he was taken to Central County General Hospital. So I came over, just to make sure—and it *was* you."

A lie drifted to the surface of his mind, but it was a kind

lie, and he said it: "I was on my way back home to see you. Hitchhiking. But I ran into a little trouble en route."

"I'm glad you decided to come back, Tom. It's been so lonely, ever since your father died, and of course Hank was married, and Marian too—it's good to see you again. I thought I never would."

He lay back, perplexed, wondering why the upwelling flood of hatred did not come. He felt only warmth toward her. He was glad to see her.

"How has it been—all these years, Tom? You haven't had it easy, I can see. I see it all over your face."

"It hasn't been easy," he said. "You know why I ran away?"

She nodded. "Because of the way you are. That thing about your mind—never forgetting. I knew. Your grandfather had it too, you know."

"My grandfather—but—"

"You got it from him. I never did tell you, I guess. He didn't get along too well with any of us. He left my mother when I was a little girl, and I never knew where he went. So I always knew you'd go away the way he did. Only you came back. Are you married?"

He shook his head.

"Time you got started, then, Tom. You're near thirty."

The room door opened, and an efficient-looking doctor appeared. "Afraid your time's up, Mrs. Niles. You'll be able to see him again later. I have to check him over, now that he's awake."

"Of course, Doctor." She smiled at him, then at Niles. "I'll see you later, Tom."

"Sure, Mother."

Niles lay back, frowning, as the doctor poked at him here and there. *I didn't hate her.* A growing wonderment rose in him, and he realized he should have come home long ago. He had changed, inside, without even knowing it.

Running away was the first stage in growing up, and a necessary one. But coming back came later, and that was the mark of maturity. He was back. And suddenly he saw he had been terribly foolish all his bitter adult life.

He had a gift, a great gift, an awesome gift. It had been too big for him until now. Self-pitying, self-tormented, he had refused to allow for the shortcomings of the forgetful people about him, and had paid the price of their hatred. But he couldn't keep running away forever. The time would have to come for him to grow big enough to contain his gift, to learn to live with it instead of moaning in dramatic self-inflicted anguish.

And now was the time. It was long overdue.

His grandfather had had the gift; they had never told him that. So it was genetically transmissible. He could marry, have children, and they, too, would never forget.

It was his duty not to let his gift die with him. Others of his kind, less sensitive, less thin-skinned, would come after, and they, too, would know how to recall a Beethoven symphony or a decade-old wisp of conversation. For the first time since that fourth birthday party he felt a hesitant flicker of happiness. The days of running were ended; he was home again. *If I learn to live with others, maybe they'll be able to live with me.*

He saw the things he yet needed: a wife, a home, children—

"—a couple of days' rest, plenty of hot liquids, and you'll be as good as new, Mr. Niles," the doctor was saying. "Is there anything you'd like me to bring you now?"

"Yes," Niles said. "Just send in the nurse, will you? Miss Carroll, I mean."

The doctor grinned and left. Niles waited expectantly, exulting in his new self. He switched on Act Three of *Die Meistersinger* as a kind of jubilant backdrop music in his mind, and let the warmth sweep up over him. When she entered the room he was smiling and wondering how to begin saying what he wanted to say.

Robert Silverberg (1935–)
A winner of two Hugo and four Nebula awards, Robert Silverberg has been, next to Isaac Asimov, the most prolific writer ever to work in the field of science fiction. So far, in addition to having edited approximately fifty anthologies, he has produced more than two hundred uncollected short stories, sixty works of non-fiction, and seventy science fiction books. From the mid-sixties on, much of his work has been extraordinarily well done. Indeed, some critics believe Dying Inside (1972) is the greatest science fiction novel ever written.

MOTIVATION

RUNAROUND
Isaac Asimov

It was one of Gregory Powell's favorite platitudes that nothing was to be gained from excitement, so when Mike Donovan came leaping down the stairs toward him, red hair matted with perspiration, Powell frowned.

"What's wrong?" he said. "Break a fingernail?"

"Yaaaah," snarled Donovan, feverishly. "What have you been doing in the sublevels all day?" He took a deep breath and blurted out, "Speedy never returned."

Powell's eyes widened momentarily and he stopped on the stairs; then he recovered and resumed his upward steps. He didn't speak until he reached the head of the flight, and then:

"You sent him after the selenium?"

"Yes."

"And how long has he been out?"

"Five hours now."

Silence! This was a devil of a situation. Here they were, on Mercury exactly twelve hours—and already up to the eyebrows in the worst sort of trouble. Mercury had long been the jinx world of the System, but this was drawing it rather strong—even for a jinx.

Powell said, "Start at the beginning, and let's get this straight."

They were in the radio room now—with its already subtly antiquated equipment, untouched for the ten years previous to their arrival. Even ten years, technologically speaking, meant so much. Compare Speedy with the type of robot they must have had back in 2005. But then, advances in robotics these days were tremendous. Powell touched a still-gleaming metal surface gingerly. The air of disuse that touched everything about the room—and the entire Station—was infinitely depressing.

Donovan must have felt it. He began: "I tried to locate him by radio, but it was no go. Radio isn't any good on the Mercury Sunside—not past two miles, anyway. That's one of the reasons the First Expedition failed. And we can't put up the ultrawave equipment for weeks yet—"

"Skip all that. What *did* you get?"

"I located the unorganized body signal in the short wave. It was no good for anything except his position. I kept track of him that way for two hours and plotted the results on the map."

There was a yellowed square of parchment in his hip pocket—a relic of the unsuccessful First Expedition—and he slapped it down on the desk with vicious force, spreading it flat with the palm of his hand. Powell, hands clasped across his chest, watched it at long range.

Donovan's pencil pointed nervously. "The red cross is the selenium pool. You marked it yourself."

"Which one is it?" interrupted Powell. "There were three that MacDougal located for us before he left."

"I sent Speedy to the nearest, naturally. Seventeen miles away. But what difference does that make?" There was tension in his voice. "There are the penciled dots that mark Speedy's position."

And for the first time Powell's artificial aplomb was shaken and his hands shot forward for the map.

"Are you serious? This is impossible."

"There it is," growled Donovan.

The little dots that marked the position formed a rough circle about the red cross of the selenium pool. And Powell's fingers went to his brown mustache, the unfailing signal of anxiety.

Donovan added: "In the two hours I checked on him, he circled that damned pool four times. It seems likely to me that he'll keep that up forever. Do you realize the position we're in?"

Powell looked up shortly, and said nothing. Oh, yes, he realized the position they were in. It worked itself out as simply as a syllogism. The photo-cell banks that alone stood between the full power of Mercury's monstrous sun and themselves were shot to hell. The only thing that could save them was selenium. The only thing that could get the selenium was Speedy. If Speedy didn't come back, no selenium. No selenium, no photo-cell banks. No photo-banks—well, death by slow broiling is one of the more unpleasant ways of being done in.

Donovan rubbed his red mop of hair savagely and expressed himself with bitterness. "We'll be the laughingstock of the System, Greg. How can everything have gone so wrong so soon? The great team of Powell and Donovan is sent out to Mercury to report on the advisability of reopening the Sunside Mining Station with modern techniques and robots and we ruin everything the first day. A purely routine job, too. We'll never live it down."

"We won't have to, perhaps," replied Powell, quietly. "If we don't do something quickly, living anything down—or even just plain living—will be out of the question."

"Don't be stupid! If you feel funny about it, Greg, I don't. It was criminal, sending us out here with only one robot. And it was your bright idea that we could handle the photo-cell banks ourselves."

"Now you're being unfair. It was a mutual decision and you know it. All we needed was a kilogram of selenium, a Stillhead Dielectrode Plate, and about three hours' time—and there are pools of pure selenium all over Sunside. MacDougal's spectroreflector spotted three for us in five minutes, didn't it? What the devil! We couldn't have waited for next conjunction."

"Well, what are we going to do? Powell, you've got an idea. I know you have, or you wouldn't be so calm. You're no more a hero than I am. Go on, spill it!"

"We can't go after Speedy ourselves, Mike—not on the Sunside. Even the new insosuits aren't good for more than twenty minutes in direct sunlight. But you know the old saying, 'Set a robot to catch a robot.' Look, Mike, maybe things aren't so bad. We've got six robots down in the sublevels, that we may be able to use, *if* they work. *If* they work."

There was a glint of sudden hope in Donovan's eyes. "You mean six robots from the First Expedition. Are you sure?

They may be subrobotic machines. Ten years is a long time as far as robot-types are concerned, you know."

"No, they're robots. I've spent all day with them and I know. They've got positronic brains: primitive, of course." He placed the map in his pocket. "Let's go down."

The robots were on the lowest sublevel—all six of them surrounded by musty packing cases of uncertain content. They were large, extremely so, and even though they were in a sitting position on the floor, legs straddled out before them, their heads were a good seven feet in the air.

Donovan whistled. "Look at the size of them, will you? The chests must be ten feet around."

"That's because they're supplied with the old McGuffy gears. I've been over the insides—crummiest set you've ever seen."

"Have you powered them yet?"

"No. There wasn't any reason to. I don't think there's anything wrong with them. Even the diaphragm is in reasonable order. They might talk."

He had unscrewed the chest plate of the nearest as he spoke, inserted the two-inch sphere that contained the tiny spark of atomic energy that was a robot's life. There was difficulty in fitting it, but he managed, and then screwed the plate back on again in laborious fashion. The radio controls of more modern models had not been heard of ten years earlier. And then to the other five.

Donovan said uneasily, "They haven't moved."

"No orders to do so," replied Powell, succinctly. He went back to the first in the line and struck him on the chest. "You! Do you hear me?"

The monster's head bent slowly and the eyes fixed themselves on Powell. Then, in a harsh, squawking voice—like that of a medieval phonograph, he grated, "Yes, Master!"

Powell grinned humorlessly at Donovan. "Did you get that? Those were the days of the first talking robots when it looked as if the use of robots on Earth would be banned. The makers were fighting that and they built good, healthy slave complexes into the damned machines."

"It didn't help them," muttered Donovan.

"No, it didn't, but they sure tried." He turned once more to the robot. "Get up!"

The robot towered upward slowly and Donovan's head craned and his puckered lips whistled.

Powell said: "Can you go out upon the surface? In the light?"

There was consideration while the robot's slow brain worked. Then, "Yes, Master."

"Good. Do you know what a mile is?"

Another consideration, and another slow answer. "Yes, Master."

"We will take you up to the surface then, and indicate a direction. You will go about seventeen miles, and somewhere in that general region you will meet another robot, smaller than yourself. You understand so far?"

"Yes, Master."

"You will find this robot and order him to return. If he does not wish to, you are to bring him back by force."

Donovan clutched at Powell's sleeve. "Why not send him for the selenium direct?"

"Because I want Speedy back, nitwit. I want to find out what's wrong with him." And to the robot, "All right, you, follow me."

The robot remained motionless and his voice rumbled: "Pardon, Master, but I cannot. You must mount first." His clumsy arms had come together with a thwack, blunt fingers interlacing.

Powell stared and then pinched at his mustache. "Uh . . . oh!"

Donovan's eyes bulged. "We've got to ride him? Like a horse?"

"I guess that's the idea. I don't know why, though. I can't see— Yes, I do. I told you they were playing up robot-safety in those days. Evidently they were going to sell the notion of safety by not allowing them to move about without a mahout on their shoulders all the time. What do we do now?"

"That's what I've been thinking," muttered Donovan. "We can't go out on the surface, with a robot or without. Oh, for the love of Pete"—and he snapped his fingers twice. He grew excited. "Give me that map you've got. I haven't studied it for two hours for nothing. This is a Mining Station. What's wrong with using the tunnels?"

The Mining Station was a black circle on the map, and the light dotted lines that were tunnels stretched out about it in spiderweb fashion.

Donovan studied the list of symbols at the bottom of the map. "Look," he said, "the small black dots are openings to the surface, and here's one maybe three miles away from the selenium pool. There's a number here—you'd think they'd write larger—13a. If the robots know their way around here—"

Powell shot the question and received the dull "Yes, Master," in reply. "Get your insosuit," he said with satisfaction.

It was the first time either had worn the insosuits—which marked one time more than either had expected to upon their arrival the day before—and they tested their limb movements uncomfortably.

The insosuits were far bulkier and far uglier than the regulation spacesuit; but withal considerably lighter, due to the fact that they were entirely nonmetallic in composition. Composed of heat-resistant plastic and chemically treated cork layers, and equipped with a desiccating unit to keep the air bone-dry, the insosuits could withstand the full glare of Mercury's sun for twenty minutes. Five to ten minutes more, as well, without actually killing the occupant.

And still the robot's hands formed the stirrup, nor did he betray the slightest atom of surprise at the grotesque figure into which Powell had been converted.

Powell's radio-harshened voice boomed out: "Are you ready to take us to Exit 13a?"

"Yes, Master."

Good, thought Powell; they might lack radio control but at least they were fitted for radio reception. "Mount one or the other, Mike," he said to Donovan.

He placed a foot in the improvised stirrup and swung upward. He found the seat comfortable; there was the humped back of the robot, evidently shaped for the purpose, a shallow groove along each shoulder for the thighs, and two elongated "ears" whose purpose now seemed obvious.

Powell seized the ears and twisted the head. His mount turned ponderously. "Lead on, Macduff." But he did not feel at all lighthearted.

The gigantic robots moved slowly, with mechanical precision, through the doorway that cleared their heads by a scant foot, so that the two men had to duck hurriedly, along a narrow corridor in which their unhurried footsteps boomed monotonously and into the air lock.

The long, airless tunnel that stretched to a pinpoint before them brought home forcefully to Powell the exact magnitude of the task accomplished by the First Expedition, with their crude robots and their start-from-scratch necessities. They might have been a failure, but their failure was a good deal better than the usual run of the System's successes.

The robots plodded onward with a pace that never varied and with footsteps that never lengthened.

Powell said: "Notice that these tunnels are blazing with lights and that the temperature is Earth-normal. It's probably been like this all the ten years that this place has remained empty."

"How's that?"

"Cheap energy; cheapest in the System. Sunpower, you know, and on Mercury's Sunside, sunpower is *something*. That's why the Station was built in the sunlight rather than in the shadow of a mountain. It's really a huge energy converter. The heat is turned into electricity, light, mechanical work, and what have you; so that energy is supplied and the Station is cooled in a simultaneous process."

"Look," said Donovan. "This is all very educational, but would you mind changing the subject? It so happens that this conversion of energy that you talk about is carried on by the photo-cell banks mainly—and that is a tender subject with me at the moment."

Powell grunted vaguely, and when Donovan broke the resulting silence, it was to change the subject completely. "Listen, Greg. What the devil's wrong with Speedy, anyway? I can't understand it."

It's not easy to shrug shoulders in an insosuit, but Powell tried it. "I don't know, Mike. You know he's perfectly adapted to a Mercurian environment. Heat doesn't mean anything to him and he's built for the light gravity and the broken ground. He's foolproof—or, at least, he should be."

Silence fell. This time, silence that lasted.

"Master," said the robot, "we are here."

"Eh?" Powell snapped out of a semidrowse. "Well, get us out of here—out to the surface."

They found themselves in a tiny substation, empty, airless, ruined. Donovan had inspected a jagged hole in the upper reaches of one of the walls by the light of his pocket flash.

"Meteorite, do you suppose?" he had asked.

Powell shrugged. "To hell with that. It doesn't matter. Let's get out."

A towering cliff of a black, basaltic rock cut off the sunlight, and the deep night shadow of an airless world surrounded them. Before them, the shadow reached out and ended in knife-edge abruptness in an all-but-unbearable blaze of white light that glittered from myriad crystals along a rocky ground.

"Space!" gasped Donovan. "It looks like snow." And it did.

Powell's eyes swept the jagged glitter of Mercury to the horizon and winced at the gorgeous brilliance.

"This must be an unusual area," he said. "The general albedo of Mercury is low and most of the soil is gray pumice. Something like the Moon, you know. Beautiful, isn't it?"

He was thankful for the light filters in their visiplates. Beautiful or not, a look at the sunlight through straight glass would have blinded them inside of half a minute.

Donovan was looking at the spring thermometer on his wrist. "Holy smokes, the temperature is eighty centigrade!"

Powell checked his and said: "Um-m-m. A little high. Atmosphere, you know."

"On Mercury? Are you nuts?"

"Mercury isn't really airless," explained Powell in absentminded fashion. He was adjusting the binocular attachments to his visiplate, and the bloated fingers of the insosuit were clumsy at it. "There is a thin exhalation that clings to its surface—vapors of the more volatile elements and compounds that are heavy enough for Mercurian gravity to retain. You know: selenium, iodine, mercury, gallium, potassium, bismuth, volatile oxides. The vapors sweep into the shadows and condense, giving up heat. It's a sort of gigantic still. In fact, if you use your flash, you'll probably find that the side of the cliff is covered with, say, hoar-sulphur, or maybe quicksilver dew.

"It doesn't matter, though. Our suits can stand a measly eighty indefinitely."

Powell had adjusted the binocular attachments, so that he seemed as eye-stalked as a snail.

Donovan watched tensely. "See anything?"

The other did not answer immediately, and when he did, his voice was anxious and thoughtful. "There's a dark spot on the horizon that might be the selenium pool. It's in the right place. But I don't see Speedy."

Powell clambered upward in an instinctive striving for better view, till he was standing in unsteady fashion upon his robot's shoulders. Legs straddled wide, eyes straining, he said: "I think . . . I think— Yes, it's definitely he. He's coming this way."

Donovan followed the pointing finger. He had no binoculars, but there was a tiny moving dot, black against the blazing brilliance of the crystalline ground.

"I see him," he yelled. "Let's get going!"

Powell had hopped down into a sitting position on the robot again, and his suited hand slapped against the Gargantuan's barrel chest. "Get going!"

"Giddy-ap," yelled Donovan, and thumped his heels, spur fashion.

The robots started off, the regular thudding of their footsteps silent in the airlessness, for the nonmetallic fabric of the insosuits did not transmit sound. There was only a rhythmic vibration just below the border of actual hearing.

"Faster," yelled Donovan. The rhythm did not change.

"No use," cried Powell, in reply. "These junk heaps are only geared to one speed. Do you think they're equipped with selective flexors?"

They had burst through the shadow, and the sunlight came down in a white-hot wash and poured liquidly about them.

Donovan ducked involuntarily. "Wow! Is it imagination or do I feel heat?"

"You'll feel more presently," was the grim reply. "Keep your eye on Speedy."

Robot SPD 13 was near enough to be seen in detail now. His graceful, streamlined body threw out blazing highlights as he loped with easy speed across the broken ground. His name was derived from his serial initials, of course, but it was apt, nevertheless, for the SPD models were among the fastest robots turned out by the United States Robot & Mechanical Men Corp.

"Hey, Speedy," howled Donovan, and waved a frantic hand.

"Speedy!" shouted Powell. "Come here!"

The distance between the men and the errant robot was being cut down momentarily—more by the efforts of Speedy than the slow plodding of the ten-year-old antique mounts of Donovan and Powell.

They were close enough now to notice that Speedy's gait included a peculiar rolling stagger, a noticeable side-to-side lurch—and then, as Powell waved his hand again and sent maximum juice into his compact head-set radio sender, in preparation for another shout, Speedy looked up and saw them.

Speedy hopped to a halt and remained standing for a

moment—with just a tiny, unsteady weave, as though he were swaying in a light wind.

Powell yelled: "All right, Speedy. Come here, boy."

Whereupon Speedy's robot voice sounded in Powell's earphones for the first time.

It said: "Hot dog, let's play games. You catch me and I catch you; no love can cut our knife in two. For I'm Little Buttercup, sweet Little Buttercup. Whoops!" Turning on his heel, he sped off in the direction from which he had come, with a speed and fury that kicked up gouts of baked dust.

And his last words as he receded into the distance were, "There grew a little flower 'neath a great oak tree," followed by a curious metallic clicking that *might* have been a robotic equivalent of a hiccup.

Donovan said weakly: "Where did he pick up the Gilbert and Sullivan? Say, Greg, he . . . he's drunk or something."

"If you hadn't told me," was the bitter response, "I'd never realize it. Let's get back to the cliff. I'm roasting."

It was Powell who broke the desperate silence. "In the first place," he said, "Speedy isn't drunk—not in the human sense—because he's a robot, and robots don't get drunk. However, there's *something* wrong with him which is the robotic equivalent of drunkenness."

"To me, he's drunk," stated Donovan, emphatically, "and all I know is that he thinks we're playing games. And we're not. It's a matter of life and very gruesome death."

"All right. Don't hurry me. A robot's only a robot. Once we find out what's wrong with him, we can fix it and go on."

"Once," said Donovan, sourly.

Powell ignored him. "Speedy is perfectly adapted to normal Mercurian environment. But this region"—and his arm swept wide—"is definitely abnormal. There's our clue. Now where do these crystals come from? They might have formed from a slowly cooling liquid; but where would you get liquid so hot that it would cool in Mercury's sun?"

"Volcanic action," suggested Donovan, instantly, and Powell's body tensed.

"Out of the mouths of sucklings," he said in a small, strange voice and remained very still for five minutes.

Then he said, "Listen, Mike, what did you say to Speedy when you sent him after the selenium?"

Donovan was taken aback. "Well damn it—I don't know. I just told him to get it."

"Yes, I know. But how? Try to remember the exact words."

"I said ... uh ... I said: 'Speedy, we need some selenium. You can get it such-and-such a place. Go get it.' That's all. What more did you want me to say?"

"You didn't put any urgency into the order, did you?"

"What for? It was pure routine."

Powell sighed. "Well, it can't be helped now—but we're in a fine fix." He had dismounted from his robot, and was sitting, back against the cliff. Donovan joined him and they linked arms. In the distance the burning sunlight seemed to wait cat-and-mouse for them, and just next them, the two giant robots were invisible but for the dull red of their photoelectric eyes that stared down at them, unblinking, unwavering and unconcerned.

Unconcerned! As was all this poisonous Mercury, as large in jinx as it was small in size.

Powell's radio voice was tense in Donovan's ear: "Now, look, let's start with the three fundamental Rules of Robotics—the three rules that are built most deeply into a robot's positronic brain." In the darkness, his gloved fingers ticked off each point.

"We have: One, a robot may not injure a human being,

or, through inaction, allow a human being to come to harm."

"Right!"

"Two," continued Powell, "a robot must obey the orders given it by human beings except where such orders would conflict with the First Law."

"Right!"

"And three, a robot must protect its own existence as long as such protection does not conflict with the First or Second Laws."

"Right! Now where are we?"

"Exactly at the explanation. The conflict between the various rules is ironed out by the different positronic potentials in the brain. We'll say that a robot is walking into danger and knows it. The automatic potential that Rule 3 sets up turns him back. But suppose you *order* him to walk into that danger. In that case, Rule 2 sets up a counterpotential higher than the previous one and the robot follows orders at the risk of existence."

"Well, I know that. What about it?"

"Let's take Speedy's case. Speedy is one of the latest models, extremely specialized, and as expensive as a battleship. It's not a thing to be lightly destroyed."

"So?"

"So Rule 3 has been strengthened—that was specifically mentioned, by the way, in the advance notices on the SPD models—so that his allergy to danger is unusually high. At the same time, when you sent him out after the selenium, you gave him his order casually and without special emphasis, so that the Rule 2 potential set-up was rather weak. Now, hold on; I'm just stating facts."

"All right, go ahead. I think I get it."

"You see how it works, don't you? There's some sort of

danger centering at the selenium pool. It increases as he approaches, and at a certain distance from it the Rule 3 potential, unusually high to start with, exactly balances the Rule 2 potential, unusually low to start with."

Donovan rose to his feet in excitement. "And it strikes an equilibrium. I see. Rule 3 drives him back and Rule 2 drives him forward—"

"So he follows a circle around the selenium pool, staying on the locus of all points of potential equilibrium. And unless we do something about it, he'll stay on that circle forever, giving us the good old runaround." Then, more thoughtfully: "And that, by the way, is what makes him drunk. At potential equilibrium, half the positronic paths of his brain are out of kilter. I'm not a robot specialist, but that seems obvious. Probably he's lost control of just those parts of his voluntary mechanism that a human drunk has. Ve-e-ery pretty."

"But what's the danger? If we knew what he was running from—"

"You suggested it. Volcanic action. Somewhere right above the selenium pool is a seepage of gas from the bowels of Mercury. Sulphur dioxide, carbon dioxide—and carbon monoxide. Lots of it—and at this temperature."

Donovan gulped audibly. "Carbon monoxide plus iron gives the volatile iron carbonyl."

"And a robot," added Powell, "is essentially iron." Then, grimly: "There's nothing like deduction. We've determined everything about our problem but the solution. We can't get the selenium ourselves. It's still too far. We can't send these robot horses, because they can't go themselves, and they can't carry us fast enough to keep us from crisping. And we can't catch Speedy, because the dope thinks we're playing games, and he can run sixty miles to our four."

"If one of us goes," began Donovan, tentatively, "and comes back cooked, there'll still be the other."

"Yes," came the sarcastic reply, "it would be a most tender sacrifice—except that a person would be in no condition to give orders before he ever reached the pool, and I don't think the robots would ever turn back to the cliff without orders. Figure it out! We're two or three miles from the pool—call it two—the robot travels at four miles an hour; and we can last twenty minutes in our suits. It isn't only the heat, remember. Solar radiation out here in the ultraviolet and below is *poison*."

"Um-m-m," said Donovan, "ten minutes short."

"As good as an eternity. And another thing. In order for Rule 3 potential to have stopped Speedy where it did, there must be an appreciable amount of carbon monoxide in the metal-vapor atmosphere—and there must be an appreciable corrosive action therefore. He's been out hours now—and how do we know when a knee joint, for instance, won't be thrown out of kilter and keel him over. It's not only a question of thinking—we've got to think *fast!*"

Deep, dark, dank, dismal silence!

Donovan broke it, voice trembling in an effort to keep itself emotionless. He said: "As long as we can't increase Rule 2 potential by giving further orders, how about working the other way? If we increase the danger, we increase Rule 3 potential and drive him backward."

Powell's visiplate had turned toward him in a silent question.

"You see," came the cautious explanation, "all we need to do to drive him out of his rut is to increase the concentration of carbon monoxide in his vicinity. Well, back at the Station there's a complete analytical laboratory."

"Naturally," assented Powell. "It's a Mining Station."

"All right. There must be pounds of oxalic acid for calcium precipitations."

"Holy space! Mike, you're a genius."

"So-so," admitted Donovan, modestly. "It's just a case of remembering that oxalic acid on heating decomposes into carbon dioxide, water, and good old carbon monoxide. College chem, you know."

Powell was on his feet and had attracted the attention of one of the monster robots by the simple expedient of pounding the machine's thigh.

"Hey," he shouted, "can you throw?"

"Master?"

"Never mind." Powell damned the robot's molasses-slow brain. He scrabbled up a jagged brick-size rock. "Take this," he said, "and hit the patch of bluish crystals just across the crooked fissure. You see it?"

Donovan pulled at his shoulder. "Too far, Greg. It's almost half a mile off."

"Quiet," replied Powell. "It's a case of Mercurian gravity and a steel throwing arm. Watch, will you?"

The robot's eyes were measuring the distance with machinely accurate stereoscopy. His arm adjusted itself to the weight of the missile and drew back. In the darkness, the robot's motions went unseen, but there was a sudden thumping sound as he shifted his weight, and seconds later the rock flew blackly into the sunlight. There was no air resistance to slow it down, nor wind to turn it aside—and when it hit the ground it threw up crystals precisely in the center of the "blue patch."

Powell yelled happily and shouted, "Let's go back after the oxalic acid, Mike."

And as they plunged into the ruined substation on the way back to the tunnels, Donovan said grimly: "Speedy's been hanging about on this side of the selenium pool, ever since we chased after him. Did you see him?"

"Yes."

"I guess he wants to play games. Well, we'll play him games!"

They were back hours later, with three-liter jars of the white chemical and a pair of long faces. The photo-cell banks were deteriorating more rapidly than had seemed likely. The two steered their robots into the sunlight and toward the waiting Speedy in silence and with grim purpose.

Speedy galloped slowly toward them. "Here we are again. Whee! I've made a little list, the piano organist; all people who eat peppermint and puff it in your face."

"We'll puff something in your face," muttered Donovan. "He's limping, Greg."

"I noticed that," came the low, worried response. "The monoxide'll get him yet, if we don't hurry."

They were approaching cautiously now, almost sidling, to refrain from setting off the thoroughly irrational robot. Powell was too far off to tell, of course, but even already he could have sworn the crack-brained Speedy was setting himself for a spring.

"Let her go," he gasped. "Count three! One—two—"

Two steel arms drew back and snapped forward simultaneously and two glass jars whirled forward in towering parallel arcs, gleaming like diamonds in the impossible sun. And in a pair of soundless puffs, they hit the ground behind Speedy in crashes that sent the oxalic acid flying like dust.

In the full heat of Mercury's sun, Powell knew it was fizzing like soda water.

Speedy turned to stare, then backed away from it slowly

—and as slowly gathered speed. In fifteen seconds, he was leaping directly toward the two humans in an unsteady canter.

Powell did not get Speedy's words just then, though he heard something that resembled, "Lover's professions when uttered in Hessians."

He turned away. "Back to the cliff, Mike. He's out of the rut and he'll be taking orders now. I'm getting hot."

They jogged toward the shadow at the slow monotonous pace of their mounts, and it was not until they had entered it and felt the sudden coolness settle softly about them that Donovan looked back. "Greg!"

Powell looked and almost shrieked. Speedy was moving slowly now—so slowly—and in the *wrong direction*. He was drifting; drifting back into his rut; and he was picking up speed. He looked dreadfully close, and dreadfully unreachable, in the binoculars.

Donovan shouted wildly, "After him!" and thumped his robot into its pace, but Powell called him back.

"You won't catch him, Mike—it's no use." He fidgeted on his robot's shoulders and clenched his fist in tight impotence. "Why the devil do I see these things five seconds after it's all over? Mike, we've wasted hours."

"We need more oxalic acid," declared Donovan, stolidly. "The concentration wasn't high enough."

"Seven tons of it wouldn't have been enough—and we haven't the hours to spare to get it, even if it were, with the monoxide chewing him away. Don't you see what it is, Mike?"

And Donovan said flatly, "No."

"We were only establishing new equilibriums. When we create new monoxide and increase Rule 3 potential, he moves backward till he's in balance again—and when the monoxide drifted away, he moved forward, and again there was balance."

Powell's voice sounded thoroughly wretched. "It's the same old runaround. We can push at Rule 2 and pull at Rule 3 and we can't get anywhere—we can only change the position of balance. We've got to get outside both rules." And then he pushed his robot closer to Donovan's so that they were sitting face to face, dim shadows in the darkness, and he whispered, "Mike!"

"Is it the finish?"—dully. "I suppose we go back to the Station, wait for the banks to fold, shake hands, take cyanide, and go out like gentlemen." He laughed shortly.

"Mike," repeated Powell earnestly, "we've got to get Speedy."

"I know."

"Mike," once more, and Powell hesitated before continuing. "There's always Rule 1. I thought of it—earlier—but it's desperate."

Donovan looked up and his voice livened. "We're desperate."

"All right. According to Rule 1, a robot can't see a human come to harm because of his own inaction. Two and 3 can't stand against it. They can't, Mike."

"Even when the robot is half cra— Well, he's drunk. You know he is."

"It's the chances you take."

"Cut it. What are you going to do?"

"I'm going out there now and see what Rule 1 will do. If it won't break the balance, then what the devil—it's either now or three-four days from now."

"Hold on, Greg. There are human rules of behavior, too. You don't go out there just like that. Figure out a lottery, and give me my chance."

"All right. First to get the cube of fourteen goes." And almost immediately, "Twenty-seven forty-four!"

Donovan felt his robot stagger at a sudden push by Powell's mount and then Powell was off into the sunlight. Donovan opened his mouth to shout, and then clicked it shut. Of course, the damn fool had worked out the cube of fourteen in advance, and on purpose. Just like him.

The sun was hotter than ever and Powell felt a maddening itch in the small of his back. Imagination, probably, or perhaps hard radiation beginning to tell even through the insosuit.

Speedy was watching him, without a word of Gilbert and Sullivan gibberish as greeting. Thank God for that! But he daren't get too close.

He was three hundred yards away when Speedy began backing, a step at a time, cautiously—and Powell stopped. He jumped from his robot's shoulders and landed on the crystalline ground with a light thump and a flying of jagged fragments.

He proceeded on foot, the ground gritty and slippery to his steps, the low gravity causing him difficulty. The soles of his feet tickled with warmth. He cast one glance over his shoulder at the blackness of the cliff's shadow and realized that he had come too far to return—either by himself or by the help of his antique robot. It was Speedy or nothing now, and the knowledge of that constricted his chest.

Far enough! He stopped.

"Speedy," he called. "Speedy!"

The sleek, modern robot ahead of him hesitated and halted his backward steps, then resumed them.

Powell tried to put a note of pleading into his voice, and found it didn't take much acting. "Speedy, I've got to get back to the shadow or the sun'll get me. It's life or death, Speedy. I need you."

Speedy took one step forward and stopped. He spoke, but at the sound Powell groaned, for it was, "When you're lying awake with a dismal headache and repose is tabooed—" It trailed off there, and Powell took time out for some reason to murmur, "*Iolanthe.*"

It was roasting hot! He caught a movement out of the corner of his eye, and whirled dizzily; then stared in utter astonishment, for the monstrous robot on which he had ridden was moving—moving toward him, and without a rider.

He was talking: "Pardon, Master. I must not move without a Master upon me, but you are in danger."

Of course, Rule 1 potential above everything. But he didn't want that clumsy antique; he wanted Speedy. He walked away and motioned frantically: "I order you to stay away. I order you to stop!"

It was quite useless. You could not beat Rule 1 potential. The robot said stupidly, "You are in danger, Master."

Powell looked about him desperately. He couldn't see clearly. His brain was in a heated whirl; his breath scorched when he breathed, and the ground all about him was a shimmering haze.

He called a last time, desperately: "*Speedy!* I'm dying, damn you! Where are you? Speedy, I *need* you."

He was still stumbling backward in a blind effort to get away from the giant robot he didn't want, when he felt steel fingers on his arms, and a worried, apologetic voice of metallic timbre in his ears.

"Holy smokes, boss, what are you doing here? And what am *I* doing—I'm so confused—"

"Never mind," murmured Powell, weakly. "Get me to

the shadow of the cliff—and hurry!" There was one last feeling of being lifted into the air and a sensation of rapid motion and burning heat, and he passed out.

He woke with Donovan bending over him and smiling anxiously. "How are you, Greg?"

"Fine!" came the response. "Where's Speedy?"

"Right here. I sent him out to one of the other selenium pools—with orders to get that selenium at all cost this time. He got it back in forty-two minutes and three seconds. I timed him. He still hasn't finished apologizing for the runaround he gave us. He's scared to come near you for fear of what you'll say."

"Drag him over," ordered Powell. "It wasn't his fault." He held out a hand and gripped Speedy's metal paw. "It's O.K., Speedy." Then, to Donovan, "You know, Mike, I was just thinking—"

"Yes!"

"Well"—he rubbed his face—the air was so delightfully cool—"you know that when we get things set up here and Speedy put through his Field Tests, they're going to send us to the Space Stations next—"

"No!"

"Yes! At least that's what old lady Calvin told me just before we left, and I didn't say anything about it, because I was going to fight the whole idea."

"Fight it?" cried Donovan. "But—"

"I know. It's all right with me now. Two hundred seventy-three degrees centigrade below zero. Won't it be a pleasure?"

"Space Station," said Donovan, "here I come."

Isaac Asimov (1920–)
Considered the world's leading author of science for the nonspecialist, Isaac Asimov began his career as a science fiction writer. His first adult novels, I Robot *(1950)*, The Foundation Trilogy *(1951–53)*, and The Caves of Steel *(1954)*, are all considered classics in the field. Yet they were simply a prelude to more than 150 important works of non-fiction. A winner of four Hugo and two Nebula awards, Asimov has also been the recipient of the Blakeslee Award for non-fiction *(1960)*, the American Chemical Society James T. Grady Award *(1965)*, and the American Association for the Advancement of Science–Westinghouse Writing Award *(1967)*.

INTELLIGENCE

ABSALOM
Henry Kuttner

At dusk Joel Locke came home from the university where he held the chair of psychonamics. He came quietly into the house, by a side door, and stood listening, a tall, tight-lipped man of forty with a faintly sardonic mouth and cool gray eyes. He could hear the precipitron humming. That meant that Abigail Schuler, the housekeeper, was busy with her duties. Locke smiled slightly and turned toward a panel in the wall that opened at his approach.

The small elevator took him noiselessly upstairs.

There, he moved with curious stealth. He went directly to a door at the end of the hall and paused before it, his head bent, his eyes unfocused. He heard nothing. Presently he opened the door and stepped into the room.

Instantly the feeling of unsureness jolted back, freezing him where he stood. He made no sign, though his mouth tightened. He forced himself to remain quiet as he glanced around.

It could have been the room of a normal twenty-year-old, not a boy of eight. Tennis racquets were heaped in a disorderly fashion against a pile of book records. The thiaminizer was turned on, and Locke automatically clicked the switch over. Abruptly he turned. The televisor screen was blank, yet he could have sworn that eyes had been watching him from it.

This wasn't the first time it had happened.

After a while Locke turned again and squatted to examine the book reels. He picked out one labeled BRIAFF ON ENTROPIC LOGIC and turned the cylinder over in his hands, scowling. Then he replaced it and went out of the room, with a last, considering look at the televisor.

Downstairs Abigail Schuler was fingering the Mastermaid switchboard. Her prim mouth was as tight as the severe bun of gray-shot hair at the back of her neck.

"Good evening," Locke said. "Where's Absalom?"

"Out playing, Brother Locke," the housekeeper said formally. "You're home early. I haven't finished the living room yet."

"Well, turn on the ions and let 'em play," Locke said. "It won't take long. I've got some papers to correct, anyway."

He started out, but Abigail coughed significantly.

"Well?"

"He's looking peaked."

"Then outdoor exercise is what he needs," Locke said shortly. "I'm going to send him to a summer camp."

"Brother Locke," Abigail said, "I don't see why you don't let him go to Baja California. He's set his heart on it. You let him study all the hard subjects he wanted before. Now you put your foot down. It's none of my affair, but I can tell he's pining."

"He'd pine worse if I said yes. I've my reasons for not wanting him to study entropic logic. Do you know what it involves?"

"I don't—you know I don't. I'm not an educated woman, Brother Locke. But Absalom is bright as a button."

Locke made an impatient gesture.

"You have a genius for understatement," he said. "Bright as a button!"

Then he shrugged and moved to the window, looking down at the play court below where his eight-year-old son played handball. Absalom did not look up. He seemed engrossed in his game. But Locke, watching, felt a cool, stealthy terror steal through his mind, and behind his back his hands clenched together.

A boy who looked ten, whose maturity level was twenty, and yet who was still a child of eight. Not easy to handle. There were many parents just now with the same problem —something was happening to the graph curve that charts the percentage of child geniuses born in recent times. Something had begun to stir lazily far back in the brains of the coming generations and a new species, of a sort, was coming slowly into being. Locke knew that well. In his own time he, too, had been a child genius.

Other parents might meet the problem in other ways, he thought stubbornly. Not himself. He *knew* what was best for Absalom. Other parents might send their genius children to one of the crèches where they could develop among their own kind. Not Locke.

"Absalom's place is here," he said aloud. "With me,

where I can—" He caught the housekeeper's eye and shrugged again, irritably, going back to the conversation that had broken off. "Of course he's bright. But not bright enough yet to go to Baja California and study entropic logic. Entropic logic! It's too advanced for the boy. Even you ought to realize that. It isn't like a lollypop you can hand the kid—first making sure there's castor oil in the bathroom closet. Absalom's immature. It would actually be dangerous to send him to the Baja California University now to study with men three times his age. It would involve mental strain he isn't fit for yet. I don't want him turned into a psychopath."

Abigail's prim mouth pursed up sourly.

"You let him take calculus."

"Oh, leave me alone." Locke glanced down again at the small boy on the play court. "I think," he said slowly, "that it's time for another rapport with Absalom."

The housekeeper looked at him sharply, opened her thin lips to speak, and then closed them with an almost audible snap of disapproval. She didn't understand entirely, of course, how a rapport worked or what it accomplished. She only knew that in these days there were ways in which it was possible to enforce hypnosis, to pry open a mind willy-nilly and search it for contraband thoughts. She shook her head, lips pressed tight.

"Don't try to interfere in things you don't understand," Locke said. "I tell you, I know what's best for Absalom. He's in the same place I was thirty-odd years ago. Who could know better? Call him in, will you? I'll be in my study."

Abigail watched his retreating back, a pucker between her brows. It was hard to know what was best. The mores of the day demanded rigid good conduct, but sometimes a person had trouble deciding in her own mind what was the right thing to do. In the old days, now, after the atomic wars, when license ran riot and anybody could do anything he pleased, life must have been easier. Nowadays, in the violent backswing to a Puritan culture, you were expected to think twice and search your soul before you did a doubtful thing.

Well, Abigail had no choice this time. She clicked over the wall microphone and spoke into it.

"Absalom?"

"Yes, Sister Schuler?"

"Come in. Your father wants you."

In his study Locke stood quiet for a moment, considering. Then he reached for the house microphone.

"Sister Schuler, I'm using the televisor. Ask Absalom to wait."

He sat down before his private visor. His hands moved deftly.

"Get me Dr. Ryan, the Wyoming Quizkid Crèche. Joel Locke calling."

Idly as he waited he reached out to take an old-fashioned cloth-bound book from a shelf of antique curiosa. He read:

> But Absalom sent spies throughout all the tribes of Israel, saying, As soon as ye hear the sound of the trumpet, then ye shall say, Absalom reigneth in Hebron. . . .

"Brother Locke?" the televisor asked.

The face of a white-haired, pleasant-featured man showed on the screen. Locke replaced the book and raised his hand in greeting.

"Dr. Ryan. I'm sorry to keep bothering you."

"That's all right," Ryan said. "I've plenty of time. I'm supposed to be supervisor at the Crèche, but the kids are running it to suit themselves." He chuckled. "How's Absalom?"

"There's a limit," Locke said sourly. "I've given the kid his head, outlined a broad curriculum, and now he wants to study entropic logic. There are only two universities that handle the subject, and the nearest's in Baja California."

"He could commute by copter, couldn't he?" Ryan asked, but Locke grunted disapproval.

"Take too long. Besides, one of the requirements is in-boarding, under a strict regime. The discipline, mental and physical, is supposed to be necessary in order to master entropic logic. Which is spinach. I got the rudiments at home, though I had to use the tri-disney to visualize it."

Ryan laughed.

"The kids here are taking it up. Uh—are you sure you understood it?"

"Enough, yeah. Enough to realize it's nothing for a kid to study until his horizons have expanded."

"We're having no trouble with it," the doctor said. "Don't forget that Absalom's a genius, not an ordinary youngster."

"I know. I know my responsibility, too. A normal home environment has to be maintained to give Absalom some sense of security—which is one reason I don't want the boy to live in Baja California just now. I want to be able to protect him."

"We've disagreed on that point before. All the quizkids are pretty self-sufficient, Locke."

"Absalom's a genius, and a child. Therefore he's lacking in a sense of proportion. There are more dangers for him to avoid. I think it's a grave mistake to give the quizkids their heads and let them do what they like. I refused to send Absalom to a crèche for an excellent reason. Putting all the boy geniuses in a batch and letting them fight it out. Completely artificial environment."

"I'm not arguing," Ryan said. "It's your business. Apparently you'll never admit that there's a sine curve of geniuses these days. A steady increase. In another generation—"

"I was a child genius myself, but I got over it," Locke said irritably. "I had enough trouble with my father. He was a tyrant, and if I hadn't been lucky, he'd have managed to warp me psychologically way out of line. I adjusted, but I had trouble. I don't want Absalom to have that trouble. That's why I'm using psychonamics."

"Narcosynthesis? Enforced hypnotism?"

"It's not enforced," Locke snapped. "It's a valuable mental catharsis. Under hypnosis, he tells me everything that's on his mind, and I can help him."

"I didn't know you were doing that," Ryan said slowly. "I'm not at all sure it's a good idea."

"I don't tell you how to run your Crèche."

"No. But the kids do. A lot of them are smarter than I am."

"Immature intelligence is dangerous. A kid will skate on thin ice without making a test first. Don't think I'm holding Absalom back. I'm just running tests for him first. I make sure the ice will hold him. Entropic logic I can understand, but he can't, yet. So he'll have to wait on that."

"Well?"

Locke hesitated. "Uh—do you know if your boys have been communicating with Absalom?"

"I don't know," Ryan said. "I don't interfere with their lives."

"All right, I don't want them interfering with mine, or with Absalom's. I wish you'd find out if they're getting in touch with him."

There was a long pause. Then Ryan said slowly:

"I'll try. But if I were you, Brother Locke, I'd let Absalom go to Baja California if he wants to."

"I know what I'm doing," Locke said, and broke the beam. His gaze went toward the Bible again.

Entropic logic!

Once the boy reached maturity, his somatic and physiological symptoms would settle toward the norm, but meanwhile the pendulum still swung wildly. Absalom needed strict control, for his own good.

And, for some reason, the boy had been trying to evade the hypnotic rapports lately. There was something going on.

Thoughts moved chaotically through Locke's mind. He forgot that Absalom was waiting for him, and remembered only when Abigail's voice, on the wall transmitter, announced the evening meal.

At dinner Abigail Schuler sat like Atropos between father and son, ready to clip the conversation whenever it did not suit her. Locke felt the beginnings of a long-standing irritation at Abigail's attitude that she had to protect Absalom against his father. Perhaps conscious of that, Locke himself finally brought up the subject of Baja California.

"You've apparently been studying the entropic logic thesis." Absalom did not seem startled. "Are you convinced yet that it's too advanced for you?"

"No, Dad," Absalom said. "I'm not convinced of that."

"The rudiments of calculus might seem easy to a youngster. But when he got far enough into it . . . I went over that entropic logic, son, through the entire book, and it was difficult enough for me. And I've a mature mind."

"I know you have. And I know I haven't, yet. But I still don't think it would be beyond me."

"Here's the thing," Locke said. "You might develop psychotic symptoms if you studied that thing, and you might not be able to recognize them in time. If we could have a rapport every night, or every other night, while you were studying—"

"But it's in Baja California!"

"That's the trouble. If you want to wait for my Sabbatical, I can go there with you. Or one of the nearer universities may start the course. I don't want to be unreasonable. Logic should show you my motive."

"It does," Absalom said. "That part's all right. The only difficulty's an intangible, isn't it? I mean, you think my mind couldn't assimilate entropic logic safely, and I'm convinced that it could."

"Exactly," Locke said. "You've the advantage of knowing yourself better than I could know you. You're handicapped by immaturity, lack of a sense of proportion. And I've had the advantage of more experience."

"Your own, though, Dad. How much would such values apply to me?"

"You must let me be the judge of that, son."

"Maybe," Absalom said. "I wish I'd gone to a quizkid crèche, though."

"Aren't you happy here?" Abigail asked, hurt, and the boy gave her a quick, warm look of affection.

"Sure I am, Abbie. You know that."

"You'd be a lot less happy with dementia praecox," Locke said sardonically. "Entropic logic, for instance, presupposes a grasp of temporal variations being assumed for problems involving relativity."

"Oh, that gives me a headache," Abigail said. "And if you're so worried about Absalom's overtraining his mind, you shouldn't talk to him like that." She pressed buttons and slid the cloisonné metal dishes into the compartment. "Coffee, Brother Locke . . . milk, Absalom . . . and I'll take tea."

Locke winked at his son, who merely looked solemn.

Abigail rose with her teacup and headed toward the fireplace. Seizing the little hearth broom, she whisked away a few ashes, relaxed amid cushions, and warmed her skinny ankles by the wood fire. Locke patted back a yawn.

"Until we settle this argument, son, matters must stand. Don't tackle that book on entropic logic again. Or anything else on the subject. Right?"

There was no answer.

"Right?" Locke insisted.

"I'm not sure," Absalom said after a pause. "As a matter of fact, the book's already given me a few ideas."

Looking across the table, Locke was struck by the incongruity of that incredibly developed mind in the childish body.

"You're still young," he said. "A few days won't matter. Don't forget that legally I exercise control over you, though I'll never do that without your agreement that I'm acting justly."

"Justice for you may not be justice for me," Absalom said, drawing designs on the tablecloth with his fingernail.

Locke stood up and laid his hand on the boy's shoulder. "We'll discuss it again, until we've thrashed it out right. Now I've some papers to correct."

He went out.

"He's acting for the best, Absalom," Abigail said.

"Of course he is, Abbie," the boy agreed. But he remained thoughtful.

The next day Locke went through his classes in an absent-minded fashion and, at noon, he televised Dr. Ryan at the Wyoming Quizkid Crèche. Ryan seemed entirely too casual and noncommittal. He said he had asked the quizkids if they had been communicating with Absalom, and they had said no.

"But they'll lie at the drop of a hat, of course, if they

think it advisable," Ryan added, with inexplicable amusement.

"What's so funny?" Locke inquired.

"I don't know," Ryan said. "The way the kids tolerate me. I'm useful to them at times, but—originally I was supposed to be supervisor here. Now the boys supervise me."

"Are you serious?"

Ryan sobered.

"I've a tremendous respect for the quizkids. And I think you're making a very grave mistake in the way you're handling your son. I was in your house once, a year ago. It's your house. Only one room belongs to Absalom. He can't leave any of his possessions around anywhere else. You're dominating him tremendously."

"I'm trying to help him."

"Are you sure you know the right way?"

"Certainly," Locke snapped. "Even if I'm wrong, does that mean I'm committing fil—filio—"

"That's an interesting point," Ryan said casually. "You could have thought of the right words for matricide, parricide, or fratricide easily enough. But it's seldom one kills his son. The word doesn't come to the tongue quite as instantly."

Locke glared at the screen. "What the devil do you mean?"

"Just be careful," Ryan said. "I believe in the mutant theory, after running this Crèche for fifteen years."

"I was a child genius myself," Locke repeated.

"Uh-huh," Ryan said, his eyes intent. "I wonder if you know that the mutation's supposed to be cumulative? Three generations ago, two percent of the population were child geniuses. Two generations ago, five percent. One generation—a sine curve, Brother Locke. And the I.Q. mounts proportionately. Wasn't your father a genius too?"

"He was," Locke admitted. "But a maladjusted one."

"I thought so. Mutations take time. The theory is that the transition is taking place right now, from Homo sapiens to Homo superior."

"I know. It's logical enough. Each generation of mutations—this dominant mutation at least—taking another step forward till Homo superior is reached. What that will be—"

"I don't think we'll ever know," Ryan said quietly. "I don't think we'd understand. How long will it take, I wonder? The next generation? I don't think so. Five more generations, or ten or twenty? And each one taking another step, realizing another buried potentiality of *Homo*, until the summit is reached. Superman, Joel."

"Absalom isn't a superman," Locke said practically. "Or a superchild, for that matter."

"Are you sure?"

"Good Lord! Don't you suppose I know my own son?"

"I won't answer that," Ryan said. "I'm certain that I don't know all there is to know about the quizkids in my Crèche. Beltram, the Denver Crèche supervisor, tells me the same thing. These quizkids are the next step in the mutation. You and I are members of a dying species, Brother Locke."

Locke's face changed. Without a word he clicked off the televisor.

The bell was ringing for his next class. But Locke stayed motionless, his cheeks and forehead slightly damp.

Presently, his mouth twisted in a curiously unpleasant smile, he nodded and turned from the televisor . . .

He got home at five. He came in quietly, by the side entrance, and took the elevator upstairs. Absalom's door was closed, but voices were coming through it faintly. Locke listened for a time. Then he rapped sharply on the panel.

"Absalom. Come downstairs. I want to talk to you."

In the living room he told Abigail to stay out for a while. With his back to the fireplace, he waited until Absalom came.

The enemies of my lord the king, and all that rise against thee to do thee hurt, be as that young man is. . . .

The boy entered without obvious embarrassment. He came forward and he faced his father, the boy-face calm and untroubled. He had poise, Locke saw, no doubt of that.

"I overheard some of your conversation, Absalom," Locke said.

"It's just as well," Absalom said coolly. "I'd have told you tonight anyway. I've got to go on with that entropic course."

Locke ignored that. "Who were you vising?"

"A boy I know. Malcolm Roberts, in the Denver Quizkid Crèche."

"Discussing entropic logic with him, eh? After what I'd told you?"

"You'll remember that I didn't agree."

Locke put his hands behind him and interlaced his fingers.

"Then you'll also remember that I mentioned I had legal control over you."

"Legal," Absalom said, "yes. Moral, no."

"This has nothing to do with morals."

"It has, though. And with ethics. Many of the youngsters—younger than I—at the quizkid crèches are studying entropic logic. It hasn't harmed them. I must go to a crèche, or to Baja California. I must."

Locke bent his head thoughtfully.

"Wait a minute," he said. "Sorry, son. I got emotionally tangled for a moment. Let's go back on the plane of pure logic."

"All right," Absalom said, with a quiet, imperceptible withdrawal.

"I'm convinced that that particular study might be dangerous for you. I don't want you to be hurt. I want you to have every possible opportunity, especially the ones I never had."

"No," Absalom said, a curious note of maturity in his high voice. "It wasn't lack of opportunity. It was incapability."

"What?" Locke said.

"You could never allow yourself to be convinced I could safely study entropic logic. I've learned that. I've talked to other quizkids."

"Of private matters?"

"They're of my race," Absalom said. "You're not. And please don't talk about filial love. You broke that law yourself long ago."

"Keep talking," Locke said quietly, his mouth tight. "But make sure it's logical."

"It is. I didn't think I'd ever have to do this for a long time, but I've got to now. You're holding me back from what I've got to do."

"The step mutation. Cumulative. I see."

The fire was too hot. Locke took a step forward from the hearth. Absalom made a slight movement of withdrawal. Locke looked at him intently.

"It *is* a mutation," the boy said. "Not the complete one, but Grandfather was one of the first steps. You, too—further along than he was. And I'm further than you. My children will be closer toward the ultimate mutation. The only psychonamic experts worth anything are the child geniuses of your generation."

"Thanks."

"You're afraid of me," Absalom said. "You're afraid of me and jealous of me."

Locke started to laugh. "What about logic now?"

The boy swallowed. "It *is* logic. Once you were convinced that the mutation was cumulative, you couldn't bear to think I'd displace you. It's a basic psychological warp in you. You had the same thing with Grandfather, in a different way. That's why you turned to psychonamics, where you were a small god, dragging out the secret minds of your students, molding their brains as Adam was molded. You're afraid that I'll outstrip you. And I will."

"That's why I let you study anything you wanted, I suppose?" Locke asked. "With this exception?"

"Yes, it is. A lot of child geniuses work so hard they burn themselves out and lose their mental capacities entirely. You wouldn't have talked so much about the danger if—under these circumstances—it hadn't been the one thing paramount in your mind. Sure you gave me my head. And, subconsciously, you were hoping I *would* burn myself out, so I wouldn't be a possible rival any more."

"I see."

"You let me study math, plane geometry, calculus, non-Euclidean, but you kept pace with me. If you didn't know the subject already, you were careful to bone up on it, to assure yourself that it was something you *could* grasp. You made sure I couldn't outstrip you, that I wouldn't get any knowledge you couldn't get. And that's why you wouldn't let me take entropic logic."

There was no expression on Locke's face.

"Why?" he asked coldly.

"You couldn't understand it yourself," Absalom said. "You tried it, and it was beyond you. You're not flexible. Your logic isn't flexible. It's founded on the fact that a second-hand registers sixty seconds. You've lost the sense of wonder. You've translated too much from abstract to concrete. I *can* understand entropic logic. I can understand it!"

"You've picked this up in the last week," Locke said.

"No. You mean the rapports. A long time ago I learned to keep part of my mind blanked off under your probing."

"That's impossible!" Locke said, startled.

"It is for you. I'm a further step in the mutation. I have a lot of talents you don't know anything about. And I know this—I'm not far enough advanced for my age. The boys in the crèches are ahead of me. Their parents followed natural laws—it's the role of any parent to protect its young. Only the immature parents are out of step—like you."

Locke was still quite impassive.

"I'm immature? And I hate you? I'm jealous of you? You've quite settled on that?"

"Is it true or not?"

Locke didn't answer. "You're still inferior to me mentally," he said, "and you will be for some years to come. Let's say, if you want it that way, that your superiority lies in your—flexibility—and your Homo superior talents. Whatever they are. Against that, balance the fact that I'm a physically mature adult and you weigh less than half of what I do. I'm legally your guardian. And I'm stronger than you are."

Absalom swallowed again, but said nothing. Locke rose a little higher, looking down at the boy. His hand went to his middle, but found only a lightweight zipper.

He walked to the door. He turned.

"I'm going to prove to you that you're my inferior," he said coldly and quietly. "You're going to admit it to me."

Absalom said nothing.

Locke went upstairs. He touched the switch on his bureau, reached into the drawer, and withdrew an elastic Lucite belt. He drew its cool, smooth length through his fingers once. Then he turned to the dropper again.

His lips were white and bloodless by now.

At the door of the living room he stopped, holding the belt. Absalom had not moved, but Abigail Schuler was standing beside the boy.

"Get out, Sister Schuler," Locke said.

"You're not going to whip him," Abigail said, her head held high, her lips purse-string tight.

"Get out."

"I won't. I heard every word. And it's true, all of it."

"Get out, I tell you!" Locke screamed.

He ran forward, the belt uncoiled in his hand. Absalom's nerve broke at last. He gasped with panic and dashed away, blindly seeking escape where there was none.

Locke plunged after him.

Abigail snatched up the little hearth broom and thrust it at Locke's legs. The man yelled something inarticulate as he lost his balance. He came down heavily, trying to brace himself against the fall with stiff arms.

His head struck the edge of a chair seat. He lay motionless.

Over his still body, Abigail and Absalom looked at each other. Suddenly the woman dropped to her knees and began sobbing.

"I've killed him," she forced out painfully. "I've killed him—but I couldn't let him whip you, Absalom! I couldn't!"

The boy caught his lower lip between his teeth. He came forward slowly to examine his father.

"He's not dead."

Abigail's breath came out in a long, shuddering sigh.

"Go on upstairs, Abbie," Absalom said, frowning a little. "I'll give him first aid. I know how."

"I can't let you—"

"Please, Abbie," he coaxed. "You'll faint or something. Lie down for a bit. It's all right, really."

At last she took the dropper upstairs. Absalom, with a thoughtful glance at his father, went to the televisor.

He called the Denver Crèche. Briefly he outlined the situation.

"What had I better do, Malcolm?"

"Wait a minute." There was a pause. Another young face showed on the screen. "Do this," an assured, high-pitched voice said, and there followed certain intricate instructions. "Got that straight, Absalom?"

"I have it. It won't hurt him?"

"He'll live. He's psychotically warped already. This will just give it a different twist, one that's safe for you. It's projection. He'll externalize all his wishes, feelings, and so forth. On you. He'll get his pleasure only out of what you do, but he won't be able to control you. You know the psychonamic key of his brain. Work with the frontal lobe chiefly. Be careful of Broca's area. We don't want aphasia. He must be made harmless to you, that's all. Any killing would be awkward to handle. Besides, I suppose you wouldn't want that."

"No," Absalom said. "H-he's my father."

"All right," the young voice said. "Leave the screen on. I'll watch and help."

Absalom turned toward the unconscious figure on the floor.

For a long time the world had been shadowy now. Locke was used to it. He could still fulfill his ordinary functions, so he was not insane, in any sense of the word. Nor could he tell the truth to anyone. They had created a psychic block. Day after day he went to the university and taught psychonamics and came home and ate and waited in hopes that Absalom would call him on the televisor.

And when Absalom called, he might condescend to tell something of what he was doing in Baja California. What he had accomplished. What he had achieved. For those things mattered now. They were the only things that mattered. The projection was complete.

Absalom was seldom forgetful. He was a good son. He called daily, though sometimes, when work was pressing, he had to make the call short. But Joel Locke could always work at his immense scrapbooks, filled with clippings and photographs about Absalom. He was writing Absalom's biography, too.

He walked otherwise through a shadow world, existing in flesh and blood, in realized happiness, only when Absalom's face appeared on the televisor screen. But he had not forgotten anything. He hated Absalom, and hated the horrible, unbreakable bond that would forever chain him to his own flesh—the flesh that was not quite his own, but one step further up the ladder of the new mutation.

Sitting there in the twilight of unreality, his scrapbooks spread before him, the televisor set never used except when Absalom called, but standing ready before his chair, Joel Locke nursed his hatred and a quiet, secret satisfaction that had come to him.

Some day Absalom would have a son. Some day. Some day.

Henry Kuttner (1914–1958)
Henry Kuttner and Catherine L. Moore were science fiction's best husband-and-wife writing team. Virtually everything they produced from the time they were married in 1940 until Kuttner's death by heart attack was to some extent a collaboration. However, Kuttner had published extensively before their marriage, beginning with a series of stories in Weird Tales. Because of his facility for mimicry, some claim he lacked an individual style. But such criticism tends to ignore his mature work, as well as his preoccupation with wacky robots, talented children, and time-traveling madmen.

PERSONALITY

WINGS OUT OF SHADOW
Fred Saberhagen

In Malori's first and only combat mission the berserker came to him in the image of a priest of the sect into which Malori had been born on the planet Yaty. In a dreamlike vision that was the analogue of a very real combat he saw the robed figure standing tall in a deformed pulpit, eyes flaming with malevolence, lowering arms winglike with the robes they stretched. With their lowering, the lights of the universe were dimming outside the windows of stained glass and Malori was being damned.

Even with his heart pounding under damnation's terror Malori retained sufficient consciousness to remember the

173

real nature of himself and of his adversary and that he was not powerless against him. His dream-feet walked him timelessly toward the pulpit and its demon-priest while all around him the stained-glass windows burst, showering him with fragments of sick fear. He walked a crooked path, avoiding the places in the smooth floor where, with quick gestures, the priest created snarling, snapping stone mouths full of teeth. Malori seemed to have unlimited time to decide where to put his feet. *Weapon*, he thought, a surgeon instructing some invisible aide. *Here—in my right hand.*

From those who had survived similar battles he had heard how the inhuman enemy appeared to each in different form, how each human must live the combat through in terms of a unique nightmare. To some a berserker came as a ravening beast, to others as devil or god or man. To still others it was some essence of terror that could never be faced or even seen. The combat was a nightmare experienced while the subconscious ruled, while the waking mind was suppressed by careful electrical pressures on the brain. Eyes and ears were padded shut so that the conscious mind might be more easily suppressed, the mouth plugged to save the tongue from being bitten, the nude body held immobile by the defensive fields that kept it whole against the thousands of gravities that came with each movement of the one-man ship while in combat mode. It was a nightmare from which mere terror could never wake one; waking came only when the fight was over, came only with death or victory or disengagement.

Into Malori's dream-hand there now came a meat cleaver keen as a razor, massive as a guillotine blade. So huge it was that had it been what it seemed it would have been far too cumbersome to even lift. His uncle's butcher shop on Yaty was gone, with all other human works of that planet. But the cleaver came back to him now, magnified, perfected to suit his need.

He gripped it hard in both hands and advanced. As he drew near, the pulpit towered higher. The carved dragon on its front, which should have been an angel, came alive, blasting him with rosy fire. With a shield that came from nowhere he parried the splashing flames.

Outside the remnants of the stained-glass windows the lights of the universe were almost dead now. Standing at the base of the pulpit, Malori drew back his cleaver as if to strike overhand at the priest who towered above his reach. Then, without any forethought at all, he switched his aim at the top of his backswing and laid the blow crashing against the pulpit's stem. It shook, but resisted stoutly. Damnation came.

Before the devils reached him, though, the energy was draining from the dream. In less than a second of real time it was no more than a fading visual image, a few seconds after that a dying memory. Malori, coming back to consciousness with eyes and ears still sealed, floated in a soothing limbo. Before post-combat fatigue and sensory deprivation could combine to send him into psychosis, attachments on his scalp began to feed his brain with bursts of pins-and-needles noise. It was the safest signal to administer to a brain that might be on the verge of any of a dozen different kinds of madness. The noise made a whitish roaring scattering of light and sound that seemed to fill his head and at the same time somehow outlined for him the positions of his limbs.

His first fully conscious thought: he had just fought a berserker and survived. He had won—or had at least achieved a stand-off—or he would not be here. It was no mean achievement.

Berserkers were like no other foe that Earth-descended human beings had ever faced. They had cunning and intelligence and yet were not alive. Relics of some interstellar war over long ages since, automated machines, warships for the most part, they carried as their basic programming the command to destroy all life wherever it could be found. Yaty was only the latest of many Earth-colonized planets to suffer a berserker attack, and it was among the luckiest; nearly all its people had been successfully evacuated. Malori and others now fought in deep space to protect the *Hope*, one of the enormous evacuation ships. The *Hope* was a sphere several kilometers in diameter, large enough to contain a good proportion of the planet's population stored tier on tier in defense-field stasis. A trickle-relaxation of the fields allowed them to breathe and live with slowed metabolism.

The voyage to a safe sector of the galaxy was going to take several months because most of it, in terms of time spent, was going to be occupied in traversing an outlying arm of the great Taynarus nebula. Here gas and dust were much too thick to let a ship duck out of normal space and travel faster than light. Here even the speeds attainable in normal space were greatly restricted. At thousands of kilometers per second, manned ship or berserker machine could alike be smashed flat against a wisp of gas far more tenuous than human breath.

Taynarus was a wilderness of uncharted plumes and tendrils of dispersed matter, laced through by corridors of relatively empty space. Much of the wilderness was completely shaded by interstellar dust from the light of all the suns outside. Through dark shoals and swamps and tides of nebula the *Hope* and her escort *Judith* fled, and a berserker pack pursued. Some berserkers were even larger than the *Hope*, but those that had taken up this chase were much smaller. In regions of space so thick with matter, a race went to the small as well as to the swift; as the impact cross-section of a ship increased, its maximum practical speed went inexorably down.

The *Hope*, ill-adapted for this chase (in the rush to evacuate, there had been no better choice available), could not expect to outrun the smaller and more maneuverable enemy. Hence the escort carrier *Judith*, trying always to keep herself between *Hope* and the pursuing pack. *Judith* mothered the little fighting ships, spawning them out whenever the enemy came too near, welcoming survivors back when the threat had once again been beaten off. There had been fifteen of the one-man ships when the chase began. Now there were nine.

The noise injections from Malori's life support equipment slowed down, then stopped. His conscious mind once more sat steady on its throne. The gradual relaxation of his defense fields he knew to be a certain sign that he would soon rejoin the world of waking men.

As soon as his fighter, Number Four, had docked itself inside the *Judith* Malori hastened to disconnect himself from the tiny ship's systems. He pulled on a loose coverall and let himself out of the cramped space. A thin man with knobby joints and an awkward step, he hurried along a catwalk through the echoing hangar-like chamber, noting that three or four fighters besides his had already returned and were resting in their cradles. The artificial gravity was quite steady, but Malori stumbled and almost fell in his haste to get down the short ladder to the operations deck.

Petrovich, commander of the *Judith*, a bulky, iron-faced man of middle height, was on the deck apparently waiting for him.

"Did—did I make my kill?" Malori stuttered eagerly as he came hurrying up. The forms of military address were little observed aboard the *Judith*, as a rule, and Malori was really a civilian anyway. That he had been allowed to take out a fighter at all was a mark of the commander's desperation.

Scowling, Petrovich answered bluntly. "Malori, you're a disaster in one of these ships. Haven't the mind for it at all."

The world turned a little gray in front of Malori. He hadn't understood until this moment just how important to him certain dreams of glory were. He could find only weak and awkward words. "But . . . I thought I did all right." He tried to recall his combat-nightmare. Something about a church.

"Two people had to divert their ships from their original combat objectives to rescue you. I've already seen their gun-camera tapes. You had Number Four just sparring around with that berserker as if you had no intention of doing it any damage at all." Petrovich looked at him more closely, shrugged, and softened his voice somewhat. "I'm not trying to chew you out, you weren't even aware of what was happening, of course. I'm just stating facts. Thank probability the *Hope* is twenty AU deep in a formaldehyde cloud up ahead. If she'd been in an exposed position just now they would have got her."

"But—" Malori tried to begin an argument but the commander simply walked away. More fighters were coming in. Locks sighed and cradles clanged, and Petrovich had plenty of more important things to do than stand here arguing with him. Malori stood there alone for a few moments, feeling deflated and defeated and diminished. Involuntarily he cast a yearning glance back at Number Four. It was a short, windowless cylinder, not much more than a man's height in diameter, resting in its metal cradle while technicians worked about it. The stubby main laser nozzle, still hot from firing, was sending up a wisp of smoke now that it was back in atmosphere. There was his two-handed cleaver.

No man could direct a ship or a weapon with anything like the competence of a good machine. The creeping slowness of human nerve impulses and of conscious thought disqualified humans from maintaining direct control of their ships in any space fight against berserkers. But the human subconscious was not so limited. Certain of its processes could not be correlated with any specific synaptic activity within the brain, and some theorists held that these processes took place outside of time. Most physicists stood aghast at this view—but for space combat it made a useful working hypothesis.

In combat, the berserker computers were coupled with sophisticated randoming devices, to provide the flair, the unpredictability that gained an advantage over an opponent who simply and consistently chose the maneuver statistically most likely to bring success. Men also used computers to drive their ships, but had now gained an edge over the best randomizers by relying once more on their own brains, parts of which were evidently freed of hurry and dwelt outside of time, where even speeding light must be as motionless as carved ice.

There were drawbacks. Some people (including Malori, it now appeared) were simply not suitable for the job, their subconscious minds seemingly uninterested in such temporal matters as life or death. And even in suitable minds the subconscious was subject to great stress. Connection to external computers loaded the mind in some way not yet understood. One after another, human pilots returning from combat were removed from their ships in states of catatonia or hysterical excitement. Sanity might be restored, but the man or woman was worthless thereafter as a combat-computer's teammate. The system was so new that the importance of these drawbacks was just coming to light aboard the *Judith* now. The trained operators of the fighting ships had been used up, and so had their replacements. Thus it was that Ian Malori, historian, and others were sent out, untrained, to fight. But using their minds had bought a little extra time.

From the operations deck Malori went to his small single cabin. He had not eaten for some time, but he was not hungry. He changed clothes and sat in a chair looking at his bunk, looking at his books and tapes and violin, but he did not try to rest or to occupy himself. He expected that he would promptly get a call from Petrovich. Because Petrovich now had nowhere else to turn.

He almost smiled when the communicator chimed, bringing a summons to meet with the commander and other officers at once. Malori acknowledged and set out, taking with him a brown leather-like case about the size of a briefcase but differently shaped, which he selected from several hundred similar cases in a small room adjacent to his cabin. The case he carried was labeled CRAZY HORSE.

Petrovich looked up as Malori entered the small planning room in which the handful of ship's officers were already gathered around a table. The commander glanced at the case Malori was carrying, and nodded. "It seems we have no choice, historian. We are running out of people, and we are going to have to use your pseudopersonalities. Fortunately we now have the necessary adapters installed in all the fighting ships."

"I think the chances of success are excellent." Malori spoke mildly as he took the seat left vacant for him and set his case out in the middle of the table. "These of course have no real subconscious minds, but as we agreed in our earlier discussions, they will provide more sophisticated randoming devices than are available otherwise. Each has a unique, if artificial, personality."

One of the other officers leaned forward. "Most of us missed these earlier discussions you speak of. Could you fill us in a little?"

"Certainly." Malori cleared his throat. "These personae, as we usually call them, are used in the computer simulation of historical problems. I was able to bring several hundred of them with me from Yaty. Many are models of military men." He put his hand on the case before him. "This is a reconstruction of the personality of one of the most able cavalry leaders on ancient Earth. It's not one of the group we have selected to try first in combat. I just brought it along to demonstrate the interior structure and design for any of you who are interested. Each persona contains about four million sheets of two-dimensional matter."

Another officer raised a hand. "How can you accurately reconstruct the personality of someone who must have died long before any kind of direct recording techniques were available?"

"We can't be positive of accuracy, of course. We have only historical records to go by, and what we deduce from computer simulations of the era. These are only models. But they should perform in combat as in the historical studies for which they were made. Their choices should reflect basic aggressiveness, determination—"

The totally unexpected sound of an explosion brought the assembled officers as one body to their feet. Petrovich, reacting very fast, still had time only to get clear of his chair before a second and much louder blast resounded through the ship. Malori himself was almost at the door, heading for his battle station, when the third explosion came.

It sounded like the end of the galaxy, and he was aware that furniture was flying, that the bulkheads around the meeting room were caving in. Malori had one clear, calm thought about the unfairness of his coming death, and then for a time he ceased to think at all.

Coming back was a slow unpleasant process. He knew *Judith* was not totally wrecked for he still breathed, and the artificial gravity still held him sprawled out against the deck. It might have been pleasing to find the gravity gone, for his body was one vast, throbbing ache, a pattern of radiated pain from a center somewhere inside his skull. He did not want to pin down the source any more closely than that. To even imagine touching his own head was painful.

At last the urgency of finding out what was going on overcame the fear of pain and he raised his head and probed it. There was a large lump just above his forehead, and smaller injuries about his face where blood had dried. He must have been out for some time.

The meeting room was ruined, shattered, littered with debris. There was a crumpled body that must be dead, and there another, and another, mixed in with the furniture. Was he the only survivor? One bulkhead had been torn wide open, and the planning table was demolished. And what was that large, unfamiliar piece of machinery standing at the other end of the room? Big as a tall filing cabinet, but far more intricate. There was something peculiar about its legs, as if they might be movable . . .

Malori froze in abject terror, because the thing did move, swiveling a complex of turrets and lenses at him, and he understood that he was seeing and being seen by a functional berserker machine. It was one of the small ones, used for boarding and operating captured human ships.

"Come here," the machine said. It had a squeaky, ludicrous parody of a human voice, recorded syllables of captives' voices stuck together electronically and played back. "The badlife has awakened."

Malori in his great fear thought that the words were directed at him but he could not move. Then, stepping through the hole in the bulkhead, came a man Malori had never seen before—a shaggy and filthy man wearing a grimy coverall that might once have been part of some military uniform.

"I see he has, sir," the man said to the machine. He spoke the standard interstellar language in a ragged voice that bore traces of a cultivated accent. He took a step closer to Malori. "Can you understand me, there?"

Malori grunted something, tried to nod, pulled himself up slowly to an awkward sitting position.

"The question is," the man continued, coming a little closer still, "how d'you want it later, easy or hard? When it comes to your finishing up, I mean. I decided a long time ago that I want mine quick and easy, and not too soon. Also that I still want to have some fun here and there along the way."

Despite the fierce pain in his head, Malori was thinking now, and beginning to understand. There was a name for humans like the man before him, who went along more or less willingly with the berserker machines. A word coined by the machines themselves. But at the moment Malori was not going to speak that name.

"I want it easy," was all he said, and blinked his eyes and tried to rub his neck against the pain.

The man looked him over in silence a little longer. "All right," he said then. Turning back to the machine, he added in a different, humble voice: "I can easily dominate this injured badlife. There will be no problems if you leave us here alone."

The machine turned one metal-cased lens toward its servant. "Remember," it vocalized, "the auxiliaries must be made ready. Time grows short. Failure will bring unpleasant stimuli."

"I will remember, sir." The man was humble and sincere. The machine looked at both of them a few moments longer and then departed, metal legs flowing suddenly into a precise and almost graceful walk. Shortly after, Malori heard the familiar sound of an airlock cycling.

"We're alone now," the man said, looking down at him. "If you want a name for me you can call me Greenleaf. Want to try to fight me? If so, let's get it over with." He was not much bigger than Malori but his hands were huge and he looked hard and very capable despite his ragged filthiness. "All right, that's a smart choice. You know, you're actually a lucky man, though you don't realize it yet. Berserkers aren't like the other masters that men have —not like the governments and parties and corporations and causes that use you up and then just let you drop and drag away. No, when the machines run out of uses for you they'll finish you off quickly and cleanly—if you've served well. I know, I've seen 'em do it that way with other humans. No reason why they shouldn't. All they want is for us to die, not suffer."

Malori said nothing. He thought perhaps he would be able to stand up soon.

Greenleaf (the name seemed so inappropriate that Malori thought it probably real) made some adjustment on a small device that he had taken from a pocket and was holding almost concealed in one large hand. He asked: "How many escort carriers besides this one are trying to protect the Hope?"

"I don't know," Malori lied. There had been only the *Judith*.

"What is your name?" The bigger man was still looking at the device in his hand.

"Ian Malori."

Greenleaf nodded, and without showing any particular emotion in his face took two steps forward and kicked Malori in the belly, precisely and with brutal power.

"That was for trying to lie to me, Ian Malori," said his captor's voice, heard dimly from somewhere above as Malori groveled on the deck, trying to breathe again. "Understand that I am infallibly able to tell when you are lying. Now, how many escort carriers are there?"

In time Malori could sit up again, and choke out words. "Only this one." Whether Greenleaf had a real lie detector, or was only trying to make it appear so by asking questions whose answers he already knew, Malori decided that from now on he would speak the literal truth as scrupulously as possible. A few more kicks like that and he would be helpless and useless and the machines would kill him. He discovered that he was by no means ready to abandon his life.

"What was your position on the crew, Malori?"

"I'm a civilian."

"What sort?"

"An historian."

"And why are you here?"

Malori started to try to get to his feet, then decided there was nothing to be gained by the struggle and stayed sitting on the deck. If he ever let himself dwell on his situation for a moment he would be too hideously afraid to think coherently. "There was a project . . . you see, I brought with me from Yaty a number of what we call historical models—blocks of programmed responses we use in historical research."

"I remember hearing about some such things. What was the project you mentioned?"

"Trying to use the personae of military men as randomizers for the combat computers on the one-man ships."

"Aha." Greenleaf squatted, supple and poised for all his raunchy look. "How do they work in combat? Better than a live pilot's subconscious mind? The machines know all about *that*."

"We never had a chance to try. Are the rest of the crew here all dead?"

Greenleaf nodded casually. "It wasn't a hard boarding. There must have been a failure in your automatic defenses. I'm glad to find one man alive and smart enough to cooperate. It'll help me in my career." He glanced at an expensive chronometer strapped to his dirty wrist. "Stand up, Ian Malori. There's work to do."

Malori got up and followed the other toward the operations deck.

"The machines and I have been looking around, Malori. These nine little fighting ships you still have on board are just too good to be wasted. The machines are sure of catching the *Hope* now, but she'll have automatic defenses, probably a lot tougher than this tub's were. The machines have taken a lot of casualties on this chase so they mean to use these nine little ships as auxiliary troops—no doubt you have some knowledge of military history?"

"Some." The answer was perhaps an understatement, but it seemed to pass as truth. The lie detector, if it was one, had been put away. But Malori would still take no more chances than he must.

"Then you probably know how some of the generals on

old Earth used their auxiliaries. Drove them on ahead of the main force of trusted troops, where they could be killed if they tried to retreat, and were also the first to be used up against the enemy."

Arriving on the operations deck, Malori saw few signs of damage. Nine tough little ships waited in their launching cradles, re-armed and retuned and refueled for combat. All that would have been taken care of within minutes of their return from their last mission.

"Malori, from looking at these ships' controls while you were unconscious, I gather that there's no fully automatic mode in which they can be operated."

"Right. There has to be some controlling mind, or randomizer, connected on board."

"You and I are going to get them out as berserker auxiliaries, Ian Malori." Greenleaf glanced at his timepiece again. "We have less than an hour to think of a good way and only a few hours more to complete the job. The faster the better. If we delay we are going to be made to suffer for it." He seemed almost to relish the thought. "What do you suggest we do?"

Malori opened his mouth as if to speak, and then did not.

Greenleaf said: "Installing any of your military personae is of course out of the question, as they might not submit well to being driven forward like mere cannon-fodder. I assume they are leaders of some kind. But have you perhaps any of these personae from different fields, of a more docile nature?"

Malori, sagging against the operations officer's empty combat chair, forced himself to think very carefully before he spoke. "As it happens, there are some personae aboard in which I have a special personal interest. Come."

With the other following closely, Malori led the way to his small bachelor cabin. Somehow it was astonishing that nothing had been changed inside. There on the bunk was his violin, and on the table were his music tapes and a few books. And here, stacked neatly in their leather-like curved cases, were some of the personae that he liked best to study.

Malori lifted the top case from the stack. "This man was a violinist, as I like to think I am. His name would probably mean nothing to you."

"Musicology was never my field. But tell me more."

"He was an Earthman, who lived in the twentieth century c.e.—quite a religious man, too, as I understand. We can plug the persona in and ask it what it thinks of fighting, if you are suspicious."

"We had better do that." When Malori had shown him the proper receptacle beside the cabin's small computer console, Greenleaf snapped the connections together himself. "How does one communicate with it?"

"Just talk."

Greenleaf spoke sharply toward the leather-like case. "Your name?"

"Albert Ball." The voice that answered from the console speaker sounded more human by far than the berserker's had.

"How does the thought of getting into a fight strike you, Albert?"

"A detestable idea."

"Will you play the violin for us?"

"Gladly." But no music followed.

Malori put in: "More connections are necessary if you want actual music."

"I don't think we'll need that." Greenleaf unplugged the Albert Ball unit and began to look through the stack of others, frowning at unfamiliar names. There were twelve or fifteen cases in all. "Who are these?"

"Albert Ball's contemporaries. Performers who shared

his profession." Malori let himself sink down on the bunk for a few moments' rest. He was not far from fainting. Then he went to stand with Greenleaf beside the stack of personae. "This is a model of Edward Mannock, who was blind in one eye and could never have passed the physical examination necessary to serve in any military force of his time." He pointed to another. "This man served briefly in the cavalry, as I recall, but he kept getting thrown from his horse and was soon relegated to gathering supplies. And this one was a frail, tubercular youth who died at twenty-three standard years of age."

Greenleaf gave up looking at the cases and turned to size up Malori once again. Malori could feel his battered stomach muscles trying to contract, anticipating another violent impact. It would be too much, it was going to kill him if it came like that again. . . .

"All right." Greenleaf was frowning, checking his chronometer yet again. Then he looked up with a little smile. Oddly, the smile made him look like a hell of a good fellow. "All right! Musicians, I suppose, are the antithesis of the military. If the machines approve, we'll install them and get the ships sent out. Ian Malori, I may just raise your pay." His pleasant smile broadened. "We may just have bought ourselves another standard year of life if this works out as well as I think it might."

When the machine came aboard again a few minutes later, Greenleaf, bowing before it, explained the essence of the plan, while Malori in the background, in an agony of terror, found himself bowing too.

"Proceed, then," the machine approved. "If you are not quick, the ship infected with life may find concealment in the storms that rise ahead of us." Then it went away again quickly. Probably it had repairs and refitting to accomplish on its own robotic ship.

With two men working, installation went very fast. It was only a matter of opening a fighting ship's cabin, inserting an uncased persona in the installed adapter, snapping together standard connectors and clamps, and closing the cabin hatch again. Since haste was vital to the berserkers' plans, testing was restricted to listening for a live response from each persona as it was activated inside a ship. Most of the responses were utter banalities about nonexistent weather or ancient food or drink, or curious phrases that Malori knew were only phatic social remarks.

All seemed to be going well, but Greenleaf was having some last-minute misgivings. "I hope these sensitive gentlemen will stand up under the strain of finding out their true situation. They will be able to grasp that, won't they? The machines won't expect them to fight well, but we don't want them going catatonic, either."

Malori, close to exhaustion, was tugging at the hatch of Number Eight, and nearly fell off the curved hull when it came open suddenly. "They will apprehend their situation within a minute after launching, I should say. At least in a general way. I don't suppose they'll understand it's interstellar space around them. You have been a military man, I suppose. If they should be reluctant to fight—I leave to you the question of how to deal with recalcitrant auxiliaries."

When they plugged the persona into ship Number Eight, its test response was: "I wish my craft to be painted red."

"At once, sir," said Malori quickly, and slammed down the ship's hatch and started to move on to Number Nine.

"What was that all about?" Greenleaf frowned, but looked at his timepiece and moved along.

"I suppose the maestro is already aware that he is about to embark in some kind of a vehicle. As to why he might like it painted red . . ." Malori grunted, trying to open up Number Nine, and let his answer trail away.

At last all the ships were ready. With his finger on the launching switch, Greenleaf paused. For one last time his eyes probed Malori's. "We've done very well, timewise. We're in for a reward, as long as this idea works at least moderately well." He was speaking now in a solemn near-whisper. "It had better work. Have you ever watched a man being skinned alive?"

Malori was gripping a stanchion to keep erect. "I have done all I can."

Greenleaf operated the launching switch. There was a polyphonic whisper of airlocks. The nine ships were gone, and simultaneously a holographic display came alive above the operations officer's console. In the center of the display the *Judith* showed as a fat green symbol, with nine smaller green dots moving slowly and uncertainly nearby. Farther off, a steady formation of red dots represented what was left of the berserker pack that had so long and so relentlessly pursued the *Hope* and her escort. There were at least fifteen red berserker dots, Malori noted gloomily.

"The trick," Greenleaf said as if to himself, "is to make them more afraid of their own leaders than they are of the enemy." He keyed the panel switches that would send his voice out to the ships. "Attention, units One through Nine!" he barked. "You are under the guns of a vastly superior force, and any attempt at disobedience or escape will be severely punished . . ."

He went on browbeating them for a minute, while Malori observed in the screen that the dirty weather the berserker had mentioned was coming on. A sleet of atomic particles was driving through this section of the nebula, across the path of the *Judith* and the odd hybrid fleet that moved with her. The *Hope*, not in view on this range scale, might be able to take advantage of the storm to get away entirely unless the berserker pursuit was swift.

Visibility on the operations display was failing fast and Greenleaf cut off his speech as it became apparent that contact was being lost. Orders in the berserkers' unnatural voices, directed at auxiliary ships One through Nine, came in fragmentarily before the curtain of noise became an opaque white-out. The pursuit of the *Hope* had not yet been resumed.

For a while all was silent on the operations deck, except for an occasional crackle of noise from the display. All around them the empty launching cradles waited.

"That's that," Greenleaf said at length. "Nothing to do now but worry." He gave his little transforming smile again, and seemed to be almost enjoying the situation.

Malori was looking at him curiously. "How do you—manage to cope so well?"

"Why not?" Greenleaf stretched and got up from the now-useless console. "You know, once a man gives up his old ways, badlife ways, admits he's really dead to them, the new ways aren't so bad. There are even women available from time to time, when the machines take prisoners."

"Goodlife," said Malori. Now he had spoken the obscene, provoking epithet. But at the moment he was not afraid.

"Goodlife yourself, little man." Greenleaf was still smiling. "You know, I think you still look down on me. You're in as deep as I am now, remember?"

"I think I pity you."

Greenleaf let out a little snort of laughter, and shook his own head pityingly. "You know, I may have ahead of me a longer and more pain-free life than most of humanity has ever enjoyed—you said one of the models for the personae died at twenty-three. Was that a common age of death in those days?"

Malori, still clinging to his stanchion, began to wear a strange, grim little smile. "Well, in his generation, in the continent of Europe, it was. The First World War was raging at the time."

"But he died of some disease, you said."

"No. I said he *had* a disease, tuberculosis. Doubtless it would have killed him eventually. But he died in battle, in 1917 C.E., in a place called Belgium. His body was never found, as I recall, an artillery barrage having destroyed it and his aircraft entirely."

Greenleaf was standing very still. "Aircraft! What are you saying?"

Malori pulled himself erect, somewhat painfully, and let go of his support. "I tell you now that Georges Guynemer—that was his name—shot down fifty-three enemy aircraft before he was killed. Wait!" Malori's voice was suddenly loud and firm, and Greenleaf halted his menacing advance in sheer surprise. "Before you begin to do anything violent to me, you should perhaps consider whether your side or mine is likely to win the fight outside."

"The fight . . ."

"It will be nine ships against fifteen or more machines, but I don't feel too pessimistic. The personae we have sent out are not going to be meekly slaughtered."

Greenleaf stared at him a moment longer, then spun around and lunged for the operations console. The display was still blank white with noise and there was nothing to be done. He slowly sank into the padded chair. "What have you done to me?" he whispered. "That collection of invalid musicians—you couldn't have been lying about them all."

"Oh, every word I spoke was true. Not all World War I fighter pilots were invalids, of course. Some were in perfect health, indeed fanatical about staying that way. And I did not say they were all musicians, though I certainly meant you to think so. Ball had the most musical ability among the aces, but was still only an amateur. He always said he loathed his real profession."

Greenleaf, slumped in the chair now, seemed to be aging visibly. "But one was blind . . . it isn't possible."

"So his enemies thought, when they released him from an internment camp early in the war. Edward Mannock, blind in one eye. He had to trick an examiner to get into the army. Of course the tragedy of these superb men is that they spent themselves killing one another. In those days they had no berserkers to fight, at least none that could be attacked dashingly, with an aircraft and a machine gun. I suppose men have always faced berserkers of some kind."

"Let me make sure I understand." Greenleaf's voice was almost pleading. "We have sent out the personae of nine fighter pilots?"

"Nine of the best. I suppose their total of claimed aerial victories is more than five hundred. Such claims were usually exaggerated, but still . . ."

There was silence again. Greenleaf slowly turned his chair back to face the operations display. After a time the storm of atomic noise began to abate. Malori, who had sat down on the deck to rest, got up again, this time more quickly. In the hologram a single glowing symbol was emerging from the noise, fast approaching the position of the *Judith*.

The approaching symbol was bright red.

"So there we are," said Greenleaf, getting to his feet. From a pocket he produced a stubby little handgun. At first he pointed it toward the shrinking Malori, but then he smiled his nice smile and shook his head. "No, let the machines have you. That will be much worse."

When they heard the airlock begin to cycle, Greenleaf raised the weapon to point at his own skull. Malori could not tear his eyes away. The inner door clicked and Greenleaf fired.

Malori bounded across the intervening space and pulled the gun from Greenleaf's dead hand almost before the body had completed its fall. He turned to aim the weapon at the airlock as its inner door sighed open. The berserker standing there was the one he had seen earlier, or the same type at least. But it had just been through violent alterations. One metal arm was cut short in a bright bubbly scar, from which the ends of truncated cables flapped. The whole metal body was riddled with small holes, and around its top there played a halo of electrical discharge.

Malori fired, but the machine ignored the impact of the force-packet. They would not have let Greenleaf keep a gun with which they could be hurt. The battered machine ignored Malori too, for the moment, and lurched forward to bend over Greenleaf's nearly decapitated body.

"Tra-tra-tra-treason," the berserker squeaked. "Ultimate unpleasant ultimate unpleasant stum-stum-stimuli. Bad-life badlife bad—"

By then Malori had moved up close behind it and thrust the muzzle of the gun into one of the still-hot holes where Albert Ball or perhaps Frank Luke or Werner Voss or one of the others had already used a laser to good effect. Two force-packets beneath its armor and the berserker went down, as still as the man who lay beneath it. The halo of electricity died.

Malori backed off, looking at them both, then spun

around to scan the operations display again. The red dot was drifting away from the *Judith*, the vessel it represented now evidently no more than inert machinery.

Out of the receding atomic storm a single green dot was approaching. A minute later, Number Eight came in alone, bumping to a gentle stop against its cradle pads. The laser nozzle at once began smoking heavily in the atmosphere. The craft was scarred in several places by enemy fire.

"I claim four more victories," the persona said as soon as Malori opened the hatch. "Today I was given fine support by my wingmen, who made great sacrifices for the Fatherland. Although the enemy outnumbered us by two to one, I think that not a single one of them escaped. But I must protest bitterly that my aircraft still has not been painted red."

"I will see to it at once, *mein Herr*," murmured Malori, as he began to disconnect the persona from the fighting ship. He felt a little foolish for trying to reassure a piece of hardware. Still, he handled the persona gently as he carried it to where the little formation of empty cases were waiting on the operations deck, their labels showing plainly:

    ALBERT BALL
    WILLIAM AVERY BISHOP
    RENÉ PAUL FONCK
    GEORGES MARIE GUYNEMER
    FRANK LUKE
    EDWARD MANNOCK
    CHARLES NUNGESSER
    MANFRED VON RICHTHOFEN
    WERNER VOSS

They were English, American, German, French. They were Jew, violinist, invalid, Prussian, rebel, hater, bon vivant, Christian. Among the nine of them they were many other things besides. Maybe there was only the one word—man —which could include them all.

Right now the nearest living humans were many millions of kilometers away, but still Malori did not feel quite alone. He put the persona back into its case gently, even knowing that it would be undamaged by ten thousand more gravities than his hands could exert. Maybe it would fit into the cabin of Number Eight with him, when he made his try to reach the *Hope*.

"Looks like it's just you and me now, Red Baron." The human being from which it had been modeled had been not quite twenty-six when he was killed over France, after less than eighteen months of success and fame. Before that, in the cavalry, his horse had thrown him again and again.

Fred Saberhagen (1930–)
A writer who began publishing short stories in the early 1960's, Fred Saberhagen is perhaps most noted for his "Berserker" stories, featuring alien robot war machines that try to destroy all organic life. Since the late 1960's, however, he has been branching out into fantasy novels, producing The Empire of the East (1979) trilogy, as well as an ongoing series of Dracula tales: The Dracula Tape (1975), The Holmes-Dracula File (1978), An Old Friend of the Family (1979), and A Matter of Taste (1980).

ABNORMAL PSYCHOLOGY

IN CASE OF FIRE
Randall Garrett

In his office apartment, on the top floor of the Terran Embassy Building in Occeq City, Bertrand Malloy leafed casually through the dossiers of the four new men who had been assigned to him. They were typical of the kind of men who were sent to him, he thought. Which meant, as usual, that they were atypical. Every man in the Diplomatic Corps who developed a twitch or a quirk was shipped to Saarkkad IV to work under Bertrand Malloy, Permanent Terran Ambassador to His Utter Munificence, the Occeq of Saarkkad.

Take this first one, for instance. Malloy ran his fingers down the columns of complex symbolism that showed the complete psychological analysis of the man. Psychopathic paranoia. The man wasn't technically insane; he could be as lucid as the next man most of the time. But he was morbidly suspicious that every man's hand was turned against him. He trusted no one, and was perpetually on his guard against imaginary plots and persecutions.

Number two suffered from some sort of emotional block that left him continually on the horns of one dilemma or another. He was psychologically incapable of making a decision if he was faced with two or more possible alternatives of any major importance.

Number three . . .

Malloy sighed and pushed the dossiers away from him. No two men were alike, and yet there sometimes seemed to be an eternal sameness about all men. He considered himself an individual, for instance, but wasn't the basic similarity there, after all?

He was—how old? He glanced at the Earth calendar dial that was automatically correlated with the Saarkkadic calendar just above it. Fifty-nine next week. Fifty-nine years old. And what did he have to show for it besides flabby muscles, sagging skin, a wrinkled face, and gray hair?

Well, he had an excellent record in the Corps, if nothing else. One of the top men in his field. And he had his memories of Diane, dead these ten years, but still beautiful and alive in his recollections. And—he grinned softly to himself—he had Saarkkad.

He glanced up at the ceiling, and mentally allowed his gaze to penetrate it to the blue sky beyond it.

Out there was the terrible emptiness of interstellar space —a great, yawning, infinite chasm capable of swallowing men, ships, planets, suns, and whole galaxies without filling its insatiable void.

Malloy closed his eyes. Somewhere out there, a war was

raging. He didn't even like to think of that, but it was necessary to keep it in mind. Somewhere out there, the ships of Earth were ranged against the ships of the alien Karna in the most important war that Mankind had yet fought.

And, Malloy knew, his own position was not unimportant in that war. He was not in the battle line, nor even in the major production line, but it was necessary to keep the drug supply lines flowing from Saarkkad, and that meant keeping on good terms with the Saarkkadic government.

The Saarkkada themselves were humanoid in physical form—if one allowed the term to cover a wide range of differences—but their minds just didn't function along the same lines.

For nine years, Bertrand Malloy had been Ambassador to Saarkkad, and for nine years, no Saarkkada had ever seen him. To have shown himself to one of them would have meant instant loss of prestige.

To their way of thinking, an important official was aloof. The greater his importance, the greater must be his isolation. The Occeq of Saarkkad himself was never seen except by a handful of picked nobles, who, themselves, were never seen except by their underlings. It was a long, roundabout way of doing business, but it was the only way Saarkkad would do any business at all. To violate the rigid social setup of Saarkkad would mean the instant closing off of the supply of biochemical products that the Saarkkadic laboratories produced from native plants and animals—products that were vitally necessary to Earth's war, and which could be duplicated nowhere else in the known universe.

It was Bertrand Malloy's job to keep the production output high and to keep the materiel flowing towards Earth and her allies and outposts.

The job would have been a snap cinch in the right circumstances; the Saarkkada weren't difficult to get along with. A staff of top-grade men could have handled them without half trying.

But Malloy didn't have top-grade men. They couldn't be spared from work that required their total capacity. It's inefficient to waste a man on a job that he can do without half trying where there are more important jobs that will tax his full output.

So Malloy was stuck with the culls. Not the worst ones, of course; there were places in the galaxy that were less important than Saarkkad to the war effort. Malloy knew that, no matter what was wrong with a man, as long as he had the mental ability to dress himself and get himself to work, useful work could be found for him.

Physical handicaps weren't at all difficult to deal with. A blind man can work very well in the total darkness of an infrared-film darkroom. Partial or total losses of limbs can be compensated for in one way or another.

The mental disabilities were harder to deal with, but not totally impossible. On a world without liquor, a dipsomaniac could be channeled easily enough; and he'd better not try fermenting his own on Saarkkad unless he brought his own yeast—which was impossible, in view of the sterilization regulations.

But Malloy didn't like to stop at merely thwarting mental quirks; he liked to find places where they were *useful*.

The phone chimed. Malloy flipped it on with a practiced hand.

"Malloy here."

"Mr. Malloy?" said a careful voice. "A special communication for you has been teletyped in from Earth. Shall I bring it in?"

"Bring it in, Miss Drayson."

Miss Drayson was a case in point. She was uncommunicative. She liked to gather in information, but she found it difficult to give it up once it was in her possession. Malloy had made her his private secretary. Nothing—but *nothing*—got out of Malloy's office without his direct order. It had taken Malloy a long time to get it into Miss Drayson's head that it was perfectly all right—even desirable—for her to keep secrets from everyone except Malloy.

She came in through the door, a rather handsome woman in her middle thirties, clutching a sheaf of papers in her right hand as though someone might at any instant snatch it from her before she could turn it over to Malloy.

She laid them carefully on the desk. "If anything else comes in, I'll let you know immediately, sir," she said. "Will there be anything else?"

Malloy let her stand there while he picked up the communiqué. She wanted to know what his reaction was going to be; it didn't matter because no one would ever find out from her what he had done unless she was ordered to tell someone.

He read the first paragraph, and his eyes widened involuntarily.

"Armistice," he said in a low whisper. "There's a chance that the war may be over."

"Yes, sir," said Miss Drayson in a hushed voice.

Malloy read the whole thing through, fighting to keep his emotions in check. Miss Drayson stood there calmly, her face a mask; her emotions were a secret.

Finally, Malloy looked up. "I'll let you know as soon as I reach a decision, Miss Drayson. I think I hardly need say that no news of this is to leave this office."

"Of course not, sir."

Malloy watched her go out the door without actually

seeing her. The war was over—at least for a while. He looked down at the papers again.

The Karna, slowly being beaten back on every front, were suing for peace. They wanted an armistice conference—immediately.

Earth was willing. Interstellar war is too costly to allow it to continue any longer than necessary, and this one had been going on for more than thirteen years now. Peace was necessary. But not peace at any price.

The trouble was that Karna had a reputation for losing wars and winning at the peace table. They were clever, persuasive talkers. They could twist a disadvantage to an advantage, and make their own strengths look like weaknesses. If they won the armistice, they'd be able to retrench and rearm, and the war would break out again within a few years.

Now—at this point in time—they could be beaten. They could be forced to allow supervision of the production potential, forced to disarm, rendered impotent. But if the armistice went to their own advantage . . .

Already, they had taken the offensive in the matter of the peace talks. They had sent a full delegation to Saarkkad V, the next planet out from the Saarkkad sun, a chilly world inhabited only by low-intelligence animals. The Karna considered this to be fully neutral territory, and Earth couldn't argue the point very well. In addition, they demanded that the conference begin in three days, Terrestrial time.

The trouble was that interstellar communication beams travel a devil of a lot faster than ships. It would take more than a week for the Earth government to get a vessel to Saarkkad V. Earth had been caught unprepared for an armistice. They objected.

The Karna pointed out that the Saarkkad sun was just

as far from Karn as it was from Earth, that it was only a few million miles from a planet which was allied with Earth, and that it was unfair for Earth to take so much time in preparing for an armistice. Why hadn't Earth been prepared? Did they intend to fight to the utter destruction of Karn?

It wouldn't have been a problem at all if Earth and Karn had fostered the only two intelligent races in the galaxy. The sort of grandstanding the Karna were putting on had to be played to an audience. But there were other intelligent races throughout the galaxy, most of whom had remained as neutral as possible during the Earth-Karn war. They had no intention of sticking their figurative noses into a battle between the two most powerful races in the galaxy.

But whoever won the armistice would find that some of the now-neutral races would come in on their side if war broke out again. If the Karna played their cards right, their side would be strong enough next time to win.

So Earth had to get a delegation to meet with the Karna representatives within the three-day limit or lose what might be a vital point in the negotiations.

And that was where Bertrand Malloy came in.

He had been appointed Minister and Plenipotentiary Extraordinary to the Earth-Karn peace conference.

He looked up at the ceiling again. "What can I do?" he said softly.

On the second day after the arrival of the communiqué, Malloy made his decision. He flipped on his intercom and said: "Miss Drayson, get hold of James Nordon and Kylen Braynek. I want to see them both immediately. Send Nordon in first, and tell Braynek to wait."

"Yes, sir."

"And keep the recorder on. You can file the tape later."

"Yes, sir."

Malloy knew the woman would listen in on the intercom anyway, and it was better to give her permission to do so.

James Nordon was tall, broad-shouldered, and thirty-eight. His hair was graying at the temples, and his handsome face looked cool and efficient.

Malloy waved him to a seat.

"Nordon, I have a job for you. It's probably one of the most important jobs you'll ever have in your life. It can mean big things for you—promotion and prestige if you do it well."

Nordon nodded slowly. "Yes, sir."

Malloy explained the problem of the Karna peace talks.

"We need a man who can outthink them," Malloy finished, "and judging from your record, I think you're that man. It involves risk, of course. If you make the wrong decisions, your name will be mud back on Earth. But I don't think there's much chance of that, really. Do you want to handle small-time operations all your life? Of course not.

"You'll be leaving within an hour for Saarkkad V."

Nordon nodded again. "Yes, sir; certainly. Am I to go alone?"

"No," said Malloy, "I'm sending an assistant with you—a man named Kylen Braynek. Ever heard of him?"

Nordon shook his head. "Not that I recall, Mr. Malloy. Should I have?"

"Not necessarily. He's a pretty shrewd operator, though. He knows a lot about interstellar law, and he's capable of spotting a trap a mile away. You'll be in charge, of course, but I want you to pay special attention to his advice."

"I will, sir," Nordon said gratefully. "A man like that can be useful."

"Right. Now, you go into the anteroom over there. I've prepared a summary of the situation, and you'll have to study it and get it into your head before the ship leaves. That isn't much time, but it's the Karna who are doing the pushing, not us."

As soon as Nordon had left, Malloy said softly: "Send in Braynek, Miss Drayson."

Kylen Braynek was a smallish man with mouse-brown hair that lay flat against his skull, and hard, penetrating, dark eyes that were shadowed by heavy, protruding brows. Malloy asked him to sit down.

Again Malloy went through the explanation of the peace conference.

"Naturally, they'll be trying to trick you every step of the way," Malloy went on. "They're shrewd and underhanded; we'll simply have to be more shrewd and more underhanded. Nordon's job is to sit quietly and evaluate the data; yours will be to find the loopholes they're laying out for themselves and plug them. Don't antagonize them, but don't baby them, either. If you see anything underhanded going on, let Nordon know immediately."

"They won't get anything by me, Mr. Malloy."

By the time the ship from Earth got there, the peace conference had been going on for four days. Bertrand Malloy had full reports on the whole parley, as relayed to him through the ship that had taken Nordon and Braynek to Saarkkad V.

Secretary of State Blendwell stopped off at Saarkkad IV before going on to V to take charge of the conference. He was a tallish, lean man with a few strands of gray hair on the top of his otherwise bald scalp, and he wore a hearty, professional smile that didn't quite make it to his calculating eyes.

He took Malloy's hand and shook it warmly. "How are you, Mr. Ambassador?"

"Fine, Mr. Secretary. How's everything on Earth?"

"Tense. They're waiting to see what is going to happen on V. So am I, for that matter." His eyes were curious. "You decided not to go yourself, eh?"

"I thought it better not to. I sent a good team, instead. Would you like to see the reports?"

"I certainly would."

Malloy handed them to the secretary, and as he read, Malloy watched him. Blendwell was a political appointee —a good man, Malloy had to admit, but he didn't know all the ins and outs of the Diplomatic Corps.

When Blendwell looked up from the reports at last, he said: "Amazing! They've held off the Karna at every point! They've beaten them back! They've managed to cope with and outdo the finest team of negotiators the Karna could send."

"I thought they would," said Malloy, trying to appear modest.

The secretary's eyes narrowed. "I've heard of the work you've been doing here with . . . ah . . . sick men. Is this one of your . . . ah . . . successes?"

Malloy nodded. "I think so. The Karna put us in a dilemma, so I threw a dilemma right back at them."

"How do you mean?"

"Nordon had a mental block against making decisions. If he took a girl out on a date, he'd have trouble making up his mind whether to kiss her or not until she made up his mind for him, one way or the other. He's that kind of guy. Until he's presented with one, single, clear decision which admits of no alternatives, he can't move at all.

"As you can see, the Karna tried to give us several choices on each point, and they were all rigged. Until they backed down to a single point and proved that it wasn't rigged, Nordon couldn't possibly make up his mind. I drummed into him how important this was, and the more importance there is attached to his decisions, the more incapable he becomes of making them."

The Secretary nodded slowly. "What about Braynek?"

"Paranoid," said Malloy. "He thinks everyone is plotting against him. In this case, that's all to the good because the Karna are plotting against him. No matter what they put forth, Braynek is convinced that there's a trap in it somewhere, and he digs to find out what the trap is. Even if there isn't a trap, the Karna can't satisfy Braynek, because he's convinced that there *has* to be—somewhere. As a result, all his advice to Nordon, and all his questioning on the wildest possibilities, just serves to keep Nordon from getting unconfused.

"These two men are honestly doing their best to win at the peace conference, and they've got the Karna reeling. The Karna can see that we're not trying to stall; our men are actually working at trying to reach a decision. But what the Karna don't see is that those men, as a team, are unbeatable because, in this situation, they're psychologically incapable of losing."

Again the Secretary of State nodded his approval, but there was still a question in his mind. "Since you know all that, couldn't you have handled it yourself?"

"Maybe, but I doubt it. They might have gotten around me some way by sneaking up on a blind spot. Nordon and Braynek have blind spots, but they're covered with armor. No, I'm glad I couldn't go; it's better this way."

The Secretary of State raised an eyebrow. "*Couldn't* go, Mr. Ambassador?"

Malloy looked at him. "Didn't you know? I wondered why you appointed me, in the first place. No, I couldn't go. The reason why I'm here, cooped up in this office, hiding from the Saarkkada the way a good Saarkkadic bigshot should, is because I *like* it that way. I suffer from agoraphobia and xenophobia.

"I have to be drugged to be put on a spaceship because I can't take all that empty space, even if I'm protected from it by a steel shell." A look of revulsion came over his face. "And I can't *stand* aliens!"

Randall Garrett (1927-)
Author of ten science fiction novels and over two hundred short stories, Randall Garrett was a mainstay of Analog during the 1960's. Indeed, some accused him of being nothing more than the fictional voice of John W. Campbell, Jr., the magazine's strong-willed editor. Paradoxically, however, Analog also proved to be the developing ground for Garrett's most famous creation, Lord Darcy. The works of this series include Too Many Magicians (1967), Murder & Magic (1981), and Lord Darcy Investigates (1981). The success of these works has led to a critical reevaluation and the issuance of his first collection, called The Best of Randall Garrett (1982).

THERAPY

WHAT FRIENDS ARE FOR
John Brunner

After Tim killed and buried the neighbors' prize terrier the Pattersons took him to the best-reputed—and most expensive—counselor in the state: Dr. Hend.

They spent forty of the fifty minutes they had purchased snapping at each other in the waiting room outside his office, breaking off now and then when a scream or a smashing noise eluded the soundproofing, only to resume more fiercely a moment later.

Eventually Tim was borne out, howling, by a strong male nurse who seemed impervious to being kicked in the belly with all the force an eight-year-old can muster, and the Pattersons were bidden to take his place in Dr. Hend's presence. There was no sign of the chaos the boy had caused. The counselor was a specialist in such cases, and there were smooth procedures for eliminating incidental mess.

"Well, doctor?" Jack Patterson demanded.

Dr. Hend studied him thoughtfully for a long moment, then glanced at his wife, Lorna, reconfirming the assessment he had made when they arrived. On the male side: expensive clothing, bluff good looks, a carefully constructed image of success. On the female: the most being made of what had to begin with been a somewhat shallow prettiness, even more expensive clothes, plus ultrafashionable hair style, cosmetics, and perfume.

He said at last, "That son of yours is going to be in court very shortly. Even if he is only eight, chronologically."

"What?" Jack Patterson erupted. "But we came here to—"

"You came here," the doctor cut in, "to be told the truth. It was your privilege to opt for a condensed-development child. You did it after being informed of the implications. Now you must face up to your responsibilities."

"No, we came here for help!" Lorna burst out. Her husband favored her with a scowl: *Shut up!*

"You have seven minutes of my time left," Dr. Hend said wearily. "You can spend it wrangling or listening to me. Shall I proceed?"

The Pattersons exchanged sour looks, then both nodded.

"*Thank* you. I can see precisely one alternative to having your child placed in a public institution. You'll have to get him a Friend."

"What? And show the world we can't cope?" Jack Patterson rasped. "You must be out of your mind!"

Dr. Hend just gazed at him.

"They're—they're terribly expensive, aren't they?" Lorna whispered.

The counselor leaned back and set his fingertips together. "As to being out of my mind . . . Well, I'm in good company. It's customary on every inhabited planet we know of to entrust the raising of the young to Friends programmed by a consensus of opinion among other intelligent races. There was an ancient proverb about not seeing the forest for the trees; it is well established that the best possible advice regarding optimum exploitation of juvenile talent comes from those who can analyze the local society in absolute, rather than committed, terms. And the habit is growing commoner here. Many families, if they can afford to, acquire a Friend from choice, not necessity.

"As to expense—yes, Mrs. Patterson, you're right. Anything which has had to be shipped over interstellar distances can hardly be cheap. But consider: this dog belonging to your neighbors was a show champion with at least one best-of-breed certificate, quite apart from being the boon companion of their small daughter. I imagine the courts will award a substantial sum by way of damages . . . Incidentally, did Tim previously advance the excuse that he couldn't stand the noise it made when it barked?"

"Uh . . ." Jack Patterson licked his lips. "Yes, he did."

"I suspected it might have been rehearsed. It had that kind of flavor. As did his excuse for breaking the arm of the little boy who was the best batter in your local junior ball team, and the excuse for setting fire to the school's free-fall gymnasium, and so forth. You have to accept the fact, I'm afraid, that thanks to his condensed-development therapy your son is a total egocentric. The universe has never yet proved sufficiently intractable to progress him out of the emotional stage most infants leave behind about the time they learn to walk. Physically he is ahead of the average for his age. Emotionally, he is concerned about nothing but his own gratification. He's incapable of empathy, sympathy, worrying about the opinions of others. He is a classic case of arrested personal development."

"But we've done everything we can to—"

"Yes, indeed you have. And it is not enough." Dr. Hend allowed the comment to rankle for a few seconds, then resumed.

"We were talking about expense. Well, let me remind you that it costs a lot of money to maintain Tim in the special school you've been compelled to send him to because he made life hell for his classmates at a regular school. The companionship of a Friend is legally equivalent to a formal course of schooling. Maybe you weren't aware of that."

"Sure!" Jack snapped. "But—oh, hell! I simply don't fancy the idea of turning my son over to some ambulating alien artifact!"

"I grant it may seem to you to be a radical step, but juvenile maladjustment is one area where the old saw remains true, about desperate diseases requiring desperate measures. And have you considered the outcome if you don't adopt a radical solution?"

It was clear from their glum faces that they had, but he spelled it out for them nonetheless.

"By opting for a modified child, you rendered yourselves liable for his maintenance and good behavior for a minimum period of twenty years, regardless of divorce or other legal interventions. If Tim is adjudged socially incorrigible, you will find yourselves obliged to support him indefinitely in a state institution. At present the annual cost of keeping one patient in such an establishment is thirty thousand dollars. Inflation at the current rate will double that by the twenty-year mark, and in view of the extensive alterations you insisted on having made in Tim's heredity I think it unlikely that any court would agree to discontinue your liability as early as twelve years from now. I put it to you that the acquisition of a Friend is your only sensible course of action—whatever you may think of the way alien intelligences have evaluated our society. Besides, you don't have to buy one. You can always rent."

He glanced at his desk clock. "I see your time is up. Good morning. My bill will be faxed to you this afternoon."

That night there was shouting from the living area of the Patterson house. Tim heard it, lying in bed with the door ajar, and grinned from ear to shell-like ear. He was an extremely beautiful child, with curly fair hair, perfectly proportioned features, ideally regular teeth, eyes blue and deep as mountain pools, a sprinkling of freckles as per specification to make him a trifle less angelic, a fraction more boylike, and—naturally—he was big for his age. That had been in the specification, too.

Moreover, his vocabulary was enormous compared to an unmodified kid's—as was his IQ, theoretically, though he had never cooperated on a test which might have proved the fact—and he fully understood what was being said.

"You and your goddamn vanity! Insisting on all those special features like wavy golden hair and baby-blue eyes and—and, my God, *freckles!* And now the little devil is apt to drive us into bankruptcy! Have you *seen* what it costs to rent a Friend, even a cheap one from Procyon?"

"Oh, stop trying to lay all the blame on me, will you? They warned you that your demand for tallness and extra strength might be incompatible with the rest, and you took not a blind bit of notice—"

"But he's a boy, dammit, a boy, and if you hadn't wanted him to look more like a girl—"

"I did not, I did not! I wanted him to be *handsome* and you wanted to make him into some kind of crazy beefcake type, loaded down with useless muscles! Just because you never made the college gladiator squad he was condemned before birth to—"

"One more word about what I *didn't* do, and I'll smash your teeth down your ugly throat! How about talking about what I *have* done for a change? Youngest area manager in the corporation, tipped to be the youngest-ever vice-president . . . small thanks to you, of course. When I think where I might have gotten to by now if you hadn't been tied around my neck—"

Tim's grin grew so wide it was almost painful. He was becoming drowsy because that outburst in the counselor's office had expended a lot of energy, but there was one more thing he could do before he dropped off to sleep. He crept from his bed, went to the door on tiptoe, and carefully urinated through the gap onto the landing carpet outside. Then, chuckling, he scrambled back under the coverlet and a few minutes later was lost in colorful dreams.

The doorbell rang when his mother was in the bathroom and his father was calling on the lawyers to see whether the matter of the dog could be kept out of court after all.

At once Lorna yelled, "Tim, stay right where you are—I'll get it!"

But he was already heading for the door at a dead run. He liked being the first to greet a visitor. It was such fun to show himself stark naked and shock puritanical callers, or scream and yell about how Dad had beaten him mercilessly, showing off bruises collected by banging into furniture and blood trickling from cuts and scratches. But today an even more inspired idea came to him, and he made a rapid detour through the kitchen and raided the garbage pail as he passed.

He opened the door with his left hand and delivered a soggy mass of rotten fruit, vegetable peelings, and coffee grounds with his right, as hard as he could and at about face height for a grownup.

Approximately half a second later the whole loathsome mass splattered over him, part on his face so that his open mouth tasted the foulness of it, part on his chest so that it dropped inside his open shirt. And a reproachful voice said, "Tim! I'm your Friend! And that's no way to treat a friend, is it?"

Reflex had brought him to the point of screaming. His lungs were filling, his muscles were tensing, when he saw what had arrived on the threshold and his embryo yell turned into a simple gape of astonishment.

The Friend was humanoid, a few inches taller than himself and a great deal broader, possessed of two legs and two arms and a head with eyes and a mouth and a pair of ears ... but it was covered all over in shaggy fur of a brilliant emerald green. Its sole decoration—apart from a trace of the multicolored garbage it had caught and heaved back at him, which still adhered to the palm of its left hand—was a belt around its waist bearing a label stamped in bright red letters—AUTHORIZED AUTONOMIC ARTIFACT (SELF-DELIVERING)—followed by the Patterson family's address.

"Invite me in," said the apparition. "You don't keep a friend standing on the doorstep, you know, and I am your Friend, as I just explained."

"Tim! *Tim!*" At a stumbling run, belting a robe around her, his mother appeared from the direction of the bathroom, a towel clumsily knotted over her newly washed hair. On seeing the nature of the visitor, she stopped dead.

"But the rental agency said not to expect you until—" She broke off. It was the first time in her life she had spoken to an alien biofact, although she had seen many both live and on tri-vee.

"We were able to include more than the anticipated quantity in the last shipment from Procyon," the Friend said. "There has been an advance in packaging methods. Permit me to identify myself." It marched past Tim and removed its belt, complete with label, and handed it to Lorna. "I trust you will find that I conform to your requirements."

"You stinking bastard! I won't have you fucking around in my home!" Tim shrieked. He had small conception of what the words he was using meant, except in a very abstract way, but he was sure of one thing: they always made his parents good and mad.

The Friend, not sparing him a glance, said, "Tim, you should have introduced me to your mother. Since you did not I am having to introduce myself. Do not compound your impoliteness by interrupting, because that makes an even worse impression."

"Get out!" Tim bellowed, and launched himself at the Friend in a flurry of kicking feet and clenched fists. At once he found himself suspended a foot off the floor with the waistband of his pants tight in a grip like a crane's.

To Lorna the Friend said, "All you're requested to do is thumbprint the acceptance box and fax the datum back to the rental company. That is, if you do agree to accept me."

She looked at it, and her son, for a long moment, and then firmly planted her thumb on the reverse label.

"Thank you. Now, Tim!" The Friend swiveled him around so that it could look directly at him. "I'm sorry to see how dirty you are. It's not the way one would wish to find a friend. I shall give you a bath and a change of clothes."

"I had a bath!" Tim howled, flailing arms and legs impotently.

Ignoring him, the Friend continued, "Mrs. Patterson, if you'll kindly show me where Tim's clothes are kept, I'll attend to the matter right away."

A slow smile spread over Lorna's face. "You know something?" she said to the air. "I guess that counselor was on the right track after all. Come this way—uh . . . Say! What do we call you?"

"It's customary to have the young person I'm assigned to select a name for me."

"If I know Tim," Lorna said, "he'll pick something so filthy it can't be used in company!"

Tim stopped screaming for a moment. That was an idea which hadn't occurred to him.

"But," Lorna declared, "we'll avoid that, and just call you Buddy right from the start. Is that okay?"

"I shall memorize the datum at once. Come along, Tim!"

"Well, I guess it's good to find such prompt service these days," Jack Patterson muttered, looking at the green form of Buddy curled up by the door of Tim's bedroom. Howls, yells, and moans were pouring from the room, but during the past half-hour they had grown less loud, and sometimes intervals of two or three minutes interrupted the racket, as though exhaustion was overcoming the boy. "I still hate to think what the neighbors are going to say, though. It's about the most public admission of defeat that parents can make, to let their kid be seen with one of those things at his heels!"

"Stop thinking about what the neighbors will say and

think about how I feel for once!" rapped his wife. "You had an easy day today—"

"The hell I did! Those damned lawyers—"

"You were sitting in a nice quiet office! If it hadn't been for Buddy, I'd have had more than even my usual kind of hell! I think Dr. Hend had a terrific idea. I'm impressed."

"Typical!" Jack grunted. "You can't cope with this, buy a machine; you can't cope with that, buy another machine . . . Now it turns out you can't even cope with your own son. *I'm* not impressed!"

"Why, you goddamn—"

"Look, I paid good money to make sure of having a kid who'd be bright and talented and a regular all-around guy, and I got one. But who's been looking after him? You have! You've screwed him up with your laziness and bad temper!"

"How much time do you waste on helping to raise him?" She confronted him, hands on hips and eyes aflame. "Every evening it's the same story, every weekend it's the same— 'Get this kid off my neck because I'm worn out!' "

"Oh, shut up. It sounds as though he's finally dropped off. Want to wake him again and make things worse? I'm going to fix a drink. I need one."

He spun on his heel and headed downstairs. Fuming, Lorna followed him.

By the door of Tim's room, Buddy remained immobile except that one of his large green ears swiveled slightly and curled over at the tip.

At breakfast next day Lorna served hot cereal—to Buddy as well as Tim, because among the advantages of this model of Friend was the fact that it could eat anything its assigned family was eating.

Tim picked up his dish as soon as it was set before him

and threw it with all his might at Buddy. The Friend caught it with such dexterity that hardly a drop splashed on the table.

"Thank you, Tim," it said, and ate the lot in a single slurping mouthful. "According to my instructions you like this kind of cereal, so giving it to me is a very generous act. Though you might have delivered the dish somewhat more gently."

Tim's semiangelic face crumpled like a mask made of wet paper. He drew a deep breath, and then flung himself forward across the table, aiming to knock everything off it onto the floor. Nothing could break—long and bitter experience had taught the Pattersons to buy only resilient plastic utensils—but spilling the milk, sugar, juice, and other items could have made a magnificent mess.

A hair's breath away from the nearest object, the milk bottle, Tim found himself pinioned in a gentle but inflexible clutch.

"It appears that it is time to begin lessons for the day," Buddy said. "Excuse me, Mrs. Patterson. I shall take Tim into the backyard, where there is more space."

"To begin lessons?" Lorna echoed. "Well—uh . . . But he hasn't had any breakfast yet!"

"If you'll forgive my saying so, he has. He chose not to eat it. He is somewhat overweight, and one presumes that lunch will be served at the customary time. Between now and noon it is unlikely that malnutrition will claim him. Besides, this offers an admirable opportunity for a practical demonstration of the nature of mass, inertia, and friction."

With no further comment Buddy rose and, carrying Tim in effortless fashion, marched over to the door giving access to the yard.

"So how has that hideous green beast behaved today?" Jack demanded.

"Oh, it's fantastic! I'm starting to get the hang of what it's designed to do." Lorna leaned back in her easy chair with a smug expression.

"Yes?" Jack's face by contrast was sour. "Such as what?"

"Well, it puts up with everything Tim can do—and that's a tough job because he's pulling out all the stops he can think of—and interprets it in the most favorable way it can. It keeps insisting that it's Tim's Friend, so he's doing what a friend ought to do."

Jack blinked at her. "What the hell are you talking about?" he rasped.

"If you'd listen, you might find out!" she snapped back. "He threw his breakfast at Buddy, so Buddy ate it and said thank you. Then because he got hungry he climbed up and got at the candy jar, and Buddy took that and ate the lot and said thank you again, and . . . Oh, it's all part of a pattern, and very clever."

"Are you crazy? You let this monstrosity eat not only Tim's breakfast but all his candy, and you didn't try and stop it?"

"I don't think you read the instructions," Lorna said.

"Quit needling me, will you? Of course I read the instructions!"

"Then you know that if you interfere with what a Friend does, your contract is automatically void and you have to pay the balance of the rental in a lump sum!"

"And how is it interfering to give your own son some more breakfast in place of what the horrible thing took?"

"But Tim threw his dish at—"

"If you gave him a decent diet he'd—"

It continued. Above, on the landing outside Tim's door,

Buddy kept his furry green ears cocked, soaking up every word.

"Tim!"

"Shut up, you fucking awful nuisance!"

"Tim, if you climb that tree past the first fork, you will be on a branch that's not strong enough to bear your weight. You will fall about nine feet to the ground, and the ground is hard because the weather this summer has been so dry."

"*Shut up!* All I want is to get away from you!"

Crack!

"What you are suffering from is a bruise, technically called a subcutaneous hemorrhage. That means a leak of blood under the skin. You also appear to have a slight rupture of the left Achilles tendon. That's this sinew here, which . . ."

"In view of your limited skill in swimming, it's not advisable to go more than five feet from the edge of this pool. Beyond that point the bottom dips very sharply."

"*Shut up!* I'm trying to get away from you, so—*glug!*"

"Insufficient oxygen is dissolved in water to support an air-breathing creature like a human. Fish, on the other hand, can utilize the oxygen dissolved in water, because they have gills and not lungs. Your ancestors . . ."

"Why, there's that little bastard Tim Patterson! And look at what he's got trailing behind him! Hey, Tim! Who said you had to live with this funny green teddy bear? Did you have to go have your head shrunk?"

Crowding around him, a dozen neighborhood kids, both sexes, various ages from nine to fourteen.

"Tim's head, as you can doubtless see, is of normal proportions. I am assigned to him as his Friend."

"Hah! Don't give us that shit! Who'd want to be a friend of Tim's? He busted my brother's arm and laughed about it!"

"He set fire to the gym of my school!"

"He killed my dog—he killed my Towser!"

"So I understand. Tim, you have the opportunity to say you were sorry, don't you?"

"Ah, he made that stinking row all the time, barking his silly head off—"

"You bastard! *You killed my dog!*"

"Buddy, help! *Help!*"

"As I said, Tim, you have an excellent opportunity to say how sorry you are . . . No, little girl: please put down that rock. It's extremely uncivil, and also dangerous, to throw things like that at people."

"*Shut up!*"

"Let's beat the hell out of him! Let him go whining back home and tell how all those terrible kids attacked him, and see how he likes his own medicine!"

"Kindly refrain from attempting to inflict injuries on my assigned charge."

"I told you to shut up, greenie!"

"I did caution you, as you'll recall. I did say that it was both uncivil and dangerous to throw rocks at people. I believe what I should do is inform your parents. Come. Tim."

"No!"

"Very well, as you wish. I shall release this juvenile to continue the aggression with rocks."

"No!"

"But, Tim, your two decisions are incompatible. Either

you come with me to inform this child's parents of the fact that rocks were thrown at you, or I shall have to let go and a great many more rocks will probably be thrown—perhaps more than I can catch before they hit you."

"I—uh . . . I—I'm sorry that I hurt your dog. It just made me so mad that he kept on barking and barking all the time, and never shut up!"

"But he didn't bark all the time! He got hurt—he cut his paw and he wanted help!"

"He did *so* bark all the time!"

"He did not! You just got mad because he did it that one time!"

"I—uh . . . Well, I guess maybe . . ."

"To be precise, there had been three complaints recorded about your dog's excessive noise. On each occasion you had gone out and left him alone for several hours."

"Right! Thank you, Buddy! See?"

"But you didn't have to kill him!"

"Correct, Tim. You did not. You could have become acquainted with him, and then looked after him when it was necessary to leave him by himself."

"Ah, who'd want to care for a dog like that shaggy brute?"

"Perhaps someone who never was allowed his own dog?"

"Okay. Okay! Sure I wanted a dog, and they never let me have one! Kept saying I'd—I'd torture it or something! So I said fine, if that's how you think of me, let's go right ahead! You always like to be proven right!"

"Kind of quiet around here tonight," Jack Patterson said. "What's been going on?"

"You can thank Buddy," Lorna answered.

"Can I now? So what's he done that I can't do, this time?"

"Persuaded Tim to go to bed on time and without yelling his head off, that's what!"

"Don't feed me that line! 'Persuaded'! Cowed him, don't you mean?"

"All I can say is that tonight's the first time he's let Buddy sleep inside the room instead of on the landing by the door."

"You keep saying I didn't read the instructions—now it turns out *you* didn't read them! Friends don't sleep, not the way we do at any rate. They're supposed to be on watch twenty-four hours per day."

"Oh, stop it! The first peaceful evening we've had in heaven knows how long, and you're determined to ruin it!"

"I am not!"

"Then why the hell don't you keep quiet?"

Upstairs, beyond the door of Tim's room, which was as ever ajar, Buddy's ears remained alert with their tips curled over to make them acoustically ultrasensitive.

"Who—? Oh! I know you! You're Tim Patterson, aren't you? Well, what do you want?"

"... I ..."

"Tim wishes to know whether your son would care to play ball with him, madam."

"You have to be joking! I'm not going to let Teddy play with Tim after the way Tim broke his elbow with a baseball bat!"

"It did happen quite a long time ago, madam, and—"

"No! That's final! No!"

Slam!

"Well, thanks for trying, Buddy. It would have been kind of fun to . . . Ah, well!"

"That little girl is ill-advised to play so close to a road carrying fast traffic— Oh, dear. Tim, I shall need help in coping with this emergency. Kindly take off your belt and place it around her leg about *here* . . . That's correct. Now pull it tight. See how the flow of blood is reduced? You've put a tourniquet on the relevant pressure point, that's to say a spot where a large artery passes near the skin. If much blood were allowed to leak, it might be fatal. I note there is a pen in the pocket of her dress. Please write a letter T on her forehead, and add the exact time; you see, there's a clock over there. When she gets to the hospital the surgeon will know how long the blood supply to her leg has been cut off. It must not be restricted more than twenty minutes."

"Uh . . . Buddy, I can't write a T. And I can't tell the time either."

"How old did you say you were?"

"Well . . . Eight. And a half."

"Yes, Tim. I'm actually aware both of your age and of your incompetence. Give me the pen, please . . . There. Now go to the nearest house and ask someone to telephone for an ambulance. Unless the driver, who I see is backing up, has a phone right in his car."

"Yes, what do you want?" Jack Patterson stared at the couple who had arrived without warning on the doorstep.

"Mr. Patterson? I'm William Vickers, from up on the 1100 block, and this is my wife, Judy. We thought we ought to call around after what your boy, Tim, did today. Louise—that's our daughter—she's still in the hospital, of course, but . . . Well, they say she's going to make a quick recovery."

"What the hell is that about Tim?" From the living area Lorna emerged, glowering and reeking of gin. "Did you say Tim put your daughter in the hospital? Well, that finishes it! Jack Patterson, I'm damned if I'm going to waste any more of my life looking after your goddamn son! I am through with him and you both—d'you hear it? *Through!*"

"But you've got it all wrong," Vickers protested feebly. "Thanks to his quick thinking, and that Friend who goes with him everywhere, Louise got off amazingly lightly. Just some cuts, and a bit of blood lost—nothing serious. Nothing like as badly hurt as you'd expect a kid to be when a car had knocked her down."

Lorna's mouth stood half-open like that of a stranded fish. There was a pause; then Judy Vickers plucked at her husband's sleeve.

"Darling, I—uh—think we came at a bad moment. We ought to get home. But . . . Well, you do understand how grateful we are, don't you?"

She turned away, and so, after a bewildered glance at both Jack and Lorna, did her husband.

"You stupid bitch!" Jack roared. "Why the hell did you have to jump to such an idiotic conclusion? Two people come around to say thanks to Tim for—for whatever the hell he did, and you have to assume the worst! Don't you have any respect for your son at all . . . or any love?"

"Of course I love him! I'm his mother! I do care about him!" Lorna was returning to the living area, crabwise because her head was turned to shout at Jack over her shoulder. "For you, though, he's nothing but a possession, a status symbol, a—"

"A correction, Mrs. Patterson," a firm voice said. She

gasped and whirled. In the middle of the living area's largest rug was Buddy, his green fur making a hideous clash with the royal blue of the oblong he was standing on.

"Hey! What are you doing down here?" Jack exploded. "You're supposed to be up with Tim!"

"Tim is fast asleep and will remain so for the time being," the Friend said calmly. "Though I would suggest that you keep your voices quiet."

"Now look here! I'm not going to take orders from—"

"Mr. Patterson, there is no question of orders involved. I simply wish to clarify a misconception on your wife's part. While she has accurately diagnosed your attitude toward your son—as she just stated, you have never regarded him as a person, but only as an attribute to bolster your own total image, which is that of the successful corporation executive—she is still under the misapprehension that she, quote unquote, 'loves' Tim. It would be more accurate to say that she welcomes his intractability because it offers her the chance to vent her jealousy against you. She resents—No, Mrs. Patterson, I would not recommend the employment of physical violence. I am engineered to a far more rapid level of nervous response than human beings enjoy."

One arm upraised, with a heavy cut-crystal glass in it poised ready to throw, Lorna hesitated, then sighed and repented.

"Yeah, okay. I've seen you catch everything Tim's thrown at you . . . But you shut up, hear me?" With a return of her former rage. "It's no damned business of yours to criticize me! Nor Jack either!"

"Right!" Jack said. "I've never been so insulted in my life!"

"Perhaps it would have been salutary for you to be told some unpleasant truths long ago," Buddy said. "My assignment is to help actualize the potential which—I must remind you—you arranged to build into Tim's genetic endowment. He did not ask to be born the way he is. He did not ask to come into the world as the son of parents who were so vain they could not be content with a natural child, but demanded the latest luxury model. You have systematically wasted his talents. No child of eight years and six months with an IQ in the range of 160–175 should be incapable of reading, writing, telling the time, counting, and so forth. This is the predicament you've wished on Tim."

"If you don't shut up I'll—"

"Mr. Patterson, I repeat my advice to keep your voice down."

"I'm not going to take advice or any other kind of nonsense from you, you green horror!"

"Nor am I!" Lorna shouted. "To be told I don't love my own son, and just use him as a stick to beat Jack with—"

"Right, right! And I'm not going to put up with being told I treat him as some kind of ornament, a . . . What did you call it?"

Prompt, Buddy said, "An attribute to bolster your image."

"That's it— Now just a second!" Jack strode toward the Friend. "You're mocking me, aren't you?"

"And me!" Lorna cried.

"Well, I've had enough! First thing tomorrow morning I call the rental company and tell them to take you away. I'm sick of having you run our lives as though we were morons unfit to look after ourselves, and above all I'm sick of my son being put in charge of— Tim! What the hell are you doing out of bed?"

"I did advise you to speak more quietly," Buddy murmured.

"Get back to your room at once!" Lorna stormed at the

small tousle-haired figure descending the stairs in blue pajamas. Tears were streaming across his cheeks, glistening in the light of the living area's lamps.

"Didn't you hear your mother?" Jack bellowed. "Get back to bed this minute!"

But Tim kept on coming down, with stolid determined paces, and reached the floor level and walked straight toward Buddy and linked his thin pink fingers with Buddy's green furry ones. Only then did he speak.

"You're not going to send Buddy away! This is my friend!"

"Don't use that tone to your father! I'll do what the hell I like with that thing!"

"No, you won't." Tim's words were full of finality. "You aren't allowed to. I read the contract. It says you can't."

"What do you mean, you 'read the contract'?" Lorna rasped. "You can't read anything, you little fool!"

"As a matter of fact, he can," Buddy said mildly. "I taught him to read this afternoon."

"You—you what?"

"I taught him to read this afternoon. The skill was present in his mind but had been rendered artificially latent, a problem which I have now rectified. Apart from certain inconsistent sound-to-symbol relationships, Tim should be capable of reading literally anything in a couple of days."

"And I did so read the contract!" Tim declared. "So I know Buddy can be with me for ever and ever!"

"You exaggerate," Buddy murmured.

"Oh, sure I do! But ten full years is a long time." Tim tightened his grip on Buddy's hand. "So let's not have any more silly talk, hm? And no more shouting either, please. Buddy has explained why kids my age need plenty of sleep, and I guess I ought to go back to bed. Coming, Buddy?"

"Yes, of course. Good night, Mr. Patterson, Mrs. Patterson. Do please ponder my remarks. And Tim's too, because he knows you so much better than I do."

Turning toward the stairs, Buddy at his side, Tim glanced back with a grave face on which the tears by now had dried.

"Don't worry," he said. "I'm not going to be such a handful any more. I realize now you can't help how you behave."

"He's so goddamn patronizing!" Jack Patterson exploded next time he and Lorna were in Dr. Hend's office. As part of the out-of-court settlement of the dead-dog affair they were obliged to bring Tim here once a month. It was marginally cheaper than hiring the kind of legal computer capacity which might save the kid from being institutionalized.

"Yes, I can well imagine that he must be," Dr. Hend sighed. "But, you see, a biofact like Buddy is designed to maximize the characteristics which leading anthropologists from Procyon, Regulus, Sigma Draconis, and elsewhere have diagnosed as being beneficial in human society but in dangerously short supply. Chief among these, of course, is empathy. Fellow-feeling, compassion, that kind of thing. And to encourage the development of it, one must start by inculcating patience. Which involves setting an example."

"Patience? There's nothing patient about Tim!" Lorna retorted. "Granted, he used to be self-willed and destructive and foul-mouthed, and that's over, but now he never gives us a moment's peace! All the time it's gimme this, gimme that, I want to make a boat, I want to build a model starship, I want glass so I can make a what's-it to watch ants breeding in . . . I want, I want! It's just as bad and maybe worse."

"Right!" Jack said morosely. "What Buddy's done is turn our son against us."

"On the contrary. It's turned him *for* you. However belatedly, he's now doing his best to live up to the ideals you envisaged in the first place. You wanted a child with a lively mind and a high IQ. You've got one." Dr. Hend's voice betrayed the fact that his temper was fraying. "He's back in a regular school, he's establishing a fine scholastic record, he's doing well at free-fall gymnastics and countless other subjects. Buddy has made him over into precisely the sort of son you originally ordered."

"No, I told you!" Jack barked. "He—he kind of looks down on us, and I can't stand it!"

"Mr. Patterson, if you stopped to think occasionally you might realize why that could not have been avoided."

"I say it could and should have been avoided!"

"It could not! To break Tim out of his isolation in the shortest possible time, to cure him of his inability to relate to other people's feelings, Buddy used the most practical means at hand. It taught Tim a sense of pity—a trick I often wish I could work, but I'm only human, myself. It wasn't Buddy's fault, any more than it was Tim's, that the first people the boy learned how to pity had to be you.

"So if you want him to switch over to respecting you, you'd better ask Buddy's advice. He'll explain how to go about it. After all, that's what Friends are for: to make us better at being human.

"Now you must excuse me, because I have other clients waiting. Good afternoon!"

John Brunner (1934–)
John Brunner began selling science fiction as a teenager and is now one of the most prominent science fiction writers in Great Britain. So far he has produced more than fifty novels and one hundred stories, winning several major awards, including the

Hugo, in the process. A very ambitious writer, he has consistently attempted to expand his range by tackling unusual subjects or by utilizing experimental techniques. The Squares of the City (1965), for example, transforms a classic chess game into a science fiction novel, while Stand on Zanzibar (1968) portrays the despair of a grossly overpopulated future through a mosaic style similar to John Dos Passos's.

SOCIAL PSYCHOLOGY

THE DRIVERS
Edward W. Ludwig

He took a deep breath. He withdrew his handkerchief and wiped perspiration from his forehead, his upper lip, the palms of his hands.

His mind caressed the hope: *Maybe I've failed the tests. Maybe they won't give me a license.*

He opened the door and stepped inside.

The metallic voice of a robot-receptionist hummed at him:

"Name?"

"T—Tom Rogers."

Click. "Have you an appointment?"

His gaze ran over the multitude of silver-boxed analyzers,

computers, tabulators, over the white-clad technicians and attendants, over the endless streams of taped data fed from mouths in the dome-shaped ceiling.

"Have you an appointment?" repeated the robot.

"Oh. At 4:45 P.M."

Click. "Follow the red arrow in Aisle Three, please."

Tom Rogers moved down the aisle, eyes wide on the flashing, arrow-shaped lights just beneath the surface of the quartzite floor.

Abruptly, he found himself before a desk. Someone pushed him into a foam-rubber contour chair.

"Surprised, eh, boy?" boomed a deep voice. "No robots at this stage of the game. No sir. This requires the human touch. Get me?"

"Uh-huh."

"Well, let's see now." The man settled back in his chair behind the desk and began thumbing through a file of papers. He was paunchy and bald save for a forepeak of red-brown fuzz. His gray eyes, with the dreamy look imposed by thick contact lenses, were kindly. Sweeping across his flat chest were two rows of rainbow-bright Driver's Ribbons. Two of the bronze accident stars were flanked by smaller stars which indicated limb replacements.

Belatedly, Tom noticed the desk's aluminum placard which read *Harry Hayden, Final Examiner—Human.*

Tom thought, *Please, Harry Hayden, tell me I failed. Don't lead up to it. Please come out and say I failed the tests.*

"Haven't had much time to look over your file," mused Harry Hayden. "Thomas Darwell Rogers. Occupation: journalism student. Unmarried. No siblings. Height, five-eleven. Weight, one-sixty-three. Age, twenty."

Harry Hayden frowned. "Twenty?" he repeated, looking up.

Oh, God, here it comes again.

"Yes, sir," said Tom Rogers.

Harry Hayden's face hardened. "You've tried to enlist before? You were turned down?"

"This is my first application."

Sudden hostility swept aside Harry Hayden's expression of kindliness. He scowled at Tom's file. "Born July 18, 2020. This is July 16, 2041. In two days you'll be twenty-one. We don't issue new licenses to people over twenty-one."

"I—I know, sir. The psychiatrists believe you adjust better to Driving when you're young."

"In fact," glowered Harry Hayden, "in two days you'd have been classified as an enlistment evader. Our robostatistics department would have issued an automatic warrant of arrest."

"I know, sir."

"Then why'd you wait so long?" The voice was razor-sharp.

Tom wiped a fresh burst of sweat from his forehead. "Well, you know how one keeps putting things off. I just—"

"You don't put off things like this, boy. Why, my three sons were lined up here at five in the morning on their sixteenth birthdays. Every mother's son of 'em. They'd talked of nothing else since they were twelve. Used to play Drivers maybe six, seven hours every day . . ." His voice trailed.

"Most kids are like that," said Tom.

"Weren't you?" The hostility in Harry Hayden seemed to be churning like boiling water.

"Oh, sure," lied Tom.

"I don't get it. You say you wanted to Drive, but you didn't try to enlist."

Tom squirmed.

You can't tell him you've been scared of jetmobiles ever since you saw that crash when you were three. You can't say that, at seven, you saw your grandfather die in a jet-

mobile and that after that you wouldn't even play with a jetmobile toy. You can't tell him those things because five years of psychiatric treatment didn't get the fear out of you. If the medics didn't understand, how could Harry Hayden?

Tom licked his lips. And you can't tell him how you used to lie in bed praying you'd die before you were sixteen—or how you've pleaded with Mom and Dad not to make you enlist till you were twenty. You can't—

Inspiration struck him. He clenched his fists. "It—it was my mother, sir. You know how mothers are sometimes. Hate to see their kids grow up. Hate to see them put on a uniform and risk being killed."

Harry Hayden digested the explanation for a few seconds. It seemed to pacify him. "By golly, that's right. Esther took it hard when Mark died in a five-car bang-up out of San Francisco. And when Larry got his three summers ago in Europe. Esther's my wife—Mark was my youngest, Larry the oldest."

He shook his head. "But it isn't as bad as it used to be. Organ and limb grafts are pretty well perfected, and with electro-hypnosis operations are painless. The only fatalities now are when death is immediate, when it happens before the medics get to you. Why, no more than one out of ten Drivers died in the last four-year period."

A portion of his good nature returned. "Anyway, your personal life's none of my business. You understand the enlistment contract?"

Tom nodded. *Damn you, Harry Hayden, let me out of here. Tell me I failed, tell me I passed. But damn you, let me out.*

"Well?" said Harry Hayden, waiting.

"Oh. The enlistment contract. First enlistment is for four years. Renewal any time during the fourth year at the option of the enlistee. Minimum number of hours required per week: seven. Use of unauthorized armor or offensive weapons punishable by $5,000.00 fine or five years in prison. All accidents and deaths not witnessed by a Jetway 'copter-jet must be reported at once by visi-phone to nearest Referee and Medical Depot. Oh yes, maximum speed: 900 miles per."

"Right! You got it, boy!" Harry Hayden paused, licking his lips. "Now, let's see. Guess I'd better ask another question or two. This *is* your final examination, you know. What do you remember about the history of Driving?"

Tom was tempted to say, "Go to hell, you fat idiot," but he knew that whatever he did or said now was of no importance. The robot-training tests he'd undergone during the past three weeks, only, were of importance.

Dimly, he heard himself repeating the phrases beaten into his mind by school history-tapes:

"In the 20th Century a majority of the Earth's peoples were filled with hatreds and frustrations. Humanity was cursed with a world war every generation or so. Between wars, young people had no outlets for their energy, and many of them formed bands of delinquents. Even older people developed an alarming number of psychoses and neuroses.

"The institution of Driving was established in 1998 after automobiles were declared obsolete because of their great number. The Jetways were retained for use of young people in search of thrills."

"Right!" Harry Hayden broke in. "Now, the kids get all the excitement they need, and there are no more delinquent bands and wars. When you've spent a hitch or two killing or almost being killed, you're mature. You're ready to settle down and live a quiet life—just like most of the old-time war veterans used to do. And you're trained to think and act fast, you've got good judgment. And the weak and unfit are weeded out. Right, boy?"

Tom nodded. A thought forced its way up from the layer of fear that covered his mind. "Right—as far as it goes."

"How's that?"

Tom's voice quavered, but he said, "I mean that's part of it. The rest is that most people are bored with themselves. They think that by traveling fast they can escape from themselves. After four or eight years of racing at 800 per, they find out they can't escape after all, so they become resigned. Or, sometimes if they're lucky enough to escape death, they begin to feel important after all. They aren't so bored then because a part of their mind tells them they're mightier than death."

Harry Hayden whistled. "Hey, I never heard that before. Is that in the tapes now? Can't say I understand it too well, but it's a fine idea. Anyway, Driving's good. Cuts down on excess population, too—and with Peru putting in Jetways, it's world-wide. Yep, by golly. Yes, sir!"

He thrust a pen at Tom. "All right, boy. Just sign here."

Tom Rogers took the pen automatically. "You mean, I—"

"Yep, you came through your robot-training tests A-1. Oh, some of the psycho reports aren't too flattering. Lack of confidence, sense of inferiority, inability to adjust. But nothing serious. A few weeks of Driving'll fix you up. Yep, boy, you've passed. You're getting your license. Tomorrow morning you'll be on the Jetway. You'll be Driving, boy, Driving!"

Oh, Mother of God, Mother of God . . .

"And now," said Harry Hayden, "you'll want to see your Hornet."

"Of course," murmured Tom Rogers, swaying.

The paunchy man rose and led Tom down an aluminite

ramp and onto a small observation platform some ninety feet above the ground.

A dry summer wind licked at Tom's hair and stung his eyes. Nausea twisted at his innards. He felt as if he were perched on the edge of a slippery precipice.

"There," intoned Harry Hayden, "is the Jetway. Beautiful, eh?"

"Uh-huh."

Trembling, Tom forced his vision to the bright, smooth canyon beneath him. Its bottom was a shining white asphalt ribbon, a thousand feet wide, that cut arrow-straight through the city. Its walls were naked concrete banks a hundred feet high whose reinforced lips curved inward over the antiseptic whiteness.

Harry Hayden pointed a chubby finger downward. "And there *they* are—the Hornets. See 'em, boy? Right there in front of the assembly shop. Twelve of 'em. Brand-new DeLuxe Super-Jet '41 Hornets. Yes, sir. Going to be twelve of you initiated tomorrow."

Tom scowled at the twelve jetmobiles shaped like flattened teardrops. No sunlight glittered on their dead-black bodies. They squatted silent and foreboding, oblivious to sunlight, black bullets poised to hurl their prospective occupants into fury and horror.

Grandpa looked so very white in his coffin, so very dead—

"What's the matter, boy? You sick?"

"N—no, of course not."

Harry Hayden laughed. "I get it. You thought you'd get to *really* see one. Get in it, I mean, try it out. It's too late in the day, boy. Shop's closing. You couldn't drive one anyway. Regulation is that new drivers start in the morning when they're fresh. But tomorrow morning one of those Hornets'll be assigned to you. Delivered to the terminal nearest your home. Live far from your terminal?"

"About four blocks."

"Half a minute on the mobile-walk. What college you go to?"

"Western U."

"Lord, that's 400 miles away. You been living there?"

"No. Commuting every day on the monorail."

"Hell, that's for old women. Must have taken you over an hour to get there. Now you'll make it in almost thirty minutes. Still, it's best to take it easy the first day. Don't get 'er over 600 per. But don't let 'er fall beneath that either. If you do, some old veteran'll know you're a greenhorn and try to knock you off."

Suddenly Harry Hayden stiffened.

"Here come a couple! Look at 'em, boy!"

The low rumbling came out of the west, as of angry bees.

Twin pinpoints of black appeared on the distant white ribbon. Louder and louder the rumbling. Larger and larger the dots. To Tom, the sterile Jetway was transformed into a home of horror, an amphitheater of death.

Louder and larger—

Brooommmmmm.

Gone.

"Hey, how'ja like that, boy? They're gonna crack the sonic barrier or my name's not Harry Hayden!"

Tom's white-knuckled hands grasped a railing for support. *Christ, I'm going to be sick. I'm going to vomit.*

"But wait'll five o'clock or nine in the morning. That's when you see the traffic. That's when you *really* do some Driving!"

Tom gulped. "Is—is there a rest room here?"

"What's that, boy?"

"A—a rest room."

"What's the matter, boy? You *do* look sick. Too much excitement, maybe?"

Tom motioned frantically.

Harry Hayden pointed, slow comprehension crawling over his puffy features. "Up the ramp, to your right."

Tom Rogers made it just in time . . .

Many voices:

> "Happy Driving to You,
> Happy Driving to You,
> Happy Driving, Dear Taaaahmmm—" (pause)
> "Happy Driving to—" (flourish) "—You!"

An explosion of laughter. A descent of beaming faces, a thrusting forward of hands.

Mom reached him first. Her small face was pale under its thin coat of make-up. Her firm, rounded body was like a girl's in its dress of swishing Martian silk, yet her blue eyes were sad and her voice held a trembling fear:

"You passed, Tom?" Softly.

Tom's upper lip twitched. Was she afraid that he'd passed the tests—or that he hadn't! He wasn't sure.

Before he could answer, Dad broke in, hilariously. "Everybody passes these days except idiots and cripples!"

Tom tried to join the chorus of laughter.

Dad said, more softly, "You *did* pass, didn't you?"

"I passed," said Tom, forcing a smile. "But, Dad, I didn't want a surprise party. Really, I—"

"Nonsense." Dad straightened. "This is the happiest moment of our lives—or at least it *should* be."

Dad grinned. An understanding, intimate and gentle, flickered across his handsome, gray-thatched features. For an instant Tom felt that he was not alone.

Then the grin faded. Dad resumed his role of proud and blustering father. Light glittered on his three rows of Driver's Ribbons. The huge Blue Ribbon of Honor was in their center, like a blue flower in an evil garden of bronze accident stars, crimson fatality ribbons, and silver death's-heads.

In a moment of desperation Tom turned to Mom. The sadness was still in her face, but it seemed overshadowed by pride. What was it she'd once said? "It's terrible, Tom, to think of your becoming a Driver, but it'd be a hundred times more terrible *not* to see you become one."

He knew now that he was alone, an exile, and Mom and Dad were strangers. After all, how could one person, entrenched in his own little world of calm security, truly know another's fear and loneliness?

"Just a little celebration," Dad was saying. "You wouldn't be a Driver unless we gave you a real send-off. All our friends are here, Tom. Uncle Mack and Aunt Edith and Bill Ackerman and Lou Dorrance—"

No, Dad, Tom thought. Not our friends. Your friends. Don't you remember that a man of twenty who isn't a Driver has no friends?

A lank, loose-jowled man jostled between them. Tom realized that Uncle Mack was babbling at him.

"Knew you'd make it, Tom. Never believed what some people said 'bout you being afraid. My boy, of course, enlisted when he was only seventeen. Over thirty now, but he still Drives now and then. Got a special license, you know. Only last week—"

Dad exclaimed, "A toast to our new Driver!"

Murmurs of delight. Clinkings of glasses. Gurglings of liquid.

Someone pounded a piano chord. Voices rose:

    "A-Driving he will go,
    A-Driving he will go,

> To Hell and back in a coffin-sack
> A-Driving he will go."

Tom downed his glass of champagne. A pleasant warmth filled his belly. A satisfying numbness dulled the raw ache of fear.

He smiled bitterly.

There was kindness and gentleness within the human heart, he thought, but like tiny inextinguishable fires, there were ferocity and savageness, too. What else could one expect from a race only a few thousand years beyond the spear and stone axe?

Through his imagination passed a parade of somber scenes:

The primitive man dancing about a Paleolithic fire, chanting an invocation to strange gods who might help in tomorrow's battle with the hairy warriors from the South.

The barrel-chested Roman gladiator, with trident and net, striding into the great stone arena.

The silver-armored knight, gauntlet in gloved hand, riding into the pennant-bordered tournament ground.

The rock-shouldered fullback trotting beneath an avalanche of cheers into the 20th Century stadium.

Men needed a challenge to their wits, a test for their strength. The urge to combat and the lust for danger was as innate as the desire for life. Who was he to say that the law of Driving was unjust?

Nevertheless he shuddered.

And the singers continued:

> "A thousand miles an hour,
> A thousand miles an hour,
> Angels cry and devils sigh
> At a thousand miles an hour . . ."

The jetmobile terminal was like a den of chained, growling black tigers. White-cloaked attendants scurried from stall to stall, deft hands flying over atomic-engine controls and flooding each vehicle with surging life.

Ashen-faced, shivering in the early-morning coolness, Tom Rogers handed an identification slip to an attendant.

"Okay, kid," the rat-faced man wheezed, "there she is—Stall 17. Brand new, first time out. Good luck."

Tom stared in horror at the grumbling metal beast.

"But remember," the attendant said, "don't try to make a killing your first day. Most Drivers aren't out to get a Ribbon every day either. They just want to get to work or school, mostly, and have fun doing it."

Have fun doing it, thought Tom. *Good God.*

About him passed other black-uniformed Drivers. They paused at the heads of their stalls, donned crash-helmets and safety belts, adjusted goggles. They were like primitive warriors, like cocky Roman gladiators, like armored knights, like star fullbacks. They were formidable and professional.

Tom's imagination wandered.

By Jupiter's beard, we'll vanquish Attila and his savages. We'll prove ourselves worthy of being men and Romans . . . The Red Knight? I vow, Mother, that his blood alone shall know the sting of the lance . . . Don't worry, Dad. Those damned Japs and Germans won't lay a hand on me . . . Watch me on TV, folks. Three touchdowns today—I promise!

The attendant's voice snapped him back to reality. "What you waiting for, kid? Get in!"

Tom's heart pounded. He felt the hot pulse of blood in his temples.

The Hornet lay beneath him like an open, waiting coffin. He swayed.

"Hi, Tom!" a boyish voice called. "Bet I beat ya!"

Tom blinked and beheld a small-boned, tousled-haired lad of seventeen striding past the stall. What was his name? Miles. That was it. Larry Miles. A frosh at Western U.

A skinny, pimply-faced boy suddenly transformed into a black-garbed warrior. How could this be?

"Okay," Tom called, biting his lip.

He looked again at the Hornet. A giddiness returned to him.

You can say you're sick, he told himself. It's happened before: a hangover from the party. Sure. Tomorrow you'll feel better. If you could just have one more day, just one—

Other Hornets were easing out into the slip, sleek black cats embarking on an insane flight. One after another, grumbling, growling, spitting scarlet flame from their tail jets.

Perhaps if he waited a few minutes, the traffic would be thinner. He could have coffee, let the other nine-o'clock people go on ahead of him.

No, dammit, get it over with. If you crash, you crash. If you die, you die. You and Grandpa and a million others.

He gritted his teeth, fighting the omnipresent giddiness. He eased his body down into the Hornet's cockpit. He felt the surge of incredible energies beneath the steelite controls. Compared to this vehicle, the ancient training jets were as children's toys.

An attendant snapped down the plexite canopy. Ahead, a guide-master twirled a blue flag in a starting signal.

Tom flicked on a switch. His trembling hands tightened about the steering lever. The Hornet lunged forward, quivering as it was seized by the Jetway's electromagnetic guide-field.

He drove . . .

One hundred miles an hour, two hundred, three hundred.

Down the great asphalt valley he drove. Perspiration formed inside his goggles, steaming the glass. He tore them off. The glaring whiteness hurt his eyes.

Swish, swish swish.

Jetmobiles roared past him. The rushing wind of their passage buffeted his own car. His hands were knuckled white around the steering lever.

He recalled the advice of Harry Hayden: *Don't let 'er under 600 per. If you do, some old veteran'll know you're a greenhorn and try to knock you off.*

Lord. Six hundred.

But strangely, a measure of desperate courage crept into his fear-clouded mind. If Larry Miles, a pimply-faced kid of seventeen, could do it, so could he. Certainly, he told himself.

His foot squeezed down on the accelerator. Atomic engines hummed smoothly.

To his right, he caught a kaleidoscopic glimpse of a white gyroambulance. A group of metal beasts lay huddled on the emergency strip like black ants feeding on a carcass.

Like Grandfather, he thought. *Like those two moments out of the dark past, moments of screaming flame and black death and a child's horror.*

Swish.

The scene was gone, transformed into a cluster of black dots on his rear-vision radarscope.

His stomach heaved. For a moment he thought he was going to be sick again.

But stronger now than his horror was a growing hatred of that horror. His body tensed as if he were fighting a physical enemy. He fought his memories, tried to thrust them back into the oblivion of lost time, tried to leave them behind him just as his Hornet had left the cluster of metal beasts.

He took a deep breath. He was not going to be sick after all.

Five hundred now. Six hundred. He'd reached the speed without realizing it. Keep 'er steady. Stay on the right. If Larry Miles can do it, so can you.

Swooommmm.

God, where did *that* one come from?

Only ten minutes more. You'll be there. You'll make a right-hand turn at the college. The automatic pilot'll take care of that. You won't have to get in the fast traffic lanes.

He wiped perspiration from his forehead. Not so bad, these Drivers. Like Harry Hayden said, the killers come out on Saturdays and Sundays. Now, most of us are just anxious to get to work and school.

Six hundred, seven hundred, seven-twenty—

Did he dare tackle the sonic barrier?

The white asphalt was like opaque mist. The universe seemed to consist only of the broad expanse of Jetway.

Swooommmm.

Someone passing even at this speed! The crazy fool! And cutting in, the flame of his exhaust clouding Tom's windshield!

Tom's foot jerked off the accelerator. His Hornet slowed. The car ahead disappeared into the white distance like a black arrow.

Whew!

His legs were suddenly like ice water. He pulled over to the emergency strip. Down went the speedometer—five hundred, four, three, two, one, zero . . .

He saw the image of the approaching Hornet in his rear-vision radarscope. It was traveling fast and heading straight toward him. Heading onto the emergency strip.

A side-swiper!

Tom's heart churned. There would be no physical contact between the two Hornets—but the torrent of air from the inch-close passage would be enough to hurl his car into the Jetway bank like a storm-blown leaf.

There was no time to build enough acceleration for escape. His only chance was to frighten the attacker away. He swung his Hornet right, slammed both his acceleration and braking jet controls to full force. The car shook under the sudden release of energy. White-hot flame roared from its two dozen jets. Tom's Hornet was enclosed by a sphere of flame.

But dwarfing the roar was the thunder of the attacking Hornet. A black meteor in Tom's radarscope, it zoomed upon him. Tom closed his eyes, braced himself for the impact.

There was no impact. There was only an explosion of sound and a moderate buffeting of his car. It was as if many feet, not inches, had separated the two Hornets.

Tom opened his eyes and flicked off his jet controls.

Ahead, through the plexite canopy, he beheld the attacker.

It was far away now, like an insane, fiery black bird. Both its acceleration and braking jets flamed. It careened to the far side of the Jetway and zig-zagged up the curved embankment. Its body trembled as its momentum fought the Jetway's electromagnetic guide-field.

As if in an incredible carnival loop-the-loop, the Hornet topped the lip of the wall. It left the concrete, did a backward somersault, and gyrated through space like a flaming pinwheel.

It descended with an earth-shaking crash in the center of the gleaming Jetway.

What happened? Tom's dazed mind screamed. *In God's name, what happened?*

He saw the sleek white shape of a Referee's 'copter-jet floating to the pavement beside him. Soon he was being pulled out of his Hornet. Someone was pumping his hand and thumping his back.

"Magnificent," a voice was saying. "Simply magnificent!"

Night. Gay laughter and tinkling glasses. Above all, Dad's voice, strong and proud:

". . . and on his very first day, too. He saw the car in his rear radarscope, guessed what the devil was up to. Did he try to escape? No, he stayed right there. When the car closed in for the kill, he spun around and turned on all his jets full-blast. The killer never had a chance to get close enough to do his side-swiping. The blast roasted him like a peanut."

Dad put his arm around Tom's shoulder. All eyes seemed upon Tom's bright new crimson fatality ribbon embossed not only with a silver death's-head, but also with a sea-blue Circle of Honor.

Tom thought:

Behold the conquering hero. Attila is vanquished and Rome is saved. The Red Knight has been defeated, and the fair princess is mine. That Jap Zero didn't have a chance. A touchdown in the final five seconds of the fourth quarter —not bad, eh?

Dad went on:

"That devil really was a killer. Fellow name of Wilson. Been Driving for six years. Had thirty-three accident ribbons with twenty-one fatalities—not one of them honorable. That Wilson drove for just one purpose: to kill. He met his match in our Tom Rogers."

Applause from Uncle Mack and Aunt Edith and Bill

Ackerman and Lou Dorrance—and more important, from young Larry Miles and big Norm Powers and blond Geraldine Oliver, and cute little Sally Peters.

Tom smiled. Not only your friends tonight, Dad. Tonight it's my friends, too. My friends from Western U.

Fame was as unpredictable as the trembling of a leaf, Tom thought, as delicate as a pillar of glass. Yet the yoke of fame rested pleasantly on his shoulders. He had no inclination to dislodge it. And while a fear was still in him, it was now a fragile thing, an egg shell to be easily crushed.

Later Mom came to him. There was a proudness in her features, and yet a sadness and a fear, too. Her eyes held the thoughtful hesitancy of one for whom time and event have moved too swiftly for comprehension.

"Tomorrow's Saturday," she murmured. "There's no school, and no one'll expect you to Drive after what happened today. You'll be staying home for your birthday, won't you, Tom?"

Tom Rogers shook his head. "No," he said wistfully. "Sally Peters is giving a little party over in New Boston. It's the first time anyone like Sally ever asked me anywhere."

"I see," said Mom, as if she really didn't see at all. "You'll take the monorail?"

"No, Mom," Tom answered very softly. "I'm Driving."

Edward Ludwig (1921–)
Edward Ludwig was born in Tracy, California, and graduated from the University of the Pacific at Stockton. After serving as a Coast Guard officer during World War II, he worked as an assistant county clerk, bookseller, and chief book buyer for San Jose State College. The author of approximately twenty science

fiction stories, he is also the founder and owner of Polaris Press. For the last three years he has been writing full time and is presently at work on The Hammer of the Tyger, a short novel about man's regression to the primeval state.

NOTES

**CHARLES G. WAUGH
AND ISAAC ASIMOV**

DEVELOPMENT

IT'S A GOOD LIFE by Jerome Bixby

Developmental psychologists study the length of life and those changes that take place steadily from start to finish as a result of growing older and gaining experience. An important developmental concept is a *stage*. Each stage represents a different period in our lives, each building on the one before, and each organized around an important theme or function.

The most dramatic changes take place from birth to adolescence and, as a result, the stages during these years have received the most attention. In fact, it wasn't until about twenty-five years ago that much consideration was given to the stages that occur after adolescence.

A psychologist named Eric Erikson first suggested a comprehensive scheme for dividing our entire lives into general stages. This notion of adult stages has recently become popular enough to serve in 1976 as the subject of a best-selling book, *Passages*, by Gail Sheehy.

Most people have heard of a psychiatrist named Sigmund Freud, and much of his work focused on childhood stages. He thought children struggled through sexual stages, acquiring a conscience, and gradually turning from oral to genital pleasures. He viewed certain types of adult behavior as ways of compensating for unsuccessfully completed stages of childhood.

Jean Piaget worked out a different theory that dealt mostly with the stages in the way that children learn about themselves and the things about them. First, there is the *sensorimotor stage*, from birth to the age of two, in which the infant learns the difference between itself and other objects, discovers that objects continue to exist even when out of sight, and learns that its acts have an effect on the environment.

Second, there is the *preoperational stage*, from the age of two to seven, where the child learns to use language and to classify things and gradually emerges from the egocentric view that only its own needs count. Third, there is the *concrete operational stage*, from the age of seven to eleven, where the youth becomes capable of logical thought. Finally, there is the *formal operational stage*, beyond the age of eleven, where the adolescent begins to think beyond the everyday things he or she sees all around, and starts to consider the abstract and hypothetical.

Unfortunately for the residents of Peaksville in Jerome Bixby's "It's a Good Life," young Anthony is not only in the preoperational stage, but also possesses the psychic power to enforce his egocentric views. What he wants must be right; what offends him must be wrong . . .

SENSATION
THE SOUND MACHINE by Roald Dahl

There are countless numbers of things in the world that affect us constantly. "Sensation" is the study of how some of these, such as sound and color, are received and identified.

In addition to the *five senses* we are most familiar with—sight, hearing, touch, taste, and smell—there are additional things about ourselves and the world that we can sense. We can sense the passage of time, for instance; the presence and degree of heat; our position in space and the position of one part of the body compared to another—and a number of other things.

For example, close your eyes, stretch out an arm full length with your forefinger pointing, then bring the forefinger to your nose in one smooth gesture. How could you tell where your nose was with your eyes closed? Your *kinesthetic sense* keeps track of the position of all parts of your body.

There are, of course, matters in the world that we cannot sense because we don't have any way of receiving the signals; or because even though we can sense them, the *stimuli* that would ordinarily affect us are too far away, or too weak to affect us.

We can, for instance, see only one small part of all the light-like radiations about us—that part we call *visible light*. If we could see other radiations of the sort, we could observe the infrared light hot objects give off; we could see ultraviolet light, X rays, radio waves, and so on. Human beings have never developed these abilities because they are not needed, or because the radiations don't exist in the natural environment in more than tiny amounts. There are no X rays to speak of in the natural environment—if there were, they would damage us badly.

Each type of organism has its own sensory limitations. For example, human beings can hear sounds ranging from 20 cycles per second (cps) to 20,000 cps, but dogs can hear "ultrasonic" sounds up to 50,000 cps, bats up to 120,000 cps, and dolphins up to 150,000 cps. And although we cannot hear sounds below 20 cps, we can experience them as vibrations (as in the movie process Sensurround).

We don't usually think of plants as having senses, but, of course, they must. Leaves respond to light, roots respond to gravitational pull, and so on. It is possible we don't know the full range of plant sensation. *The Secret Life of Plants* by Peter Tomkins and Christopher Bird (1973) dealt with a bizarre range of possible plant sensations. The authors felt that, for instance, talking kindly to plants makes them grow better, and talking unkindly does the reverse. Afterward, increasingly sensational stories told of plant responses that made it seem they could even read minds.

Botanists, who have studied plants carefully, are not the least impressed by such accounts, so far. Nevertheless, suppose plants *did* experience sensations as we do. Roald Dahl, in "The Sound Machine," considers the possibility.

To be sure, a number of serious experiments show that plants are more receptive to stimuli than we might think. Talking to plants does seem to make them healthier, probably because we exhale carbon dioxide, which they need for growth. Naturally, it doesn't matter whether we speak kindly or unkindly, as long as we exhale in their direction. Also, when plants are subjected to music, the sound vibrations seem to affect them; classical music can help them grow, while rock and roll seems to damage them.

PERCEPTION
HALLUCINATION ORBIT by J. T. McIntosh

Every second, more than ten thousand sensory stimuli impinge on us. We constantly select those we believe most important, doing so in some cases deliberately, and in some cases unconsciously and without even knowing we are doing so. By selecting among the things we sense, by putting them in order, and by altering them sometimes to make them fit better, we create a picture in our minds of what we think is the reality around us. This process is influenced by our culture and by our personal experiences, so to some extent we perceive what we expect and want. Thus, our "reality" may not be someone else's "reality."

To summarize, sensation involves receiving and identifying individual elements and qualities, such as sounds and points of light. Perception involves using these elements and qualities to build up objects, actions, and events in ways that make sense to us.

To show you the difference, place both hands in front of your face: one twelve inches away and the other at arm's length. Compare them. The actual image of the far hand on the retina of your eye is less than half the size of the near hand, but they appear to you to be about the same size because you know they are.

In J. T. McIntosh's "Hallucination Orbit" we see that perceptions of reality can be wrong, and particular situations, such as deprivation and solitude, can increase the error. To operate properly, minds must receive considerable amounts of stimulation from the outside world—otherwise we will generate false stimulation from within to compensate, and we will then hallucinate (sense things that are not there and do not really exist).

Given Ord's situation in the story, the hallucinations he experiences are not unusual. Indeed, the monotony of a one-day drive caused one of our college friends to experience many of the same problems. During the last few hours of his trip he believed he was being visited by, and carrying on conversations with, some of his close friends—who, of course, were not there.

Where McIntosh goes wrong is in the assumption that only by traveling in groups of forty or more can hallucinations in space be prevented. In 1952, when this story was written, there was already good evidence that even the presence of just one additional person (for example, a driving partner) could have provided the stimulation necessary to keep a person anchored to reality.

LEARNING THE WINNER by Donald E. Westlake

Learning is defined as a relatively permanent change in behavior that occurs as a result of practice.

Learning is important to us because most of what we know, including the language we speak, is learned. The human ability to learn with ease gives us the ability to be extremely flexible in adjusting to, and thus surviving, environmental changes.

There are four ways we learn: by our own experience, by thinking things out, by observing others' experiences, or by listening to what others tell us of their experiences, observations, or thoughts.

Much of the first kind of learning consists of the formation of habits and is called *associative learning*. Most of the three other forms of learning consist of creating mental maps, thereby gaining understanding. This is called *cognitive learning.*

Practically all tasks involve both associative and cognitive learning. For example, tennis involves the gradual development of muscular skills that are needed to move rapidly in such a way as to reach the ball and then hit it over the net. But it also requires cognitive abilities to recognize when to charge the net and when to play the baseline.

All these ways of learning are illustrated in Donald Westlake's "The Winner." Revell learns from experience what impact leaving the prison compound will have on him. The interviewer learns, from observing Revell, how the embedded Guardian transmitter operates. Wordman learns, from thinking about Revell's experiences, that the Guardian's punishment will not guarantee universal obedience. Finally, new prisoners, such as Allyn, are briefed about the consequences of attempting escape.

Operant conditioning (response substitution) is the type of associative learning emphasized in this story. In such learning, an animal or human being takes some kind of action and, in return, receives either no response, or a reward, or a punishment. Actions that receive no response or a punishment tend to stop; rewarded actions tend to increase. For example, when Revell walks more than one hundred and fifty yards from the center of the compound, he receives increasing pain transmission from the Guardian transmitter. It is only natural that, to avoid this punishment, most prisoners stay near the compound almost automatically.

But as Revell's behavior suggests, competing rewards and punishments may exist for the same actions. Short-term rewards in terms of pleasurable taste may urge us toward eating chocolate eclairs and other such goodies, but that may lead to the long-term punishment of being unable to fit into one's bathing suit next summer. Do you give up the instant gratification for long-term health and looks—or not?

In Revell's case, the Guardian's punishment is not as great as the self-condemnation (another form of punishment) he would experience from ceasing to attempt to escape. Different people might differ in their fear of pain or the intensity with which they are ready to condemn themselves, so that they would react differently to the situation.

One frightening aspect of this story is that the installation of a Guardian-like device is technically possible today. That doesn't mean it will be done. Most behavioral psychologists feel that it is more efficient to use rewards, rather than punishments, in persuading people to do what responsible others want them to do.

LANGUAGE
A ROSE BY OTHER NAME by Christopher Anvil

Language is important because it forms the primary basis for one of the ways we learn—having others relay information to us, either in speech or in writing. Furthermore, language makes it possible for us to communicate with one another about complex ideas, or about things distant in time or space.

All languages consist of a series of symbols (lexicon) and a system of arranging those symbols (grammar) that can generate an indefinitely large number of meaningful messages (sentences).

There is evidence that the biological limitations of our brains determine the manner in which an intended meaning is transformed into sentences. On the other hand, the words of a lexicon seem to occur by simple historical chance. Someone assigns a label and it sticks (or does not). Had things been different, *gronk* or *snort* might be the English term for *boy*. Nor do words resemble the objects or events to which they refer. You would not recognize *Mädchen*, *devoshka*, or *ragazza* as *girl*, if you were unfamiliar with German, Russian, or Italian, respectively.

Certain words, such as "bowwow!," do, of course, attempt to resemble what they represent. Such words are exceptional, however, and at best are approximations. For example, in Finnish comics, dogs bark "Hau! Hau!"

There are two quite different views of the relationship between language and thought. Some experts feel that languages have to differ fundamentally because they developed in different environments. One even claimed that a particular tribe of Indians had no problem with stuttering because they had no word for it.

Most research, however, supports the position that thought determines the details of language. Interested enough people can develop new or more precise ways to talk about things by inventing words and phrases that suggest new ideas or another way of looking at old ideas. Hence, in "A Rose by Other Name," Christopher Anvil is correct in suggesting that avoiding words that refer to unpleasant thoughts, such as war, will simply result in the development of new words for those same unpleasant, and unavoidable, thoughts.

MEMORY

THE MAN WHO NEVER FORGOT
by Robert Silverberg

While learning is certainly one of the most valuable skills we have, memory is equally important, for information is of no use to us if it cannot be stored and retrieved.

How memory occurs is still controversial. It is known, however, that there are at least three stages.

Sensory storage is the first. It occurs when information from the eyes, for example, is stored for about a second after stimulation occurs. This seems to provide a brief period during which the brain can select information worth further processing. (One of the most important applications of this, by the way, is that it helps make movies possible. When slightly different still pictures pass before our eyes quickly enough, new images interfere with the storage of old, and we interpret these changes as movement, rather than replacement. Still, if you've ever seen film break, you know how quickly the illusion itself can break down.)

Short-term memory is the second stage. Here verbal information can be stored for about twenty seconds before needing to be recycled. That is why we sometimes repeat interesting persons' names (and perhaps phone numbers), until the repetitions fix them in *long-term memory*. Some types of stimuli (such as faces) may bypass this stage, being deposited directly in long-term memory.

Long-term memory is the final stage. As a repository for information, it seems to be virtually unlimited. Information that is stored in this way, however, is not necessarily retrievable when wanted. The primary reason for this seems to be interference, just as it is hard to locate a particular item in a room that is messy and cluttered with objects strewn about haphazardly. Other types of forgetting include repression or distortion, as when we simply refuse to think of information that disturbs us, or when we twist memories in order to support our beliefs.

So-called photographic (or *eidetic*) memories allow previously seen information to be visualized in full detail. A number of people possess this skill, and in the 1950's Teddy Nadler used it to win the "$64,000 Question" quiz show on television, and to defeat almost all opponents on the "$64,000 Challenge." The ability to remember information, however, is not the same as the ability to process it through thinking. For example, Nadler later failed an exam to become a census taker.

Some evidence suggests that the ability to store and retrieve all information received might actually interfere with the ability to think. Memories can be so many and so specific that it becomes very difficult to generalize. The world becomes a disorderly mass of very many individual items and no sense can be made out of it.

It is fair to argue, then, as Robert Silverberg does in "The Man Who Never Forgot," that a perfect memory might create indecisiveness about acknowledging others. However, someone with better-developed social skills than Tom could handle the problem more adroitly, just as strong man Arnold Schwarzenegger has learned to shake hands without crushing them, and as a professor of philosophy may learn to speak to ordinary people without using his full vocabulary.

Nor is it necessary to deal with painful memories solely through forgetting. Experience often permits us to reinterpret. Ten years later, the memory of the embarrassments we experienced on our first date may seem funny. Nor is it necessary to focus primarily on bad memories unless one secretly enjoys being morose.

Finally, Tom's children may not have perfect memories. Though his mother's father had the gift, she does not, so the responsible gene has to be recessive.

MOTIVATION RUNAROUND by Isaac Asimov

Why does Jane pull into the Golden Arches for a burger and fries? Bodily changes, such as reduced blood sugar level, produce signals causing her to feel hungry and motivating her to find some way to satisfy her desire for food.

Motivation is the cause behind our thoughts and actions. Often our motives are physiologically inspired, but even then cultural, social, and situational factors are important. No matter how hungry you were, you would hesitate to go into a fancy restaurant if you felt improperly dressed. Then, too, there may be several motives operating at the same time, a fact which could cause conflicts.

In "Runaround," by Isaac Asimov, the robot, Speedy, is caught in the trap of conflicting motivations and arrives at a point of paralysis at which he can neither go forward nor retreat. The Second Law of Robotics obligates Speedy to proceed toward the pool of selenium as his masters have requested. Yet to do so would be to put himself in jeopardy, which the Third Law of Robotics says he is not supposed to do.

Psychologists call Speedy's dilemma an *approach-avoidance conflict*. This occurs when a person confronted with a goal has conflicting feelings about attaining it. Once a goal is established, a person judges the situation and decides whether to advance or retreat. The sense of attraction, however, can at times mask a sense of avoidance, so that the person may begin approaching the goal and then, as in the case of Speedy, encounter a point at which appreciation of the negative features of the goal begin to outweigh its positive features. Speedy is able to overcome this conflict only when the First Law of Robotics, which takes precedence over the other two, is brought into play and provides him with a more compelling motive.

Though not discussed in this story, there are three other types of motivational conflicts besides approach-avoidance.

In an *approach-approach conflict*, a person is torn between two desirable alternatives, such as reading a good book or seeing a good movie, or two alternative ways of satisfying a desired motive, such as eating cake or eating pie. Such a conflict is usually quickly resolved, since approaching either of the goals increases its attractiveness while simultaneously reducing the attractiveness of the other.

In an *avoidance-avoidance conflict*, a person must choose between two undesirable alternatives, such as registering for the draft or facing possible prosecution. This type of conflict usually drags on for a while, since movement toward either alternative makes that one seem more unpleasant than the other.

In a *double approach-avoidance conflict*, a person faces two alternative goals or two alternative ways of satisfying a motive, with each alternative having both good and bad qualities. For example, John is an avid mountain climber, and one day he faces a mountain that gives him the choice of scaling either the north slope or the south slope. The north slope is easier and faster to climb but provides little in the way of a view. The south slope is steeper and more difficult to climb but offers spectacular scenery.

Whatever decision John makes, he will probably wonder, at some time, whether that was actually the decision he should have made. Often a particular situation appears more undesirable than it actually is, since a person is always highly aware of the disadvantage of the situation he is experiencing and is less aware of the disadvantages of the alternative. Thus, in "Runaround," Powell and Donovan talk about how nice things will be when they leave Mercury for the Space Station. In Dr. Asimov's follow-up story, "Reason," in his collection *I, Robot*, they discover so many problems that they wish they were back on Mercury.

INTELLIGENCE   ABSALOM by Henry Kuttner

Alfred Binet, a Frenchman, developed the intelligence test in 1905 as a means of predicting academic success. Today, many revisions later, that is still its most suitable purpose. Binet assumed bright children would achieve scores on his test similar to those of older, less bright children. For that reason, he calculated IQ (*intelligence quotient*) by dividing mental age, as determined by the test scores, by chronological age, and multiplying by 100

Fifty per cent of the population falls within what is considered the normal range of 90 to 109, with high-school graduates averaging 105, college graduates 115, and Ph.D.'s 130. IQ's of 160 or above are possessed by only 4 out of every 10,000 people.

In "Absalom," by Henry Kuttner, Absalom is said to have a mental age of twenty, though he is only eight. Thus his IQ would be an extraordinarily high 250, far surpassing the estimated brilliance of most of history's notable men, such as Thomas Jefferson (145), Wolfgang Amadeus Mozart (150), Voltaire (170), John Stuart Mill (190), and Sir Francis Galton (200). (These men never took an intelligence test, but the figures are estimated from their reported achievements in early life and are therefore highly dubious.)

It is important to realize that a high IQ does not guarantee success. Studies have shown that college students' later career success has little or nothing to do with the grades they earned in school. Within a range of 10 to 15 points, factors such as drive, personality, connections, and luck are more important than intelligence. Indeed, the world might be a better place if relatively unrelated traits such as gentleness, honesty, morality, and creativity were given more emphasis.

For a number of years, psychologists have been interested in the impact of environment on intelligence. Environment certainly can produce dramatic shifts. For example, dissection reveals that rats raised in posh surroundings end up with better-developed brains than their litter mates. In another experiment, enriched environments were provided for ten institutionalized children classified as mentally retarded. In later life, the IQ's of these aided children averaged 53(!) points higher than those of other comparable, unaided children. Most of the first group graduated from high school, married, and led normal lives. Most of the second group remained institutionalized.

PERSONALITY
WINGS OUT OF SHADOW by Fred Saberhagen

You walk into a room and sit down at a typewriter keyboard. A light flashes on. Words march across the display screen: "The doctor is in. Please begin typing your comments."

You say, "Doctor, I'm angry with my parents."

"Why do you think you are angry with your parents?" comes the reply.

"Because they won't let me drive the car next Saturday."

"Why do you think they won't let you drive the car?"

"Well, I didn't mow the lawn."

And so it goes—for a half hour, at least. You make comments and ask questions, while the doctor responds indirectly by questioning, clarifying, and rephrasing.

In this case, though, the doctor is just a computer programmed to respond to you in this manner. If you are fooled, don't feel ashamed. Studies show that people generally cannot distinguish between real therapists and the computer program. Even experienced therapists, not aware of the source of the interviews, judge them to be quite adequate.

Does this mean that Fred Saberhagen's computer simulations of historical personages in "Wings Out of Shadow" will be possible in the near future? Will there one day be machines capable of duplicating "the characteristics and ways of behaving that determine a person's unique adjustments to the environment," that is, a particular human being's personality?

No. Two formidable problems stand in the way.

First, there is the complexity of human beings. It is reported that there are over 18,000 English words referring to personal characteristics. From these, one psychologist worked out a list of sixteen underlying source traits he felt were enough to describe an individual personality adequately. Still, these hardly describe the many secondary traits that individuals possess, or the powerful effect that temporary moods and specific situations can have on behavior. For example, real therapists do many other things besides helping patients. Considering how we shift our behavior in thousands of ways to fit our perceptions of what is happening and what we need to do, we can see that it will probably be a long time before truly human-like machines can be developed.

Second, there is the problem of reconstructing historical personalities. Saberhagen's reliance on 4 million bits of historical information are surely inadequate for such reconstruction. He includes no information about the individual's inborn potential (or genetic structure). He depends upon secondhand data that may be false and are, at best, woefully incomplete.

In actual fact, the number of bits of information the average person stores in a lifetime may be as much as 250 billion times greater than that contained in the pool of information that Saberhagen uses.

Finally, Saberhagen is wrong in assuming that unconscious information processing takes place outside the boundaries of time, not being directed by nerve impulses. Since such an assumption was not necessary and only detracts from an otherwise very fine story, one wonders why it was made.

ABNORMAL PSYCHOLOGY
IN CASE OF FIRE by Randall Garrett

What is mental illness? What types are there? What causes it? Abnormal psychology searches for answers to questions like these. Certainly mental illness is a world-wide problem. In the United States, for instance, about 1 person in 4 experiences symptoms serious enough to disturb everyday life; approximately 1 in 10 will suffer from a serious mental disturbance (*psychosis*) sometime during life; and 1 in 100 will be hospitalized for therapeutic treatment sometime during life.

Still, it is hard to come by a universally accepted definition of abnormality. For one thing, behavior considered abnormal in one society may be normal in another. American bigamists would have no troubles in that respect in a Muslim nation. For another thing, a society may consider some behavior normal in certain situations and abnormal in others. Taking your clothes off in your bedroom is to be expected, but stripping in the classroom may lead others to believe you need a psychiatric examination. Finally, disturbances occur in different degrees, and opinions differ over how much impairment must take place before one should be labeled ill.

As to what causes mental illness, the best answer seems to be: several things. Some types of illness, such as schizophrenic and manic-depressive disorders, are determined to large extent by biological causes. Others, such as phobic disorders, appear to result primarily from learning. Additional causes are internal conflicts and stresses arising from the situations one is in.

It seems quite likely, too, that some disturbances may often result from several causes acting together. For example, the biological causes of schizophrenia may be more effective if the victim never develops a basic trust in the world (an internal problem) and is subjected to a great deal of pressure by an employer (a situational stress).

There are, of course, many different types of mental aberration. In Randall Garrett's "In Case of Fire," Malloy, the ambassador, suffers from two phobic disorders (irrational fears); Miss Drayson, his secretary, and James Nordon, the head negotiator, both suffer from personality disorders; and Kylen Braynek, the assistant negotiator, suffers from paranoid psychosis (delusions of persecution).

Though this story is about abnormal behavior, Malloy succeeds because of his understanding of social psychology. He appoints two negotiators, realizing that groups are usually more effective in solving problems than is an individual. They have more resources and usually make fewer errors, since members of groups tend to catch each other's mistakes. In addition, the ambassador increases his team's chances by selecting members according to the demands of the situation. This converts Nordon's indecisive leadership and Braynek's paranoia into strengths.

THERAPY
WHAT FRIENDS ARE FOR by John Brunner

How to treat mental illness depends, of course, on your definition of what it is. Until the 1700's, most explanations involved the presence of demons in those mentally ill. Consequently, the therapies most commonly used were religious exorcism, torture (to drive out the demons), and death. Asylums began during the Middle Ages, but remained little more than prisons until 1792, when the French physician Philippe Pinel took advantage of the idealism of the French Revolution to institute reforms in the treatment of the mentally ill.

Professionals involved in *psychotherapy* include psychiatrists, clinical psychologists, psychiatric social workers, and psychiatric nurses. In order, they are physicians, Ph.D.'s in psychology, advanced-degree holders in social work, and nurses, all of whom have specialized in treating mental illness.

While more than 130 different kinds of approach to therapy exist, the best hope of a patient's getting well rests with his or her desire to do so and the quality of the relationship between the therapist and the patient, regardless of the therapy used.

We have moved far ahead of torture as a means of therapy. Some types of present-day therapy, such as behavioral psychology and the use of appropriate drugs, seem quite effective for certain problems. As more is learned about causes, better therapies should be developed.

Psychotherapies strive for changes in behavior or belief by psychological methods. They include *cognitive therapies*, which emphasize talking to the patient to change behavior; *behavioral therapies*, which emphasize changing behavior directly, rather than indirectly by developing insight; and *group therapies*, which emphasize changing social roles and communication patterns.

Cognitive therapy constitutes a major portion of Buddy's approach in "What Friends Are For," by John Brunner. Much as client-centered therapy advises, Buddy patiently clarifies Tim's feelings and actions while providing him with unqualified acceptance. Further, he uses behavioral techniques such as acting as role model, punishing transgressions, and rewarding good behavior. Finally, near the end of the story, he practices some family (group) therapy when analyzing Jack's and Lorna's feelings.

Eventually Tim's new socially acceptable behavior forces his parents to consider altering their own behavior patterns to increase his likelihood of rewarding them. However, considering that the parents' behavior was largely responsible for Tim's initial problems, one wonders why Buddy did not make greater attempts to use family therapy earlier. For example, reducing Jack's vicious game playing ("If It Weren't for You" and "Now I've Got You") would have diminished Lorna's desire to embarrass him.[1]

Somatotherapies, on the other hand, strive for changes in behavior or belief by physiological methods. These methods, which can be used only by psychiatrists, include surgery, electrical stimulation or shock therapy, and chemotherapy (drugs).

Many psychoanalysts condemn somatotherapies for not getting at underlying causes, and there are complaints that they are often overused or misused. Yet shock therapy and electrical stimulation of the brain seem to be effective ways of breaking up severe depression, and that then makes it possible to use other psychotherapies more effectively.

---

[1] See Eric Berne, *Games People Play* (New York: Grove Press, 1964).

In addition, chemotherapy is the most effective treatment found for several forms of psychosis. It is almost single-handedly responsible for the dramatic reduction of in-patient mental hospital populations from 559,000 in 1955 to 193,000 in 1975.

SOCIAL PSYCHOLOGY
THE DRIVERS by Edward W. Ludwig

At first glance, social psychology seems to be a jumble of unrelated things such as pro-social behavior, affiliation, collective behavior, aggression, group processes, and persuasion. What these things and others have in common are their concern with why and how individuals influence and are influenced by social situations and each other.

Aggression, for example, is commonly defined as words or actions that are intentionally designed to harm people, and that do, in fact, harm them. War is its most violent form, and since the advent of recorded history less than two hundred individual years have passed without a war taking place somewhere. Individual violence is also widespread. The United States averages one murder every 36 minutes, one robbery every 2 minutes, and one serious crime of some sort every 7 seconds.

As technology increases, furthermore, so does the problem, for better weapons kill more people. During the 125-year period ending with World War II, it is estimated that 58 million humans were killed by other humans. This is an average of nearly one person per minute.

Everyone agrees that steps should be taken to reduce aggression. There is, however, disagreement over the nature of the steps, because there is disagreement over the causes of aggression.

Some emphasize biological causes, such as genetic predispositions, organic damage, or chemical imbalances. According to Freud, society must bottle up people's strong inborn sexual and aggressive impulses to preserve order and civilization. There must, however, be socially approved methods of release, or people will eventually explode into violence like neglected pressure cookers, Thus Freudians feel that athletics, debating, and watching horror pictures all serve society by promoting the release of aggressive impulses. The individual becomes happier and is much less likely to be aggressive in the immediate future.

Other psychologists stress the importance of environmental factors, such as gang behavior, crowding, and TV. Television, for example, shows an average of eight violent acts per hour during prime time, and aggressive acts exceed affectionate ones by a ratio of 4 to 1. After reviewing ten years of studies, the National Institute of Mental Health recently concluded that "televised violence and aggression are positively related in children." This view is that watching violence doesn't release aggressive impulses, but increases them.

Finally, there are those who emphasize psychological factors, such as attempts to bolster one's self-esteem, perceptions of unimportance, and frustration. For example, street gangs are much more likely to be composed of teenagers with low self-esteem than of those with high.

While most psychologists believe that biological causes are the least-important sources of aggression, Edward Ludwig has chosen to base "The Drivers" on Freudian theory.

Thus highway combat is offered as a socially desirable way to channel aggressive impulses and to get rid of them harmlessly. Note, though, that the device is depicted as being reinforced by environmental and psychological supports, such as kill medals, approval by one's peers, and increased feelings of competence.

Still, most evidence (such as that from TV studies) suggests that this sort of thing is, at best, of only short-term use and is strongly outweighed by the long-term bad effect of acquiring aggressive habits. In other words, punching someone in the nose may make you feel less angry, but it also increases the chances you will again punch someone in the nose in the future, in order to get rid of hostile feelings once more. That is what Tom Rogers illustrates at the end of the story by deciding to drive to his girl friend's home.

Furthermore, if Freud is wrong about sexual and aggressive impulses, and the problem is simply one of excess energy, then space exploration or mountain climbing would make a lot more sense. Both would boost self-esteem, and neither would teach aggression.